SLOW TRAIN TO GUANTÁNAMO

A Rail Odyssey through Cuba in the Last Days of the Castros

Praise for Peter Millar

Slow Train to Guantanamo
'The book gives an insight into Cuban daily life, Caribbean communism, the food, the beer, the colours, the smells (good and bad) and the realities of an artificial economy that the package deal tourists will never even glimpse. If you have ever been to Varadero and Havana (the standard package), read this book, then go back and see the real Cuba whilst you still can. If you have never been to Cuba, read this book, and if you then don't want to go to Cuba, you have no soul, and they wouldn't want you there anyway. Go to Cuba, but take your own toilet seat, and paper, the locals will understand' – J. P. Hayward

1989 The Berlin Wall
'The best read is the irreverent and engaging account by Peter Millar, who writes for the *Sunday Times* among other papers. Fastidious readers who expect reporters to be a mere lens on events will be shocked at the amount of personal detail, including the sexual antics and drinking habits of his colleagues in what now seems a Juvenalian age of dissolute British journalism. He mentions his long-suffering wife and children rather too often, but the result is full of insights and on occasion delightfully funny. The author has a knack for befriending interesting people and tracking down important ones. He weaves their words with his clear-eyed reporting of events into a compelling narrative about the end of the cruel but bungling East German regime' – *Economist*

'The most entertaining read is Peter Millar's *1989 The Berlin Wall: My Part in its Downfall*, a witty, wry, elegiac account of his time as a Reuters and *Sunday Times* correspondent in Berlin throughout most of the 1980s' – Spectator

'*1989 The Berlin Wall* is part autobiography, part history primer and part Fleet Street gossip column . . . Millar cast aside the old chestnuts and set about reporting on the reality of life under communism. In bare Stalinist apartments, at hollow party events and over cool glasses of Volker the gravedigger-cum-hippie, the Stasi seductress "Helga the Honeypot", Kurtl the accordion player whose father had been killed at Stalingrad, and the petty smuggler Manne who has been separated from his parents by the Wall . . . Energetic and passionate . . .' – *Sunday Times*

All Gone To Look for America
'Succeeds in capturing the wonder of America that the iron horse made accessible to the world' – *The Times*

'Witty yet observant . . . this book smells of train travel and will appeal to wanderlusts as well as armchair train buffs' – *Time Out*

'Fills a hole for those who love trains, microbrewery beer and the promise of big skies and wide-open spaces' – *Daily Telegraph*

The Black Madonna
'With a journalist's keen eye and ear, and a born storyteller's soul, author Millar has written a truly compelling, globetrotting thriller. Rich in history and cultural detail, *The Black Madonna* is a page-turner of a novel that flings us into the heart of the essential conflicts of our times. Look out, Dan Brown, make way for Millar' – Jeffery Deaver

Stealing Thunder
'An intelligent thriller . . . fast-paced and convincing' – Robert Harris

PETER MILLAR

SLOW TRAIN TO GUANTÁNAMO

A Rail Odyssey through Cuba in the Last Days of the Castros

ARCADIA BOOKS

Arcadia Books Ltd
139 Highlever Road
London W10 6PH
United Kingdom

www.arcadiabooks.co.uk

First published in the United Kingdom by Arcadia Books 2013
Copyright © Peter Millar 2013

Peter Millar has asserted his moral right to be identified as the author of this work in
accordance with the Copyright, Designs and Patents Act, 1988.

A catalogue record for this book is available from the British Library

ISBN 978-1-908129-50-5

Typeset in Minion by Discript Limited, Chichester
Printed and bound by CPI Group (U K) Ltd, Croydon CRO 4YY

Acknowledgements
Many thanks to my son Oscar – an artist and graphic designer – who drew
the map of Cuba for me.

Arcadia Books supports English PEN *www.englishpen.org* and
The Book Trade Charity *http://booktradecharity.wordpress.com*

Arcadia Books distributors are as follows:

in the UK and elsewhere in Europe:
Macmillan Distribution Ltd
Brunel Road
Houndmills
Basingstoke
Hants RG21 6XS

in the USA and Canada:
Dufour Editions
PO Box 7
Chester Springs
PA 19425

in Australia/New Zealand:
NewSouth Books
University of New South Wales
Sydney NSW 2052

in South Africa:
Jacana Media (Pty) Ltd
PO Box 291784
Melville 2109
Johannesburg

Prologue

It is nearly twenty-five years since all of a sudden communism keeled over and died. The *annus mirabilis* of 1989, when the Cold War caught its death, the Berlin Wall crumbled, the dominoes of the Soviet empire in Eastern Europe tumbled and in quick succession the Soviet Union itself disintegrated, seems a lifetime ago. So long, in fact, that it is hard to remember that back then it was widely considered that capitalism had won and was from now on invincible as a global economic and social system.

Five years after the great financial crash of 2008, that no longer seems such a wise conclusion.

Apart from the aberration of China's adoption of a strange form of capitalist communism, only two states remained that genuinely considered themselves dedicated to the principles of Marx and Engels: North Korea and Cuba. Both were considered, particularly by the United States, little better than pariahs, with sanctions imposed against them.

The reality, of course, was always dramatically different. While North Korea was, by and large, a cold and barren half-peninsula, Cuba is one of the most beautiful, sun-blessed islands in the Caribbean. While the North Korean people were drummed into regimental parades and marched through the streets of Pyongyang, the Cuban people drummed, played and sang themselves into and out of the bars of Havana and onto the big screen. While North Korea's leaders died and succeeded one another in dynastic fashion, Fidel Castro hung on, seemingly forever, until eventually, in 2008, in admittedly similar dynastic fashion he yielded power to his not much younger brother Raúl.

And now Cuba is changing. Raúl himself has said he will serve five more years at most. Cuba beyond the Castros is already on the horizon. What will it be like, and more to the point what is it like now, outside the luxury enclaves visited by most beach-loving foreign tourists, in the streets, buses and trains used by the ordinary people?

As someone who lived in East Germany, the Soviet Union and communist Poland and reported on life in those countries before the fall of the Iron Curtain[1] and immediately afterwards, Cuba exerted a remarkable fascination. And as someone who has travelled the length and breadth of the United States by the method of transport that created that continental nation,[2] it seemed to me there could be no better way to experience life in Cuba on the ground, literally, than by travelling the length of the island by train.

Cuba's railway is – or was, as I was about to find out – one of the first and most extensive national systems in the world. Cubans had the fifth national railway system in the world, after the United Kingdom, United States, Germany and France, before Spain or most other European countries, and it remains the only truly national system in Latin America. Although just how extensive it was I had no idea.

This is not a guidebook, not a book about politics, nor even, I regret to tell railway buffs, a book about trains. It is a book that deals with all those topics and I hope a lot more. It is a book about people and places and country on the cusp of change. It is a book about travel and why it is the best

---

1. *1989: the Berlin Wall (My part in its Downfall)*, Arcadia Books 2009.
2. *All Gone to Look for America*, Arcadia Books 2008.

education the world can offer. It is about life and living it, the Cuban way. And believe me, for all the deprivations the Cubans today still suffer, there are worse ways to live. Far worse. Ask anybody in Iraq or Afghanistan.

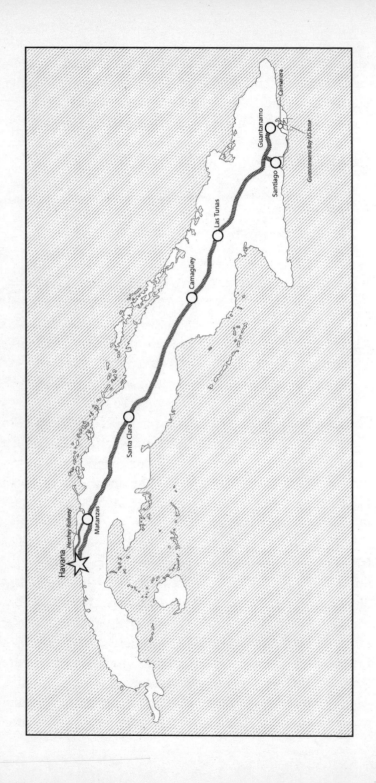

CHAPTER ONE

El Spirituario

It is 4.10 a.m. on a dark, steamy tropical morning and raindrops that look and feel like drowned bluebottles are falling from the rusting corrugated iron of the station roof. I have just been poured out of a train the Cubans nickname *El Spirituario* – an experience as close to being below decks on a seventeenth-century slave trader as a middle-aged, middle-class European man ever wants to get.

I stumble down the station steps in search of transport to where I am hoping to find a bed for what remains of the night. The options are not great: a donkey-cart with a candle burning in a jam jar as its tail light, or an ancient Soviet Lada with only one door, no windows and a patchwork quilt of badly-stitched upholstery.

This is Santa Clara, capital of the cult of Cuba's secular saint and martyr, the chess-playing, motorcycle-mad humanitarian medic and ruthless revolutionary who looked like a movie-star; his iconic image has stared from bedroom walls of generations of liberal students across the globe for more than half a century. It was here that Argentinian Ernesto 'Che' Guevara won the battle – in reality little more than a train derailment and subsequent skirmish – that would give control of the Caribbean's capitalist playground to the Communist Fidel Castro. The aftermath of the Battle of Santa Clara would make Che a household name in almost every nation on the planet.

And I hate to say it, Che, I really do, mentally addressing myself to the ghost that hovers over Santa Clara, but it looks like a crock of shit.

After four hours on an overcrowded train in 30°C heat and 80 per cent humidity, with broken seats, no windows (thankfully), compartments with no doors and endlessly flickering fluorescent corridor lights, all I want to do is sleep. I decide to leave the candle-burning donkey-cart for another time and opt for the less rustic but possibly faster option, the one-doored Lada.

I had thought that maybe one reason communism still survived in Cuba might be the weather: it's a lot easier being poor when the sun is shining, but now I'm not so sure.

Ten minutes after falling into the Lada, the rain is still beating a slow staccato on the roof and my sleep-starved brain has been addled by a ghetto blaster strapped to the passenger seat sun visor blaring at full blast as we rattle along otherwise empty and silent pre-dawn cobbled streets.

My driver is wearing rain- or sweat-soaked red shorts and torn orange T-shirt. He grins, gleefully unembarrassed by the high-volume salsa and farting Soviet exhaust pipe, as we scan the shuttered front doors behind ornate iron grilles in a street of low terraced whitewashed eighteenth-century Spanish colonial houses. One of these is the *casa particular* – a private home licensed to take in foreign guests, the Cuban equivalent of a B&B – where I have booked a room. But which one? The concept of giving houses numbers or even names, if ever common, has clearly fallen into disuse. But then as buying or selling homes has been banned for half a century, pretty much everybody knows who lives where.

I stare in bleary despair at the lack of identification when an elderly white-haired gentleman, roused to our presence by the cacophony on his doorstep, opens shuttered doors, then the elegant wrought iron-grille in front of it, and beckons me in.

The Lada driver pockets his fare and his ramshackle vehicle with under-inflated tyres, elaborate upholstery, and missing door rattles off into the predawn twilight, the tinny din from its improvised audio equipment mercifully vanishing with it as my host welcomes me into another world. Or perhaps as L. P. Hartley would have put it, another country: the past.

Beneath my feet is an ancient hardwood parquet floor, ahead of me two white Doric pillars flank the entrance to an open courtyard, like the interior of a Moroccan *riad*, with tall double doors ahead and to the right leading on into the interior of the house. Cuba's current reality intrudes here only in the form of the green corrugated plastic that covers part of the courtyard, dripping steady separated streams of rainwater.

Those who owned only one property, their home, at the time of the 1959 revolution were allowed to keep it. For those with a home big enough – ironically the middle classes which, despite belonging to them, Castro most detested – it has become not just a roof over their head but a major means of support. Toleration of foreign tourism has provided an alternative economy with access to hard currency. The communist paradise of Castro today has a vital private sector on the side.

My elderly host grandly throws open the double doors on the right to reveal a room with high ceilings, a four-bladed fan and, most importantly of all, a wide welcoming double bed.

'*Buenas noches*,' he bids me with a smile, and I collapse onto a mattress as hard as Brighton beach but more than welcome.

That old Phil Collins anthem to the homeless is running through my head as I hit what passes for a pillow: 'Oh, think twice, it's just another day for you and me in paradise.' I drift off into confused dreamland wondering just how the hell I got into this in the first place.

CHAPTER TWO

Don't stop me now . . .

Just five days earlier I had arrived in the relative luxury of a Virgin Atlantic premium economy at Havana airport, where most foreign visitors make their first acquaintance with the curious reality of life in Cuba. For most of them – whooshed off in luxury air-conditioned coaches to coastal resorts all but hermetically sealed off from the rest of the island – their last. But it is still unmistakably Cuban. For a start the security checks are on the wrong side.

Most airports are worried about you taking bombs onto airplanes; the Cubans are worried you might be bringing bombs off one. After five minutes doing my level best to give an unwavering smile in response to the unwelcoming stare of an immigration official in the shortest skirt I have ever seen on an immigration official anywhere, the woman behind the glass window handed back my passport brusquely and gestured to the scanners ahead, and said: '*Seguridad.*' Security.

Despite Ronald Reagan adding Cuba to the US State Department's list of 'state sponsors of terror', Havana's record on that score is actually better than Washington's. The White House – or at least the CIA – was behind one proxy invasion of Cuba, more than eight attempts to kill its head of state, and almost certainly one bomb which brought down an aircraft (of which more later), killing all on board. And that is without even mentioning that the greatest number of people considered terrorists by Washington itself has for several years been held on the bit of Cuban soil US armed forces still squat on, at the far end of the island: the goal of my present odyssey, Guantánamo Bay.

The dark days belong to the distant past – most incidents were in early 1960s. But the Cuban authorities, perhaps more than ever given the advanced age of their leaders and a growing sense of *fin de régime,* are not taking any chances. Anyone entering the socialist paradise of Cuba is necessarily subject to scrutiny.

Which was why half an hour after landing, and five days before being decanted into Santa Clara in the bleak hours before dawn, I found myself standing in a queue of incoming passengers watching an immensely large lady from Santo Domingo dressed in what looked like a tent arguing loudly with a stern-faced customs official in an even shorter skirt than the immigration lady had worn.

The argument, improbably enough, was as to whether or not she should be allowed to bring six one-litre cans of banana milkshake mix unopened into the Socialist Republic of Cuba. 'How do I know what's in there?' the customs lady was asking, clearly suspicious that it might be anything from gunpowder to cocaine. On an island where milk itself is usually only available on a state-issued ration card to certified mothers of small children, a large tin of powder claiming to contain banana milkshake mix is something regarded with deep suspicion.

There may be no flights or ferries to the United States (indeed US travel websites such as kayak.com or expedia.com won't even give you information about flights to Cuba, as if the huge island on their doorstep wasn't actually there). But from all over the rest of the Americas, flights pour into Havana daily, from Caracas, capital of Venezuela, which under the late – and in Cuba sorely lamented – Hugo

Chavez, had become the country's best friend, but also from Panama, from Lima, from Buenos Aires, from Santiago in Chile, from Santo Domingo in the Dominican Republic, whence the lady in front of me was trying to import the banana milkshake.

A glance at the arrivals and departures board illustrates that if the United States thinks it has cut Cuba off from the world – despite Barack Obama's softer line, the punitive embargo remains in force, and citizens of non-Cuban ethnicity are banned from visiting – it is sorely deluding itself. Cubans see themselves as part of a much broader, largely Latin American world.

They refuse to use the word *Americano* for the citizens of the big country to the north of them, preferring instead the cumbersome *Estados-Unidosenses* (roughly: United-Statesians). They see themselves as *Americanos*, like most of the other passengers arriving at or transiting through Havana airport.

That did not, however, make for much obvious tolerance for the large lady from Santo Domingo. I never did discover if she managed to import her curious cargo. She was taken aside into a separate room – possibly to be strip-searched for any other curiously flavoured corrupting capitalist comestibles – just as I was beckoned forward. To my relief my little backpack of bare necessities was rubber stamped through and I passed into the steamy, tropical, complicated chaos that is the gateway to what is probably the most magical, quixotic, complicated and confused island in the world.

Havana airport, like a lot of other things in Cuba, bears the name of José Martí, a nineteenth-century poet and idealist, revered almost as much as Che, even if he was decidedly less successful. Unlike the Argentinian revolutionary, José Martí's first glimpse of action was also his last. Aged just forty-two – three years older than Che when he was executed in the Bolivian jungle by CIA-sponsored government troops – Martí led Cuban rebels into battle against their Spanish colonial masters, heroically, romantically (and extremely stupidly) dressed in his trademark black suit, on the back of a white horse. He was immediately shot dead by a sniper.

This is one of those apocryphal but true stories that tells you a lot about Cuba. Martí was a Cuban nationalist who had a love–hate relationship with the United States, a socialist who was also a dandy, a charismatic romantic revolutionary, a poet and a nutcase. Today he is an airport.

Having sailed through immigration and security, my one moment of stress before heading for downtown Havana, was tipping the clutch of toilet ladies gathered purposefully round the door to the gents. I had 45 British pence in small change, which seemed an adequate sum though I doubted they would recognize the currency. They didn't, but all that mattered was that it was foreign. Converted into the money nearly all Cubans are paid in, that is about as much as the average worker might earn in a day. In Cuba's curious economy, the foreign currency tips alone make being a toilet cleaner at Havana airport a much sought-after profession.

Taxi drivers make more, a lot more, especially, as everywhere in the world, taxi drivers based at the airport. A ride into central Havana in what turned out by ordinary Cuban standards the height of luxury – a ten-year-old Peugeot 306 – was going to cost me, the cab driver grinned, 25 US dollars. At least, that was what he said. It wasn't actually what he meant. In Cuba, money, like everything else, is complicated.

Prior to Castro's revolution the Cuban peso was pegged to the US dollar, afterwards it was pegged to the Soviet rouble. When the USSR collapsed in 1990, the Cuban peso went into freefall, but in the bleak years after the collapse of the Soviet Union when even the Spartan supplies from the rest of the communist world dried up, the only option was to use the currency of the hated enemy. Cubans duly dragged out piles of dollars sent from relatives in the US and hidden under mattresses and for half a dozen years the *dolar* became the only money worth having.

Then, in 2004, George W. Bush decided he would do his bit to win the vote of anti-communist Cuban exiles in Miami and increased sanctions against Havana. In an admirable (if rash) fit of pique, Fidel responded by banning the use of the dollar. Its place was taken by the 'convertible peso' (already in circulation but not so widely used as the greenback). Ever since that has been the currency of necessity for foreigners and desire for Cubans. It is pegged to the US dollar, which means there are 25 ordinary (or *nacional*) pesos to every one convertible peso. The former are officially designated CUP (but universally simply called 'pesos') while the latter are designated CUCs, and usually called that too, phonetically pronounced 'kooks'.

It sounds complicated, and it is, but it can be literally a matter of life and death in Cuba. There is not a whole lot you can buy with CUPs. Most bars in Havana and shops selling a limited variety of goods you get anywhere in most other countries deal only in CUCs, which means no ordinary Cuban can afford them. A doctor earns 500 national pesos a month – the equivalent of roughly US $20 (less than my cab fare). As the US-Americans say, 'go figure'.

The important thing is not to get the two confused. If you do, despite the intrinsic honesty of most Cubans, it's not hard to get taken for a mug, or to use a word that in the vernacular is almost equally insulting: a gringo.

On the way into the city my cab driver tells a caller on his mobile phone – the latest Cuban must-have but subject to interesting restrictions – to ring back because he has a gringo in his cab. To his surprise I immediately object. My

Spanish is not great but nor is it non-existent and I resent being referred to by what I have always considered to be the contemptuous term for a US-American.

The driver looks abashed for about half a millisecond then shrugs, and says no, it's not just Yankees, it's, 'You know...' and then dries up. I suddenly realize he is struggling to avoid racial stereotypes. Eventually by a mix of body language, gestures and euphemisms he conveys his meaning: a gringo is any pale-skinned northern European-looking bloke. It is the only form of, albeit mild, racism I am to perceive in my whole Cuban adventure.

He admits to being surprised I understood. Most gringos, I gather, don't speak much Spanish. Most of the pale-skinned northern European-looking blokes he meets come from Canada, so-called snow geese fleeing the winter. They too are, however, allowed to be called *Americanos*, which must make Cuba about the only place in the world where Canadians (if they understood) might take it as a compliment.

This got us talking enough for him to point out – if only to save his embarrassment by changing the subject – that the black BMW hurtling past us on the inside belongs to the South African ambassador. He knows this because Cuban number plates have a colour code. Black is for diplomats, with a number to signal their country, white is for government ministers, red for the tourist industry including hire cars, brown for the armed forces, green for agriculture, blue for all other state-owned vehicles (which in a communist country accounts for a huge proportion), and yellow for private vehicles, which by the bizarre logic of Cuba's economy makes yellow the rarest colour.

So how is Cuba these days, I ask him, meaning, without spelling it out, post-Fidel, a world that as yet most Cubans are not quite sure has really arrived? I'm not really expecting an answer other than 'wonderful as ever', the sort of North Korean-style 'dear leader' reply that was common among the few Cubans who would talk to foreigners a decade or so ago. Since the man who *was* the Cuban revolution stood down from power in 2008 in favour of his younger brother, there have been some reforms and rumours of reforms. Change is afoot in Cuba, even if it is not exactly generational change: Raúl turns eighty-two in 2013 and Big Brother, heading for ninety, is still watching.

My driver's answer, though not exactly critical, surprises me: 'Better.' Better? I ask in astonishment. Better under Raúl than under the sainted Fidel? In what way? 'There are big changes,' he offers voluntarily. 'Now it is okay to do business.' Isn't that just the tiniest bit capitalist, I hint, using the dreaded 'c' word. He shrugs, thinks a second and gives me one of those gems of wisdom that on the right day cab drivers the world over are capable of producing: 'Greed is not good, but making money is never bad.'

Then he drops me at the corner of Plaza Vieja, and with a broad smile pockets his 25 CUC, more money than a brain surgeon would make in a month.

I am a few yards' walk from my hotel along cobbled streets too narrow for motor vehicles. The Plaza Vieja, literally Old Square, is one of the most atmospheric in all Havana, popular not least because of the Austrian joint venture brewpub in one corner, and the inevitable *trova*[3] band playing on the terrace. It is teeming with tourists: French, Spanish, German, Italian, most of them European, including a few Brits, and a goodly number of Canadians, although as it is summer, most of the snow geese have flown back up north.

La Meson de la Flota is the smallest of the hotels operated

---

3. *Trova* along with *son*, *danzón*, *salsa* and about a dozen other variations of traditional Cuban music was made famous by the 1999 film, *Buena Vista Social Club*.

by Habaguanex, the state-run company that runs most of Old Havana's hotels. La Meson in reality is little more than a pub with three upstairs rooms. It was once an old pirate haunt and now prides itself on a nightly flamenco show.

After dumping my bags and an ice-cold glass of Cristal, one of the two main Cuban beer brands aimed at those wealthy enough to be able to pay in CUCs (the other is the stronger, sweeter Bucanero), I stroll out into the warm sticky afternoon heat to reacquaint myself with a city that is forever being built and forever falling down.

Since 1982 Havana Vieja, the heart of the city founded by the Spanish and one of the most important staging points for their conquest of the New World, has been a UNESCO World Heritage site. It receives UN funds and restoration of its historic centre is a national priority, not least because since the early 1990s and the demise of the Soviet Union, one of the prime props on which Cuban communism depended, tourism has become a keystone to the economy. Or what passes for an economy.

At first glance it is hard to tell whether much of Havana is being rebuilt, restored, reconstructed, demolished or simply in the long process of crumbling. The reality is that all of those are true. One of the hardest things Havana has to cope with is its location. Most of the hurricanes which each summer smash into the south coast of the United States, from Miami to New Orleans, take a glancing blow at Cuba on the way past. In 2008 Hurricane Ike decided to stop over for a few days and all but undid a decade of painstaking restoration work.

Curiously the most striking thing about Old Havana, particularly in comparison to the rest of the city, not to mention the rest of the country, is how clean it is. There are waste bins on every corner, street cleaners sweeping religiously. And everywhere you look there are police – not secret police, we will come to them later – but tourist police: the *Policía Especializada* in neat blue-grey uniforms on both men and women, in the latter case augmented by striking black fishnet tights worn under the ubiquitous miniskirts.

These are a very different force from the mainstream national police, the *Policía Nacional Revolucionaria*, a few of whom are also in evidence. Havana is Cuba's public face, and apart from a few gated tourist resorts, all most visitors ever get to see.

The best old colonial buildings have been turned into grandiose hotels: splendid marble edifices such as the Hotel Saratoga, Palacio O'Farrill, Hotel Santa Isabel, the newly opened and immodestly named Hotel Palacio del Marqués de San Felipe y Santiago de Bejucal, and the grand if a little creaky Ambos Mundos (Both Worlds) famed for being Ernest Hemingway's hangout in the late 1930s and early 1940s. Havana is even worse than Paris when it comes to bars trading on their history as Hemingway hangouts. Perhaps all writers should leave calling cards in pubs they pop into, just on the off-chance. I'd have run out long ago.

But then Havana in its hedonistic heyday, in what it did not know at the time was the terminal stages of capitalism, was a magnet for writers fleeing demons of one sort or another. Graham Greene stayed in the huge pink slab of the Hotel Sevilla and gave the same room to James Wormold, his vacuum cleaner salesman turned reluctant secret agent in *Our Man in Havana*. The book was published in 1958 but the film starring Alec Guinness was made a year later in the immediate wake of the revolution. Castro complained it did not accurately depict the brutality of the Batista regime, but watching it today is primarily a depressing reminder of how much Havana's fabric has deteriorated since then.

Nowhere is this more evident than on the Malecón, the sweeping seaside promenade which stretches for nearly three miles in a gentle curve from Old Havana to beyond the great 1930s edifice of the Hotel Nacional. Once the headquarters of the American mafia headed by gangster Lucky Luciano and with Winston Churchill among its pre-revolutionary celebrity guests, the Nacional is now like some old dowager, rather down-at-heel but still trading on past glories. Its chief claim to fame is the regular performances of the Tropicano cabaret, which for all the *mulata* beauties and daring dress sense displayed along the Malecón, is like watching a troupe of Bolton amateur dramatics ladies pretending to be Las Vegas showgirls.

The Malecón itself is Havana's communal living-room. At four o'clock on a clammy sunny afternoon the sea wall is lined with natives armed only with a bottle or two of hooch and here and there a guitar, a trumpet or a few trombones. Cuba and its music are inseparable. Ever since Ry Cooder's celebrated film *Buena Vista Social Club* made some of its veteran artistes global names, Havana has traded on the legend.

These guys are not here for the tourists. They are making music for themselves, and anyone who cares to listen. On the rocks beyond them Cubans strip down and plunge into the waves to cool off. Boys with fishing rods made, Huckleberry Finn-style, from bamboo canes and catgut hope for a catch that will make a better meal than anything that can be bought in the CUP 'peso shops'.

Across the road a couple of young men in shorts are drinking from a bottle on a perilously insecure looking rooftop balustrade, four storeys up, their legs dangling over the edge. Once the Malecón was lined with chic cafés; today it is a panorama of neglect, peeling pastel colours, Formica-topped tables outside seedy bars busy in the evening with freelance prostitutes plying their trade. One building stands out, set a little way back: an eight-storey concrete slab which incongruously claims to be the Swiss Embassy but in reality houses the US Interests Section, Washington's representation in Havana since it broke off diplomatic relations in 1961.

Heading back towards the hotel I am shocked to find scaffolding surrounding one particular grand old building that looks almost as if it is being prepared for demolition. Surely not. If any building in Havana is sacrosanct so long as a Castro is at the helm, it has to be the Museo de la Revolución. This is the museum that boasts the exploding cigar supposedly sent by the CIA to kill Fidel, pictures of the great man himself wielding a baseball bat (in sport not violence, he was allegedly a great player in his day), rifles and prison uniforms, documents and old banknotes, and most significantly of all, housed in a glass showcase of its own, *Granma*, the 'yacht' on which Castro and his colleagues evaded coastguards to sneak back into Cuba to prepare their rebellion.

But the museum is merely having an external facelift. Just around the corner sits *Granma* in all her glory, a rather dowdy little 1940s motorboat originally owned by a sentimental sailor who named it after his grannie, never imagining that one day it would be preserved in glass and give its name to Cuba's national newspaper, a baseball team and an entire province.

Around *Granma* like an honour guard of old troopers stands a collection of military memorabilia, including a Hawker Sea Fury propeller plane and a tank used to repel the US-sponsored Bay of Pigs invasion by anti-communist Cuban exiles in April 1961. There is a surface-to-air missile and the engine of a US Lockheed U-2 spy plane shot down by one of its kind. A diligent soldier of the Fuerzas Armadas Revolucionarias (Revolutionary Armed Forces) stands guard over them.

Breathing a sign of relief that the world hasn't ended yet I decide to give La Meson a chance for dinner, more in hope than expectation. There is always the flamenco to look forward to. Culinary delights are few and far between. I am told there are great Cuban restaurants in Miami. Maybe the chefs all emigrated.

The one thing I know I am not going to eat is the lobster. This is another one of those Cuban conundrums. There is an old saying in the world of journalism that whenever more than six hacks are gathered together for dinner they all will eat lobster. Apocryphally this is because one of them is bound to order it and it being bad form to do anything but divvy up the bill equally, everybody else decides they'd better have it too.

Price is not the reason I am not going to have the lobster. Cuba is one of the cheapest places in the world to eat lobster. The waters are teeming with them. And local people are expressly banned from catching them. Precisely because of their perceived desirability as a luxury dish lobsters are sold only for CUCs, which effectively means only to foreigners, so government-licensed fishing boats are the only ones allowed to catch them, and state-owned restaurants are the only ones allowed to serve them.

For all its homeliness, La Meson is owned by Habaguanex, which is a state organization, so lobster is on the menu. I know because I can see it. There has been a lobster slowly turning over a low heat spit since I left my bags, nearly two hours ago. Which means, you will have gathered, that by now it will have at best the consistency of one of those rubber models of lobsters you might see in a low-quality fishmonger's window display.

Instead, at the waitress's suggestion, I order the grilled pork with something called 'a Cuban salad', which instinctively sounds like a contradiction in terms. I should have known better, but sometimes the hard way is the only way.

What finally arrives masquerading as a salad, is some cubes of rubbery processed cheese, accompanied by a few olives and a sprig of coriander. The Waldorf will not be worried. The pork, which turns up some time later, isn't much of an improvement. Cuba must be one of the only places in the world where seafood is grilled for hours and pork for a few seconds. My grilled kebab is a few lumps of tough pinky-white meat on a skewer by the side of a spoonful of relatively inoffensive bland rice and a few soggy plantain chips. Lurking next to it is something that looks like mashed potato and has a very similar consistency but tastes disconcertingly like banana flavour Angel Delight. I wonder vaguely to myself if the milkshake mix brought by the large lady from Santo Domingo might have made it through customs after all.

Thank God for the flamenco dancers. I have seen flamenco put on for tourists in Seville, Spain, which is supposed to be its home. Compared to this it was Ann Widdecombe on *Strictly Come Dancing*. As passion goes this is on the level of throwing a grenade into a firework factory. Two young women in their twenties strapped into corsets with dresses figure-huggingly tight to the waist then exploding into a riot of swirling satin strut, stomp and stamp their way across the raised wooden stage, whirling to twanging guitar chords and a drumbeat reminiscent of a voodoo rite. Mesmerizing. The audience, me amongst them, sits in rapt wonder, as do the Cubans standing in crowds outside – unable to afford the two CUC for a beer but taking advantage of the fact that the tropical heat means the bar is wide open to the street.

It is almost to exorcize the contagious fervour that after digesting what little I could of my dinner, I stroll through the old town up towards the Plaza de la Catedral for a glimpse of one of the New World's most glorious old buildings softly lit by floodlights under the dark tropical sky.

Described by Cuban writer Alejo Carpentier as 'music set in stone', this baroque gem was built by Jesuits in the mid-eighteenth century on the site of an older building. It is too easy for us Europeans – and many North Americans – to forget how ancient some of the great buildings of Latin America really are. Columbus landed here on his first great voyage in 1492. Havana was founded in 1519, when Henry VIII was a mere boy on the throne of England. And it is not the island's oldest city.

That honour belongs to remote Baracoa, at the opposite end of the island. It was founded nearly a decade earlier, but lost any chance of becoming the capital because for hundreds of years its location surrounded by high mountains made it inaccessible other than by sea. This situation lasted until the 1960s when putting a road through became one of the token great projects of the revolution's early days.

The nearest city of any size to distant Baracoa is the one that is the destination of my planned journey: Guantánamo. For all the evil that word has come to evoke one way or another since the United States turned the bit of Cuban land it has controversially squatted on for a century into an incarceration camp for 'enemy combatants' in its 'war on terror', for Cubans it remains primarily the subject of one of their island's most haunting and evocative melodies. Almost an alternative national anthem.

And here and now in front of one of the most beautiful cathedrals in the Americas it is that song that fills the air, played by a little chamber orchestra sat out in the warm night across the cobble-stones: *Guantanamera, guajira Guantanamera*. A 1920s song about love for a simple country girl from the remote provinces, long since fused with words from that great mad romantic José Martí's words to become Cuba's alternative sentimental national anthem: *Yo soy un hombre sincero, de donde crece la palma.* (I am an honest man from where the palm tree grows.)

It is hard to hear it in circumstances such as these – lilting strings, moonlight, a beautiful baroque cathedral illuminated by a warm yellow light, swaying palm trees while an elegant elderly black couple dressed in full colonial fig pose for cameras, he in white trousers, wide-brimmed straw hat, black jacket and silver-knobbed cane, she in full petticoated dress and bonnet – and not have the word Guantánamo conjure up anything a vision of heavenly enchantment.

Now all I have to do is work out how the hell to get there.

CHAPTER THREE

In Training

Breakfast is something of relief, primarily because the Cuban breakfast does not require much cooking. My plate of sliced pineapple, mango and papaya accompanied by thick mango juice and hot dark coffee hits the spot. The decision to take it at an outside table loses its charm when almost immediately a municipal drain clearing machine parks itself a metre way and begins sucking goop noisily from a manhole.

Nobody else seems to mind. And I am far from alone. By now the outside tables are packed with the *Policía Especializada*, puffing away on cheap cigarettes, swigging coffee – in one case at least accompanied by a tot of white rum – and joking boisterously with one another, not least because some of the female officers have difficulty maintaining a modicum of decency crossing their legs in those ridiculously short skirts. The black fishnets, it seems, are regulation issue in almost every government position.

Breakfast has a hot course too. One I am to discover is absolutely standard everywhere I go, not least because it relies on the one form of intensive farming that works: eggs. The choice does not automatically include a boiled egg. And I am more than happy with the options suggested – *revuelto* (scrambled) or *tortilla*. The latter turns up in seconds. Proving – as we Anglophones used to a myriad varieties of English know only too well – that the same word in the same language does not necessarily mean the same thing in different places, the Cuban tortilla is nothing like either Spain's thick potato omelette, or Mexico's corn-based burrito wrapper. Order a tortilla in Havana and what you get is a rich eggy omelette, as thin as a French crêpe, well seasoned, and with a bit of sliced onion on the side. Surprisingly delightful. I feel set up for the day.

And it is to be quite a day. First things first. I need to get to the railway station and find out about train timings. The Estación Central de Ferrocarriles (Central Railway Station – even though it is actually the only railway station in Havana proper) is situated to the south-west of the old town, on the other side of the main central artery that divides the ancient part of the city from the great sprawl of the districts known as Centro Havana and Vedado, much of which dates only from the nineteenth and twentieth centuries.

The great landmark that sits on the broad boulevard that is officially known as the Paseo de Martí (that man again) but everyone simply refers to as the Prado, is the Capitolio. This is a magnificent copy of the Capitol in Washington DC, one of those facts that seems to confirm the image of Cuba as an image of the United States seen in a distorted fairground mirror. It was finished in 1929 and for a mere 28 years from 1931 until the revolution in 1959 was the seat of government. It now houses the Academy of Sciences. And is open as a museum. To itself.

Wander beyond it though into the streets of Centro or Vedado and you are in the Cuba that does not receive generous UNESCO grants for restoration. The result is, well, to put it delicately: rubble. Or soon to be rubble. There is hardly a tenement block that does not appear to be made of fast crumbling concrete. Washing hangs on lines stretched across balconies that appear to defy gravity by remaining tenuously attached to the buildings they protrude from.

Cubans lean on them and shout to one another across the street. I wouldn't stand on one if you paid me.

It is hot, sticky – 29°C (84°F) and 80 per cent humidity, which is pretty much standard for Cuba most of the year round – and the streets are crowded both with pedestrians and motor vehicles, of one sort or another. Two things immediately strike me as having changed since my previous visit four years earlier. First there are no more of the idiosyncratic, slow, dirty and dangerous buses known as *camellos* for the simple reason that they were hump-backed. Instead there are now Chinese-built bendy buses that not too long ago must have been shiny. Secondly, and this has an almost tragic note, there are far fewer of the ancient iconic American automobiles that have become Cuba's accidental global trademark.

They are still there, of course, 1950s Chevrolets and Cadillacs, their bright painted colours – sometimes renewed with a lick of gloss – defying their rusting bodywork. But it is only here, in front of the Capitolio, where they line up to offer rides to tourists, that I realize how few of them I have seen compared to just four years ago. In fact, the more I think of it, the more I realize I have seen a greater number up on bricks or in final stages of decomposition by the roadside than actually on the road. It may be a sign of changing times, or it may be just that at long last these old workhorses – never designed as such but forced into the role by the US embargo and a curiously egalitarian-inspired communist ban on private car sales – may finally be coming to the end of the road. There is a limit to how long soldering irons, sewing needles and coat hangers can keep a car on the road when it lacks spare parts that, even were there no embargo, have been unavailable for more than four decades.

In their place there are, from a nostalgic romantic's point of view, a depressing number of nondescript, relatively modern, blue-number-plated Peugeots, similar to my taxi from the airport. These appear to have become the government import car of choice. Yet as one emblem of romantic nostalgia fades away, another emerges. As the elegant dinosaurs of the golden age of American capitalism slowly edge towards extinction, their place as iconic totems is being taken by the woolly mammoths of the golden age of global communism: the imports of the Soviet era. Here and there I spot an East German Trabant (its composite body signally suited to the tropical climate, as long as it doesn't go soggy in the hurricane season) or a rusty Wartburg, and a host of Moskviches and Ladas. To someone like me who lived and worked in Eastern Europe, they too are now especially evocative of a vanished world.

I am standing outside the garishly painted El Floridita, which boasts of being Havana's most famous bar and the home of the Hemingway daiquiri (it is certainly the most expensive place in Cuba to drink one), although not where it was invented (more on that later). A vehicle pulls up outside to put a smile on my face I would never have imagined, a perfect automobile incarnation of the two worlds that Cuba still schizophrenically straddles: an improvised stretch limo made up of two Russian Ladas. Amazing what the human imagination can do with a hacksaw and a welding gun.

I have another mode of transportation to the train station, however, one that suits the heat. Nowadays as visible in the wealthy metropolises of Chicago and London, the pedal-powered conveyance usually known as a bicycle rickshaw is called a *bicitaxi* in Cuba and, like so many things in this Caribbean communist anomaly, has had an evolution all of its own here. The main difference, for a start, is a general lack of proper saddles for the cyclist. The lean black guy in a red singlet and shorts I ask to take me to the station has manufactured a place for his posterior out of an ingenious crisscrossed set of bungee cords. It doesn't look comfortable but it appears to work.

The breeze caused by our motion is a blessed relief but the ride soon develops typical Cuban fairground qualities as we edge into traffic by a process of alarming wiggling turns to avoid potholes big enough to lose a leg in. All of this is accompanied by a strange series of whistles from my 'driver', not melodic, not constant, just sharp, frequent and met more often than not by similar responses from other *bicitaxi* guys. For a moment I wonder if they are communicating in some sort of code, and then as he emits a particularly strident whistle just as an elderly lady with an open basket of overripe bananas on her head steps into the street in front of us, I realize: nobody has a bell!

My driver also is as keen to chat as your average London cabbie with a foreigner in the back of his taxi. 'Where you from?' he starts in elementary English, repeating it in Spanish, a phrase I am to hear constantly over the coming weeks, '*De donde?*' I give him the easy answer, '*Inglaterra.*' 'Ah,' he says and then, just as we nearly run over a passing nun, he launches into a tirade in Spanish, disconcertingly turning his head very few seconds to make sure I understand, which I do, despite a shaky start primarily due to his subject. To my surprise, he is talking about the pope.

'You have good people in England and in Netherlands,' he says. 'I saw the pope visited your country and many people protested.'

Well yes, I think, but there were also a lot of people who turned out to welcome him. I have no idea where this is going. It is a totally unexpected conversation. He points to a tattoo on his arm which unfortunately means nothing to me and then goes on to tell me how nuns beat children and that the pope is a murderous pervert.

Whether this guy had a nasty childhood experience at the

hands of some Catholic clergy – enough people did – I have no idea, but I do know religion in Cuba is complicated to say the least, with a substantial fusion between Catholicism and old African religions. One way or another I am fairly certain that when Pope Benedict came to town in March 2012 – and even Raúl Castro turned out to meet him – this guy wasn't in the audience.

But his attention has now switched to making sure I pay him his fare (one CUC) as he deposits me outside a palatial but crumbling edifice that I take to be the central station. I can see the trains. Or at least some trains. Beautiful trains, but not trains I am going to be taking any day soon. Sadly. On traffic islands in the middle of the road behind railings sit several examples of the most wonderful nineteenth- and early twentieth-century steam locomotives, beautifully painted up and firmly out of action, relics of a distant past, a past when, I am about to learn, Cuban trains actually worked.

Right now I need to discover a timetable for those that still actually run, and how to buy a ticket. That turns out to a belief system all of its own.

The place to buy tickets, for a start, is not inside the main station building itself but in a special office just around the corner. I push open the door and find myself in what looks like the waiting-room at a British NHS hospital: filled with long lines of people sitting on plastic chairs, and not looking as if they expect to leave them any time soon. The only significant difference is that is hot as hell.

In front of them there is a line of little ticket windows, only one of which appears to be staffed. I spend a few minutes vaguely looking for timetables on the walls, or any information as to the system – in Spanish, I am not expecting anything in English – but find nothing more than a hook from which hangs a sheaf of papers that might be train numbers and times but look to me like Excel spreadsheets.

Over the next few minutes the woman at the ticket window calls two names and each time someone goes up, apparently collects a ticket or reservation and leaves. Happy. I walk up to her and attempt in halting Spanish to ask about train times. She stares at me as if I have landed from Mars and asked to be taken to her leader, and points to the end of the room, where I realize there is an open door with a policeman standing by it.

Not wholly encouraged by this I go over and realize the policeman – a burly black guy with *Policía Revolucionaria* (the ones who might actually have to deal with crime rather than just smile at tourists) on his sleeve – is also trying to buy a train ticket. From a little man sitting at a desk inside the door out of sight of everybody in the waiting-room. I do what seems sensible in the circumstances: I wait my turn.

Eventually the policeman, after displaying his identity card, goes away with a piece of paper with something written on it which, from the smile on his face I assume to be a ticket. The little man – I call him that not patronizingly but because he was one of those pale-skinned, pinched-faced, skinny characters in a waistcoat (in this heat!) who seemed to embody the global caricature of a railway clerk – looks up at me with mild bemusement on his face. Now for the hard bit.

'*Cuando* . . .' I start. I knew my Spanish was going to have to sink or swim on this trip. What I hadn't quite been prepared for was the heavier than expected Cuban accent. Happily the clerk was prepared to listen, and reply, in a close approximation of my pidgin *castellano*.

Spanish is every bit as global a language as English, and that means it's got every bit as many accents. *Castellano*, the language of Madrid and what you end up speaking if you learn Spanish in Europe, is actually quite difficult to pronounce properly, laden with lisps. For example, that most important of phrases, 'a beer please', is written '*una cerveza por favor*' but in a classic Madrid accent sounds something like '*una therbetha por fabor*'. In most of the new world, from Mexico down to the tip of Latin America it sounds more like '*una servesa por favor*'. Easier. Unless of course you have learned the other version first. And laid-back Cuba has a take on the lingo that is all its own.

But Cubans on the whole are remarkably educated people and my railway clerk has worked out that I want to know what time the trains left for the east. He has a simple answer: the train to Santiago de Cuba leaves at eight. What about the more local services? He smiles and repeated his answer. Yes, I smile back for politeness' sake, and to show him I have indeed understood what time the train to Santiago leaves, but I wasn't just asking about that one. It's not as if the train to Santiago can be the only train, can it? Can it? His response is simply to look even more amused and reply, '*Sí, el único.*' Yep, just the one.

I hadn't considered this possibility. Santiago is on my route, sort of. It is the second biggest city in Cuba, Havana's ancient rival in everything from sport to salsa. Guantánamo, the end of the line, lies beyond it. So at least getting on a train heading for Santiago is a step in the right direction. I can always get off and on along the line.

The only problem is, I don't want to leave today – I have things to sort out, like a mobile phone SIM card so I can ring ahead to book rooms – but I do want to leave in the next day or two. But most importantly I need to get back to Havana in time to catch my plane back to Britain. My plan is that having taken the slow route there, I'll take the fast route back, sampling the supposed luxury of the *tren frances,* the 'French train', supposed to be the pride of Ferrocarriles de Cuba, an overnight deluxe service direct from Santiago to

Havana. Under the circumstances booking in advance seems like a good idea, so I decide I might as well give it a go.

'Can I buy a ticket now from Santiago to Havana for the 20th?' I ask.

'To buy a ticket to Santiago, you should come back here on the 15th.'

'No, I want to buy a ticket for the train that leaves Santiago on the 20th.'

'Ah, for that you should go to the station in Santiago on the 15th.'

This is starting to look bad. I hadn't planned on getting to Santiago that long in advance. I had to get to Guantánamo first.

'Can't I buy it here, now?'

By now he's looking at me as if I've seriously lost my marbles. I'm beginning to understand the rest of the people in the waiting-room, why they were there, how long they had probably been waiting and why they'd sensibly left their brains at home.

'To buy a ticket from Santiago, you must be in Santiago,' he says, as if it were the most obvious thing in the world. He almost has me believing him too. That's the thing about Cuba: it has a logic all of its own.

'What would I do,' I ask aloud, aware that I might be getting into the realms of speculative fiction here, 'if I wanted to buy a ticket to go from here to Santiago tonight.'

He brightens up at that. 'That is not so hard. Then you should come back tonight. Two hours before the train is due to leave.'

'Could I buy a ticket now?'

'No. You must come back two hours before the train leaves. Then if there are any seats left, you can buy a ticket.'

Ah, the centavo was beginning to drop. I would be on standby. Better than nothing, but hardly reassuring.

Especially for the return journey when I would have a plane to catch.

'What if there are no seats left?' I ask, already anticipating the dreaded shrug of the shoulders so familiar to long-suffering travellers in the olden days in communist Eastern Europe. Instead I get me a beaming smile.

'You are a foreigner. You will pay in *convertibles*, CUCs, no? For CUCs there is always a seat. That is why you talk to me, see. This is desk for special travellers.'

His job, I suddenly realize, is only to deal with foreigners, and other privileged members of society. Like the large revolutionary policeman who'd picked up a ticket in front of me, who would have paid in pesos rather than CUC but would have been given priority. Everybody else had to book their journey days in advance at least, then come and queue up and wait to be told whether or not they'd got a seat.

The best joke is that they pretend we're all paying the same price. The tickets have the same face value, but which currency you are obliged to pay in, depends on who you are. As a foreigner paying in the convertible CUC rather than the CUP *peso nacional*, I would be handing over twenty-five times as much for a ticket with the same nominal face value. And even then, it seems, I can't buy a ticket now unless I want to leave this evening.

Somewhat in a daze I leave the office and wander up to the main station itself to see if I can pick up a printed copy of the national rail timetable. I'm beginning to think timetables might be rather thin on the ground, *if* – and I haven't quite got my head around this possibility which I would have considered distant but now seems to be approaching rather faster than any railway engine – such a thing as printed timetables actually exist at all.

Inside what might once have been a grand departure hall there are three information windows in a row. All boarded up. The fourth is open. Behind a cracked glass window a pretty, chubby black woman is munching something. I ask her what time the next train leaves. (I know, I had already been told the answer but my brain is reluctant to take it in: even on a slow Sunday in Britain services aren't that limited. Surely there has to be one to somewhere at some time over the next eight hours.)

'Eight o'clock,' she says. 'To Santiago.'

'That's the only one today?' She looks amused even to be asked the question. 'Have you got a timetable?' I try. She giggles and offers me some of her huge bag of popcorn.

Declining the popcorn as gracefully as possible under the circumstances, I try asking her – just in case I might get a different answer – about the *tren frances*. Does it run every night?

She shrugs. 'Every night? *Todas las noches*?' I'm starting to get desperate.

Wide eyes. 'Nooooo.'

'Alternate nights?'

'More or less.'

More or less!?! 'How do I find out? Can I buy a ticket now for a specific date?'

Her face cracks up into a beaming smile as if to say you're having a laugh, mate.

'In Santiago. They'll tell you in Santiago. Buy a ticket there.'

I give her a look of incredulity. She gives me another huge smile and a phrase I'm going to hear again and again: '*Cuba e' Cuba*.' Cuba is Cuba.

On the rows of plastic seats facing the platforms a dozen or so people are sitting staring at a few diesel locomotives that don't look as if they had any intention of moving. Ever. I have no idea whether the people staring at them might have just dropped in for a sit-down, a sort of extremely sedentary

form of trainspotting, or if they really are prospective passengers intending to sit there for another eight hours. I'm
not about to do either. Time to find a phone, or at least a
SIM card.

Mobile phones have become such a part of the modern
world that it is hard to imagine what life was like without them. In Cuba you can find out. I had deliberately not
brought my iPhone with me because it includes a GPS
tracker and it is illegal to bring any such device into Cuba
without the express permission of the military, a stipulation
about which I have to say many tourists these days never
even find out. Instead I had brought an old mobile – though
still reasonable by standards of five years ago – tri-band so
I knew it would work on whatever passed for the Cuban
network.

Under Fidel Castro mobile phones in Cuba were only for
government employees. Under his trendy octogenarian kid
brother the regulations have been opened up: now anybody
can have one. Anybody who can afford one, that is. A mobile
is the must-have accessory for young Cubans. All I had to
do, I had been told, was to buy a local SIM card and have my
phone registered to work on the local network. Easy.

Except that I had forgotten the golden rule: in Cuba
nothing is easy. A couple of the smarter hotels claimed to
offer mobile phone services, notably the Inglaterra and the
Sevilla. In the plush chintzy lobby of the Inglaterra, the one
person equipped to deal with such high technology issues
is at lunch. She would be back shortly, I'm told. I sip a cold
Cristal at the bar and wait. After 25 minutes a large and
rather severe mulatto lady arrived at the desk.

I stroll over and ask if I can buy a SIM card. She looks
at me in amazement. No, sorry that is not possible, she
says as if I've asked her for Raúl Castro's private line. She
could sell me a top-up if I already had a Cuban SIM, but

only if my phone was already registered. Which, obviously, it isn't. Can I register? No, sorry. Same look. That can only be done at an office of ETECSA, the national telecommunications agency. Preferably the main one on Obispo Street in Havana Vieja.

With that sinking feeling that this wasn't going to be as simple as I had hoped, I trudge off towards Obispo, half expecting the office to be closed. It isn't. It's open. In a very Cuban definition of the word 'open': that is to say the doors were actually closed. Locked in fact. And with a heavyset doorman standing there to make sure they stay like that until he decides there is room inside for more customers. Given that there are at least 50 people queuing up on the street outside that could be some time. Maybe several hours.

This is not good. I need a phone primarily to call ahead and book accommodation wherever it looks like I am going to end up each day. To my relief a woman in the crowd tells me there is another ETECSA office, located in a warehouse turned into a tourist art market down near the port, 'just past the Russian church'. That is no more than fifteen minutes' walk away so I head off following her rough directions. Havana sits on a large irregular bay, one of the world's natural harbours (one argument about how it got its names is that it comes for the Dutch and German words for harbour, another however is that it was named after a native chieftain). All I have to do is head for the Malecón, turn right and sooner or later I'll get there.

It turns out, as most things do, to be further than I expect. But I realize I am getting near when I spot a bizarrely incongruous golden onion dome, surrounded by four smaller undecorated ones. The building could be ageless, built in traditional style, its distinctively Russian domes topped with crosses wholly incongruous against the colonial Spanish architecture of Havana Vieja and the decrepit warehouses of the port.

It seems more than improbably out of place. I am also astonished – given years spent living in the Soviet Union and visits to countless Russian Orthodox churches – that I did not spot it on my previous visit to Cuba. It seems highly unlikely that it belongs to the old Cuban–Soviet partnership of the Cold War years; under the Kremlin's atheist communists even the churches in Moscow were falling into disrepair. Is this some far more ancient relic, of a Tsarist presence in the Caribbean? That seems no more likely.

I climb the steps and peer inside. It is empty, the whitewashed walls contrasting sharply with a magnificent golden reredos inlaid with stylized icons of the saints. A plaque on the wall tells me I am standing in the Havana Cathedral of Our Lady of Kazan, date of construction: 2006. This 'house of God' is, it would seem, the main token of reconciliation between two countries once united in their devotion to communism and atheism.

If I think the world has turned topsy-turvy, I can hardly imagine what Fidel Castro thinks. Over three decades, from the birth of Castro's revolution the 'great and powerful Soviet Union', as the words of Moscow's national anthem used to boast, kept the Cuban economy just about afloat by buying its sugar harvest in exchange for cheap oil, while Havana provided the Kremlin with a priceless communist thorn in Uncle Sam's underbelly. Until it all went belly-up in Moscow. Overnight Cuba lost 80 per cent of its export market, and 80 per cent of its imports. The 'special period', as the early 90s were known, took Cubans to the brink of starvation. The worst tales are apocryphal, such as melting condoms on top of pizza bases instead of cheese, but there genuinely were families forced to survive on little more than sugar and water.

And now at a time of fresh relations with a newly prosperous capitalist Russia, what do they give their erstwhile allies? A church. Unsurprisingly it seems Fidel came to the opening ceremony out of politeness, but made a point of leaving before the service.

That's when it dawns on me: there are, or would appear to be, no Russians in Havana. Once upon a time, back in the days when meeting a Russian on the wrong side of the Iron Curtain was as rare as a fillet steak in a Moscow butcher's there must have been thousands of them here: party officials, military men, scientists, most famously ballistic missile men. Now, when you can't walk down a street in London, Paris or Istanbul without being overwhelmed by Russians and they have virtually bought up Cyprus (only to find it was a bad bargain), there are none evident, this church notwithstanding, in Cuba. I have heard Italian, French, German, Chinese, Japanese and English in the busy streets of Old Havana, but not a word of Russian. The reason for this is obvious, of course: they still have communism here. And that is something modern Russians definitely want no part of.

This digression hasn't sorted my mobile though. Happily the directions I was given were right. The warehouse on the other side of the road, as well as being home to various garish painting of street scenes being hawked to tourists, contains a little white cabin with ETECSA on the side. And there is no queue. Well, no queue to get in and only four people waiting ahead of me inside.

When I get to the front of the queue I find out why. This ETECSA office doesn't do mobile: 'You have to go to the office on Obispo.' But there's a queue a mile long, I protest. Yes, she nods. There usually is. *Cuba e' Cuba.* 'I can sell you a phone card,' she says. 'That's what most people use.' A phone card! I dimly remember them from that odd interim period when few people had mobiles and we still had lots of phone boxes but they wouldn't take coins any more. But hey, back to the future. It's better than nothing, which is what I have now.

'They cost five pesos,' she says. I pull out a five-CUC note and she just as she is about to take it the woman behind me says, 'Do you need to call abroad?' 'No,' I say, because I don't really, not least because I know although you can call anywhere in the world from Havana the flow of information is restricted by the price. For a call to Europe, five CUCs would last about 80 seconds.

'So get a peso card,' she says. The woman behind the desk shrugs – that's the thing about everyone working for the government, it's no skin off her nose – and hands me an almost identical card. At which point I am very grateful that I also changed some of my CUCs into national pesos: I changed 10 CUC and got 250 CUP pesos. I give her a grubby five, and she hands me the card, telling me calls within Cuba cost five cents a minute (that's 'national' cents, or a twentieth of a twenty-fifth of a US dollar: less than 0.1 US cents. Virtually free!)

First I have to make sure I know how it works. Which means I have to have someone to call. But that isn't a problem. I have just found my train out of Havana, advertised on the first railway timetable I have seen, pinned on the wall opposite, next to the dock for the little ferry dock across the bay. It was a train I had heard had fallen into disuse and had little hope of being able to take. But it is allegedly still running: and not just any train, one of the most famous in all Cuba: the Hershey Train.

Back in 1922 when the global giant confectionary company that started out in Hershey, Pennsylvania, still got most of its sugar from Cuba it built a little electric railway to bring workers from the countryside to its sugar mill. The reason its timetable is by the ferry dock is that the Hershey train doesn't leave from Havana proper, but from the evocatively named suburb on the other side of the bay: Casablanca. Say it again, Sam!

The train goes to Matanzas, capital of the neighbouring province and about 80 kilometres (50 miles) east of Havana, a fine first stop on my itinerary. I have a list of *casas particulares* downloaded from the internet before I left England. Now seems to be the right time to try to ring one in the hope of making sure I have a bed for the night, assuming that the timetable is accurate and the train is indeed running. Right now I am not taking anything for granted. It turns out to be a wise move.

The instructions on the phone card tells me to scratch off the silver coating, just like on a national lottery scratch card, to find my personal code. Underneath is a 13-digit number. I lift the receiver, insert the card into the phone and immediately an officious automated voice tells me to take it out because it isn't valid. I try again. Same thing. At that point I look at the card a bit more loosely and notice there is a 'use by' date on the top. 'Use by 14 March' it says. It is now mid-June.

Annoyed at being taken for an idiot, I storm back into the cabin and point this out to the girl behind the desk. She looks at me as if I *am* an idiot, and points to the sign on the door. It says: 'Please note that all cards which say use by 14 March are valid until December.' D'uh? She shrugs and says: '*Cuba e' Cuba*'.

Back to the phone cabin again. I try the same thing but still no luck. By now there is a queue of people waiting. In despair I ask one of them what I am doing wrong. It turns out I shouldn't insert the card at all. At least not first. First I have to press a button and wait for a voice to tell me to enter the 13-digit number, *then* enter the card. Obvious really.

Except that that doesn't work either. 'No, no,' the woman waiting for her turn to use the phone, tells me, 'You do it too quick; the machine cannot keep up. Slowly.'

I do what she says, watching her smile at the foreign idiot unable to cope with technology, one button at a time, each one recognized by a beep. Suddenly I am through, at least to an automatic operator.

There is a plus side to this. The automated voice asks me if I want to change *idioma* to *inglés*. Yes please. Immediately the rather stern formal Spanish is replaced by what sounds like a sassy Florida American. 'Please dial yore numbah'. I do, only to get: '*Wrang* number, check it up.' It would be funny, except that 'wrong number' isn't what I want to hear.

Checking my phone number once again, it dawns on me that I might have forgotten to include an area code. I try again and this time a phone at the other end rings. And rings. And rings. Eventually someone at the other end picks up. A child. Sounding about five years old. But obviously a bright child who fairly quickly understands that he is talking to a gringo, and therefore has to use the sort of language you would employ when, well, talking to a child.

A few seconds later an adult voice comes on, makes the same deduction, but nonetheless takes my name and says that someone will be there to meet the Hershey Train which leaves Casablanca at midday and usually – there is a long pause before the 'usually' – gets in around 4 p.m. Yes! I put down the receiver with something approaching a glint of triumphalism. I have actually achieved something. I have a phone card, a room booked for tomorrow night and the departure time – more or less – of a train that might get me there.

And opposite me is the Museo del Ron, not just a museum of rum but a cool place to sample it with music of the old

Buena Vista boys playing in the background. I sit down and sip on an ice-cold mojito, mint and rum mingling to soothe my mood. Don't stop me now! Havana good time! I'm on the road at last.

CHAPTER FOUR

Hershey Bar

I'm not actually on the road of course, rail or otherwise. First I've got to cross the sea, or at least the bit of it that separates Havana proper from Casablanca, and the Hershey railway terminus.

This means getting up rather earlier than I had anticipated for a midday train. Guidebooks published in 2010 said the ferry across the bay goes twice an hour. The timetable down by the ferry itself, however, suggested it was once an hour at most. When I asked at the hotel, a waitress suggested it might be more like once every two hours.

Similarly the Hershey train itself, which once upon a time ran hourly, is now only three times a day, the first before 8 o'clock in the morning, which is out of the question, chiefly because that is before the first ferry.

Following my mojitos of the previous afternoon, I had decided to treat myself to a rooftop dinner at one of the private *paladares*, the confusingly-named Moneda Cubana, confusing because it definitely did not accept Cuban money, at least not the sort most ordinary Cubans have. *Moneda nacional* was not welcome. The big sign by the door made clear: 'CUC only'.

Two of the steps that have done most to make life easier for a relatively large minority of ordinary Cubans were in fact introduced in the wake of the Soviet collapse and the resultant economic hardship. When it became clear tourism was an inevitable part of the answer, the government in 1997 allowed private individuals to rent out a room to foreigners for CUCs, in exchange for them paying to the treasury a large monthly tax, also in CUCs. These *casas particulares* (literally private houses) had the advantage for visitors – and disadvantage for the government – that it meant ordinary Cubans could meet foreigners more easily. But it also for the first time provided an ample supply of accommodation beyond the spattering of official hotels.

The obvious answer to the shortage of restaurants, the other most obvious way to soak up hard currency the foreigners might otherwise be loath to part with (especially given the shortage of things to buy) was to apply the same logic: tolerate a bit of private enterprise on a family-only scale and then tax it.

From the mid 1990s onwards the government allowed ordinary Cubans to open up their living-rooms or roof terraces if they had them to serve meals to foreigners for CUCs. Bizarrely they acquired the name *paladares* not from any government decree or popular tradition but from a Brazilian soap opera, *Vale Tudo*, popular in Cuba when private restaurants were first legalized. The main character ran a chain of restaurants called *paladar*, which means 'palate' in both Spanish and Portuguese. If you want a crash course in a Mastermind special subject on South American soap operas, Cuba is the place to come. They lap up all of them.

La Moneda Cubana is one of the oldest of Havana's *paladares*. It occupies a magnificent location near the western end of the Malecón with a fine view from its rooftop eating space over the cathedral square, the bay with the old Spanish fortifications on both the Havana and Casablanca sides. It is a great spot to watch the sun go down, and enjoy the spectacle at 9 p.m. each evening of a great old cannon being fired across the bay. It helps of course if you know about that bit in advance. I didn't and ended up with a substantial splash of mojito in my lap when it went off behind me.

This time, as I was leaving in the morning and not at all sure what food would be like in the interior provinces, I broke my rule and had the lobster, or at least a small version of one in a mixed seafood platter. This was a private restaurant, after all. They could, I reasoned, be expected to be better cooks than the employees of the state-run hotels. I won't make that mistake again.

I spent the remainder of the evening, while picking bits of rubberized seafood out from between my teeth, wandering the atmospheric streets of the old town, along Obispo and Obra Pia, names redolent with ancient Catholicism – Bishop Street and Pious Works Street – now awash with rum, beer, tourists and natives swaying to bands in ever bar playing *trova*, *danzón*, *rumba*, *timba* and *son*. Cuban music traditions, with their mix of Latino tunes, jazz improvisation and heady rhythms derived from African drumming are more than worthy of a book in their own right, but nothing quite equates to just soaking it up, or taking to the floor with the Cubans.

Sometimes that can be hard to avoid. Most bars have at least a proportion of working girls – and guys – in residence. This does not mean prostitutes. Prostitution is illegal in Cuba as well as the sort of sleazy sex industry that flourished in Havana when Meyer Lansky's Jewish and Italian mafia gangs ran the girls and gambling emporia of the 1930s and later. Pimps are next to non-existent in Castro's Cuba, but ironically it is one area in which freewheeling capitalism flourishes. There are more than enough girls – and guys – in Havana willing to give a tourist a good time – by no means necessarily involving sex (since prostitution is illegal) – as long as they get to share a taste of the good life they can't otherwise afford.

Each bar will have at least one 'dance instructor' of each sex, who may well be just that – to encourage shy Canadian 'snow geese' to get up and enjoy themselves, maybe just to spend a bit more money behind the bar, maybe to splash out on a bit of 'extra fun'. Or maybe not. The latter was the option I chose when unexpectedly an extremely giggly large round black lady perched on a stool next to me and asked me if I wanted to *salsa*. When I politely declined, she suggested I might prefer something a bit more *piccante*. Maybe I would like her to be my girlfriend for my holidays. Like they used to say at the *News of the World*, I made my excuses and left.

Which is how I manage to be relatively bright-eyed and bushy-tailed heading out of La Meson de la Flota at 7.30 in the morning, strolling with a fair wind at my back (or would be if there was any wind rather than the constant oppressive tropical heat) towards the ferry terminal in time to catch the 08.00 to Casablanca. There is supposed to be a 10.00 ferry as well but nobody is willing to swear to that, and I'm gradually getting the message that getting anywhere takes a lot longer than expected.

Except now that I'm there, it doesn't look as if they're going to let me on. A fierce woman with dangly earrings, the regulation state micro-miniskirt girding her ample *derrière* above the equally obligatory fishnets, is aggressively wielding a metal detector in the direction of my rucksack.

'*Bagaje, no,*' she insists. No luggage. This is something I hadn't reckoned on. This is hardly an international flight after all, nor even a long-distance crossing. The journey time is no more than 10 minutes across the bay, and the ferry itself a single-decked square rust-bucket – little better than a motorized raft with a roof– with standing room only and place for a couple of bicycles.

But then I remember an anecdote I had heard and all but dismissed as a joke. Despite the wholly evident unseaworthiness of this dodgy looking excuse for a nautical vessel – the Woolwich ferry in South London is an ocean-going cruise liner in comparison – back in 2003 a gang of would-be emigrants hijacked one and tried to take it to Miami. It is perhaps 200 miles across the Florida Straits to Key West; these guys only got a few miles off the Cuban shore with 30 men, women and children as hostages on board before the Cuban coastguard boarded without firing a shot. The only shots that were eventually fired, were those that executed three of the hijackers.

That incident was nearly a decade ago, but it is undoubtedly still in the minds of government officials and their attitudes. On the other hand, as the routine at the airport suggested, there genuinely is in these latter, post-Fidel days of Cuban communism more of an air of official insecurity than anyone is admitting.

In the end, though, largely due to the influence of a younger woman who has already started going through my rucksack – partly I suspect in the hope of finding something worth confiscating – the tubby tyrant with the metal detector settles for giving me a brusque frisking. The only thing her colleague can find worth confiscating is my Gillette Fusion Power razor, especially after she plays for some time enthusiastically with the 'smooth glide' vibrating control. In the end her colleague insists that I remove and hand over the multi-blade razor head, clearly not suspecting (at least from a security point of view) that I might have a spare. If I really were James Bond I would have quipped, as I boarded the ferry, 'That was a close shave.'

There are only a dozen of us on board the rusty motor raft

as we pull out into the waters of Havana Bay, the cool breeze from the sea welcome in the sticky heat building already at even this hour of the morning. The fare is two pesos each, but again I am forced to pay in convertible 'CUCs' while the Cubans pay in *nacional* pesos. I am not one hundred per cent sure however that my fare is going straight to the government. Not my problem.

By 8.30 I'm clambering off the ferry onto a crumbling concrete jetty and looking up at the gleaming white giant Jesus which dominates the hillside above Casablanca. I'm actually surprised I can see him at all. I have a problem with large religious monuments. Or rather they seem to have a problem with me. It first manifested nearly 20 years ago when on a visit to Hong Kong I went out to Lantau island, home to the then newly erected world's largest statue of Buddha, a 250-tonne seated colossus more than 100 feet high. By the time I got to its base the fog was so thick I could barely make out Buddha's big toe.

Similarly on my one and only trip to Rio de Janeiro I took the funicular up the Corcovado mountain to the city's famed landmark 130-foot statue of Christ the Redeemer. By the time I reached the top, the clouds had come down. It might have felt like an allegory of the Ascension, but as far as I was concerned the Saviour was invisible.

The first time I tried to see the Sistine Chapel in Rome, I discovered I was there on the one day in the year apart from Christmas when the Vatican's treasures were off-limits to the public. As a convinced atheist, I think God is trying to tell me something.

Even on this occasion the 66-foot high Christ of Havana is clad in scaffolding, not enough to completely obscure it, though if I can see Jesus I'm not absolutely sure he can see me. Which may be just was well. This statue has a history of interventionism: it was inaugurated on Christmas Eve 1958, just 15 days before Fidel Castro entered Havana to celebrate the triumph of his revolution. As he did, a lightning bolt hit the statue knocking its head off. A mixed message at best.

Just to be sure, I tip a nod to Big Jesus – his head was subsequently restored – before making my way to a little concrete shed by the side of some rusty iron rails. This, according to the piece of scrappy white paper in the window announcing that the ticket office will open at 9.30, turns out to be Casablanca station. Not much of a place to kick your heels for nearly four hours. But I'm starting to realize that in Cuba waiting is a way of life.

There is not a great deal of local colour to take in. The station itself looks like a 1960s seaside bus shelter in peeling green paint and a slogan on the wall that reads, MI FUTURO – REVOLUCIÓN. In most of the world it seems history is condemned to repeat itself, in Cuba it would appear to be actively encouraged. Opposite me on the other side of the tracks, assuming these rusting bits of iron are actually part of a functioning railway, is a pile of concrete rubble that might once have been a house, overgrown with a crimson riot of bougainvillaea in full blossom.

My belief that a train might actually arrive is given an oblique sort of encouragement by the sight of man on a ladder doing some form of welding work near what seem to be overhead electric cables. I suspect doing welding near live cables might not fit the prescription of our own dear Health and Safety Executive, but then they probably wouldn't approve either of the fact he isn't wearing gloves or goggles, despite the flying sparks, and his ladder doesn't look awfully well secured.

The noise of the welding gun is a counterpoint to the rattle of cicadas in the trees. There is a curious laid-back exotic romanticism to it all. It occurs to me that if I were Japanese I should compose a haiku, something along the lines of

> *Above rusty rails*
> *Sparks fly, crimson flowers fade.*
> *When will my train come?*

A little pedestrian perhaps, but I think I've got the number of syllables right and the flowers are a seasonal reference, sort of. Then a cloud of dust billows down what passes for a road and one of those ancient black Chevrolets that the Russians modelled their 1960s Chaika limousines on, clunks across the tracks, does a three-point turn for no apparent reason and disappears again, swallowed up by its own sandstorm.

From out of nowhere, a scrawny, pale-faced elderly bloke with close-cropped grey hair in a black singlet hanging loosely over his emaciated frame stumbles into view, trips up on the tracks, steadies himself and then collapses onto the bench in front of me, takes a long swig from a can of Bucanero *fuerte* (the 5.7 per cent ABV variety) and belches loudly.

A few minutes later he looks over in my direction and mumbles something of which I pick up one word, *borracho*, amongst a slur of other syllables. Which is fair enough, because *borracho* means drunk, and he is at least applying it to himself. With a hiccup.

At this stage, however, I haven't had long enough to work out that rather than saying *estoy borracho* (meaning I'm drunk) he might actually have said *soy borracho* (meaning, I am a drunk). Because the latter certainly turns out to be the case.

It did not take an awful lot of the three hours we were both going to sit there waiting for a train for me to realize that. Initially, he seems harmless enough, almost pleasant even. He even has some English: 'Sorry,' he says pleasantly apologetic when he realizes that my Spanish is substantially less than perfect, and I am having difficulty understanding him. 'Please tell me if I am a problem for you,' he says, embarrassing me into the usual, 'No, no not at all' disclaimer. Disclaimers I almost immediately come to regret as he says, 'Sorry,' yet again, before completely unexpectedly and very loudly bursting into song: 'Sorry seems to be the hardest word!'

I am partial to a glass myself but 9.30 in the morning seems a bit early to be as wasted as this guy clearly is and singing to strangers in the street is definitely more than is called for.

Happily it doesn't last. After a slight intermission, during which I suspect he has briefly dozed off, he comes to, apparently slightly sobered up. For the next half hour or so, we have a conversation in which he and actually tells me interesting stuff, such as the fact that just along the coast at Las Terrazas is where Hemingway kept his boat *Pilar*. As I noticed earlier, just about everybody in Havana has a Hemingway story.

The reason for his more than adequate English, he tells me, is that he has a son in Norway, 'where everybody speaks English'. Then suddenly he goes quiet. 'They are looking at me,' he says. Who, I wonder, and then I notice a couple of policemen who have just come off the later ferry. They don't seem to me to be paying any attention to anyone much. But then I am not Cuban. Or drunk.

'When I was at the University of Havana, they said I was mad,' the drunk, who tells me his name is Miguel, says. 'Because I was an individual. You know what Stalin said, he said, one man is more of a problem than a million, a million is just a statistic. They watch me, you know.'

It is not impossible. I have lived in countries with secret police long enough to know you never know when they might be watching and when they are not. But in reality I suspect it is a long time since anyone has watched Miguel, or watched out for him. That does not mean he is paranoid.

His Stalin quote is inaccurate, the original is a lot worse: 'the death of one man is a tragedy, the death of a million is a statistic.' But the fact that he knows it suggests he might indeed at some stage have been a thorn in the communist authorities' side. It might also explain why now, in his fifties but probably not much older, he is unemployed. And a drunk. I ask him where he is going.

But the sleep-induced sobriety is wearing enough and instead of a destination I get something between poetic prophecy and drunken doggerel: 'I don't know where I'm going. No one knows, when the volcano blows.'

Over by the crumbling concrete jetty a café is opening up. A bite to eat might be a good idea. The timetable suggests the journey to Matanzas, barely 80 kilometres (50 miles) by road, will take nearly four hours as the train winds its way through the countryside and along the coast. It also gives me an excuse to escape Miguel's now melancholy drunken ramblings.

The café staff are cleaning up, sweeping the bare concrete floor and my hopes of finding something edible are not great. But then a large man in a loud checked shirt comes over an inquires if I am a foreigner : the unavoidable *de donde, amigo* question: where do you come from, my friend? I tell him and he says he is the manager, that they are just getting ready to open in half an hour. I explain that I am waiting for the train and gesture towards the station where Miguel has once again burst into song, this time serenading an elderly couple doing their best to ignore him.

The manager shakes his head. 'Take a seat, I will get you something,' just taking the time to reassure himself – politely – that I can pay in CUCs.

Ten minutes later, much to my surprise and astonished pleasure, the kitchen has rustled up a *bocadillito* – a roast pork and grilled bacon sandwich served with some freshly made potato crisps. I settle down to eat under some dried palm fronds savouring the cool breeze from the bay and a cold beer from the fridge. If I'm going to have to put up with a drunk all the way to Matanzas, I'd better take some of his medicine.

By the time I get back to the platform a few more potential passengers have arrived. The ticket office isn't open yet but there is a woman in an approximation of a uniform fussing around. I take my seat again opposite Miguel who has mercifully gone back to sleep. A woman with two children arrives and shouts the question which I have been warned is crucial etiquette in the unavoidable everyday Cuban experience, the queue: '*Quién es último?*' Who's last?

This is a remarkably civilized and in my experience uniquely Cuban attitude to queuing. Instead of having to stand in a long line for hours – and in Cuba queues frequently last for hours if not days – you find out who the person immediately ahead of you is. That way everybody is free to mill around or wander off until you see that person being called. It is a sort of chain reaction and happily, while I was feeding my face, the drunk Miguel has already established my place in it at the head of the line.

Eventually with much clanking and squealing of iron on iron an apparition which I can only construe to be our train lurches in. The drunk looks up from his sleep and says surprisingly lucidly, 'I've been waiting for this moment all my life.' I wonder for a poignant moment if he might actually mean it. Then all of a sudden he repeats the same line, at the top of his voice, in an impromptu karaoke version of Phil Collins. It seems his entire English vocabulary and syntax is a litany of pop song refrains strung together with a few conjunctions. (I suspect it was that which would put the Phil Collins line into my head arriving in the bleak Santa Clara dawn two days later.)

Glad as I am to see the train arrive, I find it hard to believe it will actually get us to Matanzas. The only time I have ever seen such rusted bodywork was in a scrapheap for ancient cars in the midst of the Montana desert. There are just two carriages and parts of the lower sections of each which look thin enough to push a finger through. The roof has long lost the bulbs supposed to fit in its horn-like headlights. The pantograph which provides the power from the overhead rails looks like if it stopped hanging from them the whole train would fall to bits.

But clearly everyone else is more optimistic. The ticket office is open. I pay my four 'CUCs' and finally get hold of my first Cuban train ticket, a little piece of paper with punched holes for each station you are allowed to stop at. I'm going all the way so it is virtually perforated.

My fellow passengers are an assorted lot: a massive handsome black guy who could be a double for the young Mohammad Ali, in a tight red T-shirt that shows off his pecs, a skinny, stereotypically Latino gangsta-looking bloke in designer sneakers and bright orange shorts with a spider tattoo climbing up his arm, a well-built mulatto woman in skin-tight day-glo pink pants and a tight low-cut top, and of course the drunk who is now giving English lessons of a sort to one of the children of the middle-aged woman who arrived last. The elderly couple I had spotted from the café apparently aren't getting on the train all day: it seems they've just come to watch.

A quick look at the train suggests, to say the least, that it lacks even the most rudimentary toilet facilities, so I really need to lose some of that beer before getting on board. The difficulty is that there is no obvious sign indicating the whereabouts of the station conveniences.

This turns out to be for the very good reason that there aren't any. Not any more. I eventually identify a blue-painted concrete block which proclaims itself the *servicios*, but both cubicles are missing doors and boarded over. In desperation I take a quick leak behind the block and get back to the platform just in time to see a bloke who appears to be the conductor in a white shirt jumping down from the train and calling at people to climb onboard.

But before we are allowed to, he fetches a bucket of water from a standpipe and splashes it over a seat, apparently his own, before wiping it dry with a cloth. Only then are we invited to clamber on board.

The seats are the most basic I have yet encountered on any form of public transport: basic plastic moulds fixed to wooden frames screwed to the floor. An old lady I hadn't noticed on the platform, coal black with the classic finely-chiselled features of the Yoruba Africans who in the nineteenth century were imported into Cuba as slaves, is helped on board by a young man, a son or nephew perhaps, and sits down opposite me. She is painfully thin with a fine lace scarf wrapped around her head, gold rings on her fingers, painted fingernails and a long cigarette holder. She is carrying a plastic bottle of a pale yellow liquid. It could be a drink, a medicine or a urine sample.

A few clanks, bumps and creaks later, we are off. Ten seconds later we stop, barely a few dozen metres from the platform. There is a long minute's silence when I wonder if that is it for today. Then the clanks and bumps again and we lurch once more into life. For a full twenty seconds this time. I am no longer surprised it will take four hours to get to Matanzas. Four weeks seems more probable.

The same procedure repeats itself a couple more times, and then finally we pick up a surge or power and are rattling away into the lush tropical landscape, hurtling along at a speed of maybe 20 miles an hour. Not that going much faster would be a good idea, given that all the doors and windows are open and we are at times so close to the rich green foliage that heavy fronds slap the fragile-looking bodywork and at times flap briefly into the carriage. Britain's Health and Safety inspectors would have heart failure, but then they would almost anywhere in Cuba; here everyone, including the conductor, thinks it's a bit of a laugh.

In the first five minutes we stop another three times. At stations. Or what pass for stations: raised concrete platforms, about six feet off the ground with steps, and scrawled in black paint names for the middle of nowhere. Penas Altas for example is little more than a junction with a road, where a couple of lorries, despite the lack of a level crossing, wait patiently for us to rattle by.

We leave the jungle and are out in a savannah area with a few shacks here and there, wooden or part breezeblocks with corrugated iron roofs, and the occasional surprisingly smart looking pastel-painted bungalow that wouldn't be overly incongruous on the outskirts of Worthing, on the English south coast. I stick my head out of the window and note fierce-looking red-headed birds of prey wheeling in the bright blue sky above us. Perhaps they know something I don't.

At times it's like being on a fairground ride as the coaches shake from side to side, almost bouncing over the rails. The conductor has to jump from one coach to the next over rusty footplates that don't interconnect. The train is beginning to fill up now as we stop at more stations. A young Revolutionary Policeman no more than twenty-two or twenty-three gets on, his blue-grey uniform perfectly pressed, his black shoes shining, and his gun firmly buttoned in to its holster. But he's just on board for the ride and gets off a couple of stops later at a hamlet with no more than three shacks, some chickens running loose and a goat tethered to a stake. I suspect it's where he lives and he's going home for lunch.

With the warm air flowing freely in from the open doors and windows and a landscape occasionally lush tropical jungle, occasionally seasonally parched savannah, the first two hours pass quickly and in no time we are pulling into the half-way point, the reason for the railway's existence in the first place: Central Hershey.

The original sugar mill was set up here by chocolate magnate Milton Hershey, who came to Cuba in 1916 and fell in love with the place to the extent that he not only brought the railway, but set up his own model town, much as his British rivals Cadbury did with Bournville, south of Birmingham, complete with its own schools, healthcare system and baseball team. In 1946, however, a year after old Mr Hershey's death, the company sold the operation to the Cuban Atlantic Sugar Company, in a deal which accounted for 60,000 acres of land as well as the railway, sugar mills and electric plant. If the old philanthropist would have regretted the loss of the Cuban connection, just thirteen years later his company must have been grateful it had got out when the business was seized by Castro and nationalized.

The town of Hershey is not called that any more of course. Since 1960 it has been called Camilo Cienfuegos, after one of Castro's comrades, a romantic figure to rival Che who died in mysterious circumstances on the eve of the revolution. But the station is still called Hershey, and despite five decades of economic hardship, still shares certain similarities in design with old pictures I have seen of its sister municipality: Hershey Chocolate Town in Pennsylvania.

This is obviously not Pennsylvania, but the municipality of Santa Cruz del Norte in the province of La Habana (Havana). For a start, the Pennsylvania town does not have views of the Santa Cruz river and the Caribbean sparkling in the distance. On the other hand nor does the Pennsylvania town have a humongous derelict sugar mill dominating the entire landscape with its decrepitude, and while Hershey Chocolate Town advertises itself as 'the sweetest place on Earth', with a theme park bolted on to the original model town, the Cuban equivalent is doing its best to stave off the twin threats of rust and dereliction. Decay happens fast in these latitudes.

Since the collapse of the Soviet Union the Castros have taken the country's once dominant sugar industry on a roller coaster of development and neglect all of their own, centrally planned and ignoring the supply and demand situation on the world's markets. Currently the state of the industry is at the unfortunate bottom of a dip. The Hershey mill closed in 2002. The fact that sugar is once again becoming a valuable cash crop is something Cuba's economic planners may only get round to recognizing when it is again on the wane.

Hershey, the town, still has its lines of little bungalows, though few have more than flaking remnants of the original regulation green paint, but the overall impression is one of stagnant tropical decay. The train crawls slowly past the ruins of the sugar mill where the only sign of life is a man in his underpants and singlet prodding a cow with a wooden switch to stop it wandering onto the tracks.

This being the centre point of the line, though, the tracks are double and we pass for the first time – not least because this is the first time it has been possible – our sister train coming in the opposite direction. It looks, if possible, marginally more decrepit than ours.

The stop is about 15 minutes which means that there is also the possibility of taking on board some refreshment. Local entrepreneurs clamber on board to offer whatever they have managed to get hold of for sale. It is not exactly a cornucopia of delights but necessity means most of it is home made. The main offerings are cheese rolls and bottles of mango juice, hand-pressed I am assured. To me it is almost embarrassing that they are sold so cheaply. A half-litre plastic bottle of fresh, thick mango juice, chilled in a bucket of ice, costs one peso. One national peso: about the equivalent of four US cents. And the smallest note I have is a 10, in itself worth barely 30 British pence. But it is gratefully accepted and I find myself waiting patiently for the smaller notes. I could say, 'keep the change', as any of my US relatives might have done, but I am British and that would be making a scene. Ordinary Cubans not involved with the tourist industry know that foreigners are a lot richer, but they have no real idea how much richer. And even those who do, prefer not to have their noses rubbed in it.

We also change conductors and drivers here, which makes a lot of sense, as with only a couple of trains a day that is the only way to make sure they can get home. There is also an invasion of schoolkids, by today's sloppy British standards, remarkably neat and tidy in their white shirts and maroon skirts or shorts, but every bit as noisy as their contemporaries anywhere, pushing and shouting. The conductor makes a point of herding them to the back of the carriage, not least to get them away from the gaping open side doors.

The landscape meanwhile has lurched back to tropical semi-jungle with trees dripping mangos. I understand why the fruit juice is so cheap. Again and again we cross small dirt-track roads without level crossings. Coming in to the halt at Mena, a hamlet of only a few dozen shacks, the driver is forced to blow his horn repeatedly before a blue open-topped truck with a family of four in the back notices us and manages to screech to a halt. It would appear at least that the railway has priority, though I am not sure why, given that pulling out of Hershey we were overtaken by a boy eagerly whipping on his horse-pulled cart.

The new conductor, a rather dapper sallow-skinned Hispanic type in smart brown slacks, a clean white shirt with a fine blue stripe (I am impressed how well those Cubans who have decent clothes look after them) and a stylish pair of thin-rimmed spectacles comes over for a chat. He has already identified me as a gringo of some description and is delighted when I tell him I come from Britain. He has a cousin in London, he says. The drunk Miguel has a son in Norway. For a country which officially makes emigration difficult for its citizens, I am increasingly surprised to find how many Cubans have relatives abroad.

He is interested in my guidebook, a functional list of the main sites and history. 'May I see?' he asks politely. I hand it over only slightly reluctantly because I have just found that the section on the Hershey train says cows have been known to stray onto the track and get killed. I am afraid he may find this unacceptably patronizing.

Inevitably his eyes go straight to that line, and he looks up at me with a serious expression in which I fear I can see reproachfulness, and says without a trace of irony: 'It is true. This train kills many cows. Sometimes people get out with their knives.'

I am just restraining the urge to burst out laughing at this ramshackle antique electric train being turned into a mobile butchery, when the driver up front issues a curse.

'Come,' says my new friend, inviting me up forward into the driver's cabin, which turns out to be a pretty open invitation, seeing as there isn't a door. We get there just in time to see the man at the wheel – or rather on the go-stop knob, usually euphemistically referred to as a dead man's handle – clambering out of the cab with a cross expression on his face.

He is a dark black giant of a man in blue jeans and a tight red T-shirt with 'Red Pride' emblazoned on the back in white letters, which turns out to refer to an (US) American football team rather than being a declaration of faith in communism. And the reason he was cursing is that we have come to a junction in the tracks where there is a set of points that once might have directed the train onto a spur line, in the days when it had spur lines. It seems the points are not pointing in the right direction and he has to get out and see to them.

But it is not that which has me gawping and the conductor next to me slapping me on the back and saying, 'I told you so'. Up ahead, just next to the points, not actually on the tracks but right next to them as if waiting to see which way the train will go before they attempt to cross, are a couple of scrawny cows. I could hardly have conjured them up more opportunely.

To our big beast of a driver, however, they are just another nuisance to be deal with. He deals with them with a few loud shoos and waves of his arms. Personally, scrawny though they are, I wouldn't have risked them charging me, but clearly he is a different matter. The cows amble off. He struggles with the points but eventually manages to deal with the matter to his satisfaction and comes back to the cab.

The conductor is still merrily faking disappointment, saying 'no burger tonight', when we jerk back into life. For the next half hour or so, at the driver's invitation I share the cab, watching over his shoulder as we trundle, faster now it must be admitted, maybe 25 m.p.h., through the ever-changing, yet somehow already disappointingly monotonous landscape.

The most surprising thing, I eventually realize, is how little it appears to be productive. There are no obvious fields, or signs of agriculture, although I have little idea what might usefully grow here, nor is there much in the way of cattle, beyond the apparently free range pair we just passed.

But I am retaking my hard wooden seat in the passenger car when we suddenly pull round a corner and the dense foliage gives way to a beautiful green scrub savannah plain in which a pair of white horses canter past a distant herd of small brown goats. In the 'real' world the rest of us inhabit it would be a scene from a television advertisement – for who knows? washing powder, an electricity provider or an instant access bank account – but then maybe I am wrong, and this is the real world.

Before I know it, lost in this exotic rural landscape, we are clattering over a bridge across a river lined with fishing boats and small cabins, then turn right and we are rattling along what I now realize has to be the estuary of the Yumurí river, which means we have arrived. This is Matanzas.

And more to my surprise, we are more or less on time. It has taken over four hours to cover what was by rail probably some 140 kilometres (90 miles), not exactly a TGV, but at least the little ramshackle eighty-year-old railway did what it said on the ticket. And that can't be all bad.

CHAPTER FIVE

Athens of Cuba

The Hershey railway station is no more in the centre of Matanzas than its counterpart at the other hand is in central Havana. But at least there isn't a ferry to catch. The station is relatively smart, in that it looks slightly more like a terminus than the dilapidated concrete hut in Casablanca. It sits discreetly in the outer suburbs of Matanzas.

This small but ancient little town is most – if not all – of what the majority of beach package holiday tourists see of real Cuba. That is because it is the mainland gateway to Varadero, a thin peninsula 10 miles long but barely half a mile across with perfect sandy beaches along its northern coast, almost completely taken up with all-inclusive hotels for foreigners only.

For that reason alone Matanzas is one of the most sought-after places, after Havana, for ordinary Cubans to live. Get a flat or just a shack in Matanzas and, if you are very, very lucky – and have the right connections – you just might get a job as a waiter or a chambermaid in Varadero. Which means tips in CUCs and that puts you, in Cuban terms, in the league of the super-rich.

The other way for Cubans to legitimately get their hands on the all-important convertible version of their currency, is to run a *casa particular*. Which is why I am slightly surprised that my host for the night has not, as promised, sent somebody to pick me up from the station. I have the address, but it is a long enough walk – a mile or two – into the town centre. Especially if I have to do it in the company of Miguel, the drunk from the station in Casablanca who, much to my surprise – and possibly to his – has just managed to stagger off the train in Matanzas. I had imagined him sleeping on it all the way back to Havana.

He looks equally surprised to see me and wants to know where I am staying the night. This appears to be genuine concern. Nonetheless I am not keen to spend the evening in the company of someone barely able to string two sentences together without bursting into a cover version of Phil Collins or Dionne Warwick.

Thankfully a battered Lada turns up and the driver confirms he is from the *casa* I telephoned from Havana, much bemused to find the Hershey train here on time. We leave Miguel the singing drunk and the suburbs behind and are soon swerving to avoid the potholes down the main street of Matanzas. All of a sudden the driver signals right and appears to be about to pull onto the kerb, when a big iron gate opens in front of us and we drive straight off the road into what appears to be somebody's living-room.

There is a television in one corner and a desk with a computer – complete with ancient cathode ray tube screen, but a computer nonetheless – a bicycle leaning against the facing wall, a fridge, and a large rocking chair in the middle of what's left of the room after being invaded by the Lada. With Cuba's warm tropical climate – temperatures never vary by more than a few degrees throughout the year – and the general state of decay of most domestic buildings, the difference between indoors and outdoors isn't quite as fixed as we imagine it.

For example, this living-room-cum-garage doesn't have four walls. Beyond the Lada and the rocking chair it opens out into a courtyard that clearly serves as a dining area with a wrought iron table and chairs, a few heavy-leafed potted plants and a well-used washing line.

The owner, a jolly, portly middle-aged lady with a beaming smile and doing her best to speak impeccable *castellano* greets me and shows me to my room, just on the other side of the courtyard. It has high ceilings, a double bed and a little bathroom with a concertina plastic door. Not exactly the Ritz, but more than adequate. It even has toilet paper.

Once settled, my first task quixotically is to find out how to leave. My experience at Havana's main station has led me to believe this train travel business may not be as simple as I had imagined. My host is more than happy to ring the station for me, only to return with the news that the next train east leaves at 12.20. In a few hours' time. Given that I've only just got here, that seems a bit soon. What about the next? He passes on the inquiry. Same time. 24 hours later. And in between? Nothing. Not all trains stop at Matanzas, it would appear, even though it is the capital of the province and has a population of nearly 150,000.

There is no alternative therefore to spending only a few hours in Matanzas or the better part of a day and a half. So I'd better make the most of it. Matanzas is home to legendary African *bata* drummers. Unfortunately they don't seem to be playing anywhere tonight. Or any time soon.

That rather depressing information comes from the waiter in the town's main bar, a cavernous wood-panelled place called Vigía, with Corinthian columns and rotating ceiling fans. A giant sepia picture behind the bar depicts highlights of the town's old colonial architecture and asserts the somewhat over-aspirational claim that Matanzas is 'the Athens of Cuba'.

For a start the classical atmosphere is somewhat diluted by the ugly protruding filaments of energy-saving bulbs.

Thanks to a deal with China, like that which replaced Havana's unloved *camellos* with new Chinese buses, Cuba probably has more energy-saving bulbs than anywhere else in the world. There is also a big green poster advertising *hamburguesas* and two large Panasonic flat-screen televisions showing baseball. It could almost be a small town somewhere in Louisiana.

Across the road is the fire station, a crumbling neo-classical stone building with a great snub-nosed Russian fire engine, built by Zil (the same state firm that made the Soviet politburo's limousines), alongside an almost identical vintage American General Motors machine. My first thought was that both were part of the 'Fire Museum' housed in the same building, but it would appear they are the current working vehicles.

But I have chosen the right place to take in the sounds and scenes. The Vigía and its veranda are Matanzas' front parlour. Sit here long enough and the world passes by, a large proportion of it in classic 1950s American automobiles, far more than I saw anywhere in Havana other than the spruced-up tourist cabs in front of the Capitolio. But there is a reason for the relative affluence, and the traffic, all of it headed the one way: over the bridge and along the highway that leads to the foreigner-filled beachside holiday haven of Varadero.

I finish a cold beer and a *bocadillo de tortilla* – a sort of tomato omelette in a sweet, greasy bun – and take a brief stroll along the road. The first step, almost literally, is to cross the Yumurí river. An iron bridge takes me over murky waters that still manage to sparkle in the bright sunlight, lined with little shacks with boats tethered by their doors. It looks like pictures of the Mekong in 1960s Vietnam.

On the other side, there are two parallel roads. The one I am walking on is all but empty, lined with little houses built of concrete breezeblocks brightly painted, music coming from every one. This gradually peters out and the surface deteriorates rapidly.

I cross rusted railway tracks – the ones I am due to leave on tomorrow? – and a wooden sign leaning at an oblique angle that actually says *crucero ferrocarril* – level crossing – although it is anything but level: deep pools of water have collected in lake-sized potholes. Two ageing lorries stand under a corrugated iron shelter supported by rusty ironwork next to what appears to be a closed tool store with red letters on a bright yellow background proclaiming how Fidel's abortive 1958 raid on an army base in Santiago, at the other end of the country, 'shows us that reverses can be turned into victories.' The optimism seems forced. The whole scene would be one of depressing decay except that the bright colours, the sea beyond and the scudding tropical storm clouds against the blue sky lend it a curious superficial beauty. If they had East Germany's climate here, communism here would have collapsed decades ago.

Across the tracks, though, things are different, here the roadway is a well-made dual carriageway which curves along the palm-tree studded Caribbean coast to the Varadero pseudo-peninsula. A splendid tail-finned Plymouth Belvedere, its turquoise paintwork a perfect match for the gleaming Caribbean waters, sits next to a windswept palm as if James Dean or Clark Gable had only just got out of it. An air-conditioned Viazul bus slows down for tourists on board to take photographs.

Close-up inspection reveals the exotic turquoise to be a faded green. A sticker on the rear windscreen proudly proclaims it boasts a rare and locally extremely coveted Pioneer hi-fi system. Whether it actually has the sound system or just the sticker isn't evident, but the road to Varadero has to be the safest place in Cuba. Along the inland side of the road is a military base. There are no troops in evidence, just a welter of the usual revolutionary slogans. A police car sits by the road, keeping an eye on the traffic, and the long lines of hitchhikers.

Varadero proper starts about 25 kilometres (15 miles) along the road, where a small bridge links what is really an island to the mainland. There is a police post there, but contrary to widespread Western belief, particularly in the United States, it is rarely manned. There is nothing to prevent ordinary Cubans getting to Varadero town, and they can even use some, if not all, of the hotels. What effectively keeps most out are the prices. Varadero is a CUC-only enclave, which is also what draws in those lucky enough to have secured employment on the peninsula. But not all of them get transport provided. Hence the long queue of hitchhikers.

I scramble over some rocks to the scrappy little patch of sand that is the town beach of Matanzas and dabble my already blistered feet in the warm but disconcertingly murky seawater. That famous radiant turquoise only starts further along the coast, near Varadero. As if the colour of the sea were charged for in hard currency too.

Along the sands two athletic looking black guys appear at first to be wrestling, one dressed entirely in black, the other in white with a red bandana around his head. I stand back as one grabs the other by the arm and appears to fling him bodily upwards, only for the other to go with the flow and turn a somersault landing perfectly on his feet. They repeat the manoeuvre, in reverse and I can only applaud. Far from local thugs, they are ballet dancers practising.

And then my attention is seized from the other direction, as borne on the rising wind a huge bird soars between the palm trees, brown-black feathers beating a downdraft only feet above the waves. I ask one of the dancers what it is, and they look bemused. *Buitre.* Vulture. These were the red-headed birds I saw from the train swooping over the savannah.

Back at the *casa*, my host has dinner waiting. I'm glad I didn't ask for the lobster. One of the most common recommendations for eating well in Cuba is to eat in private houses for a taste of 'true home cooking'. That is a phrase I've always been a bit suspicious of: a taste of real British home cooking, I imagine, might be a fairly grim experience somewhat resembling a close encounter with a microwave.

Cubans may not have vast supermarket isles stocked with ready meals. But they do have microwaves. The landlady serves me a simple salad, very simple: one radish, two slices of cucumber, a tomato and some sliced carrot. Add a spring onion, salad cream, half a boiled egg and a slice of supermarket ham and it might have been the sort of salad my mother served as 'tea' in the 1960s.

But this is only the first course. It is followed by rice with prawns, boiled and with a pale pink sauce poured over them which adds colour, but unfortunately not flavour. I wolf them down and head out to sample the Matanzas nightlife – if there is any.

My first encounter is not propitious. Miguel, the drunk from Casablanca, still clutching – the same? – can of Cristal, wandering in the middle of the road. I turn a corner sharpish to avoid him, and end up where I wanted to be anyhow: *Parque de la Libertad*, the main town square.

Through glassless windows on the street that leads into the square I glimpse men in half-lit rooms under rotating ceiling fans playing chess with timing clocks that conjure up visions of Fischer and Spassky. Another legacy of the long-dead Russian connection, maybe? A sign on the wall behind them declares this to be the premises of the Revolutionary Army Club.

The square itself that hums with activity. *Parque de la*

Libertad is the town's after-dinner sitting-room. Men in baseball caps sit playing dominoes and drinking peso beer under trees whose leaves rustle in the warm slowly rising wind. Other groups, male and female, sprawl on the concrete benches, literally shooting the breeze. Children throw balls and chase one another, shouting and laughing with no obvious sign of or need for adult supervision. Everybody knows everybody. Everybody feels responsible.

Across the square I am tempted in by one building that has clearly just recently been renovated, where a line of people are drinking at the bar. The sign by the door announces it to be the Hotel Velasco. According to my guidebook, published only six months earlier, it doesn't exist. Times are changing and things can move fast in Cuba. If they move at all.

I order a mojito. It is the best I have yet tasted, topped up with a splash of the best *añejo 15 años*, fifteen-year-old Havana Club which gives it just an extra kick and a lot more depth.

The gaggle at the bar is made up of two Canadian girls in their twenties on holiday plus a guy they seem to have picked up and a couple, the latter three to my surprise all Cuban. To my surprise only because this is a bar that accepts CUCs only. We get into a discussion, in mixed Spanish and English, and they ask where I am going and how.

When I tell them it is the Cubans who crease up with laughter. '*En tren?*', by train? Why? Because it's a great rail journey and the way most Cubans travel, isn't it? They exchange knowing looks and smile patronizingly. Yes, but not all. Meaning clearly those who can afford not to. Either because they have sufficient access to CUCs to be able to afford the air-conditioned Viazul buses or because they have cars. Either of which places them in the affluent élite of Cuban society.

Predictably all of them work in the tourist industry. Which

is why they can afford to live like tourists. I am increasingly aware that there is a middle class is slowly emerging in communist Cuba, a phenomenon gently encouraged by the younger Castro's gradual reforms, slight though they may be. Raúl – who turned 80 just a few days before I arrived – is tinkering enough with the long-established rigidly enforce structure of Cuba's economy for it to have a noticeable effect on the population.

He has already dismissed hundreds of thousands of workers from superfluous government jobs, but at the same time made it legal for the first time since 1968 (when his older brother nationalized the entire workforce from shoe-shiners to barmen) for Cubans not only to set up in business on their own, but to hire another Cuban. Soon it might be two, or even three!

The guy with the two Canadian girls tells me he runs his own guide business. Only a year or two ago he could have been doing virtually the same thing, except that he might have been considered a *jinetero*. The word literally means 'jockey', but in Cuba it has long acquired a subsidiary meaning of one who 'rides' the tourists. The sexual innuendo was deliberately intended even if in many cases the *jineteros* or *jineteras* were just acting as guides and companions; there was usually more on offer if the price was right. Now, he proudly says, he has a legitimate business, and is thinking of taking on a secretary or driver. But he makes a face when I mention taxes. It seems that if their government gives Cubans the right to earn more money, not many of them are going to be happy giving any of it back.

Instead he changes the subject and tells me I have to try a *canchanchara*, which he claims is Cuba's real national drink, Hemingway and his mojitos notwithstanding. The barman grins and starts to make me one: 'This is what we Cubans drink to give us fire in our bellies to cut the Spaniards' throats,' he says with a jolly grin. It is an odd concoction to say the least. He spoons a large dollop of thick golden honey into the bottom of a glass, tops it up with squeezed lime juice, throws in some crushed ice and then fills up the glass with a huge measure of *aguardiente*, which in Cuba is the raw spirit distilled from sugar cane. It bears the same relation to a finished rum as bootleg hooch does to fine whisky, or poteen to potato vodka. It doesn't have subtleties or nuances of flavour, but it does creep up and whack you over the head, which is of course what the Cuban rebels wanted to do to their Spanish colonial masters.

I'm wondering not just whether but *how* on earth to drink the thing, which at this stage looks an iceberg of firewater on top of a layer of brown sludge, when the Cuban laughs, orders one for himself and shows me. The trick is to stir it with a spoon to dissolve the honey while sipping up the mixture through a straw. It seems a bit effete for an army of revolutionary peasants, but it tastes delicious: a sweet and sour infusion that is the alcoholic equivalent of nitro-glycerine.

I cast my eyes, while I still have control of them, along the array of drinks displayed behind the bar. There is every variety of Havana Club of course – and the Cubans are delighted when I tell them that it has long since supplanted Bacardi as the rum of choice in London bars and clubs – plus some recondite and no doubt expensive imports that nonetheless every classy cocktail bar requires: including Lea & Perrins Worcestershire sauce and Angostura bitters.

Among the cocktail classics there is only one that has a Cuban local product substituted and at first I don't even notice that it is. The little bottle of fiery red sauce with its diamond-shaped label and green lettering looks familiar; its only on close inspection that I realize it isn't Tabasco, but a Cuban lookalike. In almost any other country it would be sued by the US manufacturer (Tabasco may be a region of

Mexico but the sauce comes from Louisiana) for 'passing off'. But as US firms are banned by their own government from trading in Cuba they can hardly complain about unfair competition.

In fact, glancing along the shelves I start to pick out a whole range of Cuban copycats I had mistaken for the originals, from *Naranja*, which looks, tastes and has packaging almost exactly like Fanta, and Tu Cola: Cuban Coke. The real thing, it's not.

I can't help thinking that the relationship between communist Cuba and its giant capitalist neighbour is remarkably similar to one of the wackier creations of DC comics. When I was a child I was reluctantly fascinated by the freakish character Bizarro, a Superman clone that had gone wrong, with cracked white skin and a childlike mentality who married a Bizarro version of Lois Lane and lived on a cube-shaped planet where everything was like on Earth but viewed through a kaleidoscope rather than a telescope.

Just to reinforce the point, the television cuts from its interminable coverage of a baseball game somewhere in Florida to yet another commercial break, this time advertising health insurance. Up until now I hadn't realized the screen in the background beyond the bar was showing what appears to be US television. The regime does not approve of its citizens watching US channels, and tries to block them, especially those run by Cuban emigrés, which broadcast anti-Castro propaganda. This, however, is ESPN *Deportes*, broadcast from Mexico City but unashamedly targeting the vast numbers of Spanish-speaking Americans in the southern states.

But anyone who might think allowing Cubans to watch adverts for the subversive luxuries of capitalism, might want to vet the content. 'You too can have total healthcare insurance in the Miami area,' the announcer is boasting (in

Spanish), 'for just $100 a month.' The Cubans beside me splutter into their *cancancharas*. 'That's $1,200 a year,' one of the girls exclaims. Far more than a top rate Cuban surgeon earns. 'Here it is free,' she says proudly. Free healthcare is one of the benefits of the revolution that no Cuban would argue with, even if the American embargo means they lack many drugs. She is no less than astonished, and more than a little sceptical, when I tell her it is free in Britain too.

I leave them mildly disbelieving to wander the few yards back to my *casa*. On the way I yet again come across Miguel the drunk for the final time, lying unconscious in a doorway. I check that he is breathing. Dark clouds are gathering over the moon. But I doubt it will be the first time he has woken up wet.

CHAPTER SIX

Little League

Sunlight streaming through the thin curtains of my room wakens me and I emerge to find the central courtyard of the house recovering from a minor flood. It has rained heavily during the night and the drains have only just coped. But the waters have receded enough for the wrought iron table to be laid for breakfast and already I can feel the sun hot on the back of my head.

It seems odd to someone brought up in the British Isles to have both rain and sun almost in one's living-room. But as I observed, Cuba's climate makes a mockery of our strict delineation between outdoors and indoors.

By 11 o'clock in the morning I'm sitting on a bench lapping up the sunlight outside the cathedral of San Carlos de Borromeo, a hulking squat slab built in 1693. It is closed – for renovation – and looks like it has been for some time. So long, in fact, that the sign that says CLOSED FOR RENOVATION, needs renewing.

So instead of enriching my cultural knowledge I am doing what people in hot climes do a lot: 'chilling'. If it were an Olympic discipline, Cubans would be gold medallists. Just about everyone I can see is practising hard, dressed for the part in flip-flops and open-necked shirts. The only exceptions are annoying groups of teenage kids who can't resist the game of 'where's the foreigner from'. *Dedonde, dedonde, quel país?* Luckily my deductions in Havana prove accurate. Reply in any language, particularly English, and you will be pestered for hours. Say *ruso* – Russian – and they gape open-mouthed for a few moments and slope off. Khrushchev must be spinning in his grave.

The thing about 'chilling' though is that after a while it wears off, especially in the heat. Matanzas may have a long and rich past dating back to the seventeenth century – when it was named (*matar* is Spanish verb 'to kill': hence the noun *matador*) for the slaughter of 30 Spanish colonists (the guy in the hotel bar wasn't kidding me) but nowadays it's a bit dull.

There is, however, a museum. And I have never seen anyone more delighted than its attendants when I walk in the door. A middle-aged woman in a tight red miniskirt looks over her glasses and almost jumps to her feet, and shouts to her two colleagues who emerge in a fluster from some dark sepulchral recesses of the interior. Beaming. All of them. Matanzas museum doesn't get many visitors.

Then comes the difficult bit. The entrance fee, the first woman tells me, is '*Dos pesos*'. Two pesos. And then she bites her lip and all but looks away, before adding, 'CUC'. Because I am a foreigner, I have to pay 25 times the local price.

It seems perfectly reasonable to me, but to them it is clearly so exorbitant they are embarrassed to ask for it. I hand her a five and immediately provoke another crisis. She can't change it. '*Momento, señor, uno momento*,' she pleads, panicking that her first foreign guest this millennium – to judge from my reception – might decide not to bother after all, and dashes out into the street to find change.

In the mean time, to make sure I don't change my mind, her colleague has already started to show me round. I don't really need or want a guided tour, and I'm in any case not sure my Spanish is up to it, but I don't want to spoil her evident enjoyment in actually having something to do for her living, even if it is only following me round and telling me where the door is to the next room.

By the time her colleague comes back with my change I am thoroughly engrossed in the history of Matanzas. And a fairly grim one it is too. The Athens of Cuba was a Mecca for slave traders, to the extent that by the middle of the nineteenth century they made up more than 62 per cent of the population, over 100,000 souls. Amidst the cane-cutting machetes, and pirates' pistols, the museum has a seemingly endless stock of leg-irons, but also some enlightening comments on the Spanish attitude to slavery: unlike in the Anglo-Saxon world, the Spanish imposed a hierarchical ladder which luckier and more industrious slaves could actually climb, to the extent of eventually not just winning their freedom but access to the ranks of the bourgeoisie. Contrary to their reputation as harsh colonial masters, the Spanish, partly aided by the turbulence back home during the early nineteenth century including the invasion of Spain by Napoleon, contributed to the growth of an educated, relatively affluent black middle class. There was a much larger degree of intermarriage than in Anglo-Saxon colonies.

The one Matanzas is most proud of is Juan Gualberto Gómez, born to slaves on a sugar plantation who were allowed to purchase his freedom allowing him to learn to read and write, and send him to school in Havana. His intelligence was such that his parents, with financial support from the owner of the sugar plantation where they worked, eventually sent him to Paris to learn to be a carriage maker.

There he lived through the traumatic events following the Franco–Prussian War, the Paris Commune and the rise of the Third Republic, becoming instead a French–Spanish translator and writing for a French newspaper. When he finally returned to Cuba, it was fate that he should bump

into and become friends with José Martí, the gadfly intellectual revolutionary. Martí made him his 'man in Havana',
but the Spanish arrested him, deported and interned him in
their north African enclave of Ceuta.

Unlike Martí therefore, he survived the wars of independence, returned to Cuba and for the next thirty years until
his death in 1933 he was a champion of the free press, campaigning against those who were ready to let Cuba slip into
America's back pocket. It is hard to know what he would
have made of the Castros' regime, but it is easy to know
what they thought of him. Like his old chum José Martí, they
made him an airport, Cuba's second biggest, at Varadero,
just up the road.

The lady showing me round the museum is also keen
that I see their other proud possession: bit of twisted metal
from the wreckage of *La Coubre*, a French freighter which
exploded in Havana harbour in March 1960, just a few
months after the revolution. The ship was carrying large
amounts of munitions ordered by the Castros from Belgium.
Not only were the arms lost but 75 people died and more
than 200 were injured, not least because a second bomb
exploded half an hour later, apparently deliberately targeting the rescue services, which included Che Guevara acting
in his trained profession as a doctor. The Cuban revolutionaries blamed it squarely on the CIA. The US government has
never commented, but acknowledges the existence of official
files on the incident, closed to the public for 150 years. Over
to you, Mr Obama?

There are more rain clouds on the horizon as I emerge
back into the blistering sunlight, leaving my three museum
ladies clucking over a one-CUC tip and smiling like they'd
just been invited to a Buckingham Palace garden party.

I look at my watch and realize that it's barely 12.30. I've
still got another 12 hours in Matanzas. Time to make the day

for one of the hordes of taxi drivers who seem to be the only group in town actively touting for business. In theory only 'official' licensed tourist taxis are supposed to take foreigners; in practice anyone does, taxi driver or not. If you have a car in Cuba, no matter how ancient, you are part of an élite. It has only just been proposed by the new regime to make it legal to buy and sell cars (and/or property); up until now if you or your family didn't have a car before 1959, you either have good contacts in the government, or you walk.

That not only explains the continuing survival of those American dinosaurs from the fifties – if it goes you can't replace it – but it makes every Cuban car owner an amateur mechanic, and a part-time taxi driver.

Opting for style rather than comfort I choose the owner of a bright red big-hooded bulbous 1958 Peugeot 403, the distant ancestor of the little models being imported for government use today. My destination is Monserrate, a nineteenth-century monastery that had fallen into disuse but has recently been restored. The main reason for visiting it, however, is the spectacular vista from the hill top over the whole city, straddling its two rivers, the Yumurí and the San Juan, a pair of glinting silver ribbons that wind their way through the lush green landscape. In the distance I can just make out a little grey-white line of the hotels in Varadero.

Aware that this is one of the few towns most beach-loving package holiday makers actually visit, the government has set up a laid-back little bar and restaurant. And mindful – up to a point – of its own citizens it also operates a second, which takes *moneda nacional*, a little down the hill, without the view. I give it a go, much to the surprise of the staff who exchange glances suggesting I should know my place and eat in the foreigners' café.

The procedure for ordering in a *moneda nacional* institution is a little different. For a start you don't really order a dish so much as compose it. Cubans get exactly what they pay for. No more and no less. And I mean exactly. Just like in the old Soviet Union, there is a weight for each piece of meat on the menu. If there's pork chops available it will say 'pork chop, 210 grams'. I order rabbit – not least because I'm surprised to see it – 160 grams – and at the waitress's prompting, add some rice (180 grams). Otherwise I'd have just got a piece of meat on its own.

Well, not quite on its own. It comes in a sauce. A quite nice sauce actually. Brown. More like a thick gravy. Its main function though is to disguise how little meat there actually is. Of that 160 grams I'd say a good 100 is bone. Which means scraping around somewhere in the brown goop for a few shreds of rabbit meat. This was one lean bunny. But what there is tastes okay and the sauce gives the rice some taste, plus there's the bonus that the whole meal costs only marginally more than the beer I wash it down with.

Cacique is one of two brands I've come across that are sold for national pesos. The name comes from the word for 'chief' in the language of the Taino tribes who were the original inhabitants of Cuba before the Spanish arrived and exterminated them, partly deliberately and partly because they introduced them to European diseases such as small-pox and the common cold. The Taino got their own back by giving the Spaniards syphilis.

The other beer is Mayabe, named after a town in the Holguin province of eastern Cuba, where there is supposed to be a drunk donkey called Pancho who lives on the beer. I suspected this story of being apocryphal but there is a YouTube video so I suppose it must be true, though the donkey looks less than desperate for another pint.

To my taste, however, Cacique is a better beer than the supposedly premium brand Bucanero sold primarily to tourists for CUCs. For a start it is lighter and more bitter without the cloying sweet taste that I suspect in Bucanero comes from putting too much sugar into the brew. Not that it's a whole heap cheaper. A can of Cacique costs 18 pesos while outside Havana you can get a Bucanero or Cristal for one CUC, which you have to remember is worth 25 'national' pesos. A substantial bit more you might say, but it still means for the average Cuban without access to CUCs (unlike most of those living in Matanzas) a can of Cacique costs a couple of days' salary.

Inevitably by the time I finish my meal and head back into town, there isn't a taxi to be found. Anywhere. It's siesta time; in fact the main way to distinguish siesta time from the rest of the time is the absence of would-be taxi drivers hawking their services. The result is that I could do with a siesta myself by the time, footsore and fried, I trudge into the town centre.

Going back to the hotel to crash for an hour or so seems a bit defeatist, especially as it seems one or two of the taxi drivers have decided to re-emerge, it is still hot as hell and a lot more humid, and there's a bit of beach a couple of miles out of town.

La Concha is not exactly Varadero, just a little crescent of sand with a bar at one end. The bar is mainly colonized by a middle-aged Italian bloke sporting a coiffed salt-and-pepper hairstyle with a Cuban girl less than half his age on one arm and a Rolex on the other, fondling them alternately. He looks like the sort of bloke who might have been a regular guest at Silvio Berlusconi's *bunga bunga* parties.

The heat is unrelenting, at least 35°C and humid enough to grow orchids in the air. After a brief swim and a seat in the shade, I realize I'm in danger of melting and reckon it's time to go back and pack my bags. Which is when I discover that the taxi drivers have packed it in for the day again.

Convoys of rusty buses and open-topped trucks are flying

by, stuffed with workers from Varadero. The ones in the trucks are jammed together, hanging on for dear life as they jolt unheedingly over 'sleeping policemen'. I envy them. Despite a sturdy straw hat salvaged from a previous trip to Mexico, I feel in danger of dropping from heatstroke. There is a total lack of shade.

On the landward side stretches a long, gently curve of neo-colonial single-storey buildings, with mock Corinthian columns, most still bearing remnants of once-bright colours while one or two have been repainted: blues, pinks, purples, yellows. Every single one is shuttered up. At one end there is a faded mural of José Martí, Camilo Cienfuegos and Fidel Castro, the Father, Son and Holy Ghost of Cuban Communism.

I am back in Bizarro World again. In front of me, in the middle of a long thin field of brown grass between the former shopping arcade – I realize now that is what this gentle colonial curve must once have been – the Cuban flag hangs limply from a flagpole. The symbol of independence from Spain since 1902, unchanged by Castro, began life – like the Capitolio, mimicking a US institution. The US 'stars and stripes' flew in Havana for three years during the 1899–1902 US intervention in the Cubans' revolt against Spain. When the Cubans adopted one that was their own design but remarkably similar: a star and stripes, five stripes and a single star.

Today the US flag flies only at the far end of the island, at Guantánamo. But the influence still hovers in the background. Cuban Spanish is littered with US-Americanisms. Hot dogs are translated literally as *perros calientes* while *los baños* a literal translation of 'bathrooms', is used here – as in Mexico – when they mean toilets (*servicios* in Spain).

Beneath the flag a group of kids in smart red uniforms are practising baseball. It could be a Little League game somewhere in Florida or the Carolinas. And all of a sudden I can visualize the little neo-colonial parade behind me festooned with inflatable toys, beach balls, flippers, hot dog stands, a picture of the finger-lickin' chicken-selling colonel, the Seattle coffee shop mermaid in her green circle and – somewhere subtly integrated into the colonial architecture – the yellow arches. And I don't know if it would make the average Cuban laugh or cry. The Cuban national anthem, much touted by the Castros, includes the lines 'to live in chains is to live in dishonour'. Will it still be true when the chains are Starbucks, KFC and McDonalds?

We could ask ourselves the same question back in Britain. I find it hard to rejoice that one of the few signs of economic expansion in the current climate of recession is that Krispy Kreme donuts are tripling their number of branches in the UK. On a recent holiday to Thailand, globally famed for its healthy cuisine, I found the natives queuing for coffee and donuts at American chains. Cuba for the moment is safe from this commercial contagion, but only because it is in an isolation ward. Fully exposed to the virus, I suspect it would succumb in a heartbeat.

The same speculation is still running through my head three hours later as I watch what passes for adverts on Cuban television: a video montage of Che Guevara smoking cigars, brandishing pistols, in a doctor's white coat treating patients, and incongruously bare-chested on a factory floor. These alternate with romantic shots of the bearded Camilo Cienfuegos riding on horseback at the head of a troop of revolutionaries, looking for all the world like the US Seventh Cavalry.

I am sitting with four other people in a line of red plastic chairs in a concrete bunker that purports to be a railway station somewhere very definitely on the wrong side of the tracks, about a mile out of the centre of Matanzas. On the wall is a photograph of Raúl Castro in his army cap beaming myopically through his glasses with what one cynic has called the 'smug smile of a self-satisfied Madrid greengrocer'. Slogans stencilled on either side proclaim, 'Unity means Strength and Victory', and, 'We have no right not to do our best'. It is easy to laugh at these faded, endlessly repeated political slogans, but western politicians regularly come out with equally glib nonsense: they just don't paint it on the walls.

But my major concern for the moment is trying to find out when my train might arrive, to little avail. It seems the reason for my extended stay in Matanzas is that being relatively close to Havana, not many trains stop here. That said, not many seem to pass without stopping either. Except for goods trains. Yet again Cuba seems to have followed a US model: the railways have become dominated by goods trains. Passengers come second best.

In theory, according to a chalk scribble on a blackboard near a doorway that leads onto what I presume is the platform, the train is timetabled at 23.20. With little faith in just how the system might actually work I'm here even earlier than the two hours before departure I was advised in Havana.

On the advice of the lady owner of my *casa*, I have asked for the *jefe de torno*, the duty manager. A thickset man in his forties claimed to fit the bill and told me he'll call me up to the ticket office at 23.00 to buy a ticket. And not before. Despite the fact that I am here two hours early.

The blackboard is the only timetable. The television, which in a European station might display train information, is there to entertain the waiting passengers, of which there is a growing number. A bloke in jeans, T-shirt, sneakers and baseball cap pulled down low over his eyes is taking surreptitious swigs from a bottle of rum. After a while he pulls out a packet of cigarettes and goes out for a smoke. For the first time I notice a red sign on the wall proclaiming *No fumar*. Even here in Cuba, home of the big cigar, the health lobby has won at least a token victory in the war against smoking. Even Fidel, once never seen without a cigar in his mouth, gave up in the 1980s.

By 10 p.m., with just an hour or so to go, things are getting livelier. Sort of. A little green lizard just ran across the floor. There are now about 15 of us waiting, most captivated by an Argentinian soap opera on the television, called *Mujeres de Nadie* (*Nobody's Wives*), which mainly revolves around a series of flirtatious affairs between female doctors, their male colleagues and various patients. The acting is histrionic to say the least, one blonde in a white coat displaying angry grimaces while waving her hands in the air. It may, of course, be true to life; I've never been in an Argentinian hospital.

The bloke with the rum bottle inside his jacket comes back in with a decent looking filled roll, which he indicates he bought outside. A woman in her sixties with a big suitcase asks me to look after it for a moment while she goes to get one too. This seems a good idea. I was so concerned with getting to the station that my only thought for provisions was a bottle of sparkling water. I go to the door to find a guy with a rasta hairdo selling ham rolls from a big cardboard box. They aren't cheap by Cuban standards, or maybe it is just that he has twigged I am a foreigner that he demands one CUC. Or because we are in Matanzas, Varadero's backyard?

It is just gone 23.05 and I am watching the ticket counter avidly for any sign of the man who has just appeared behind the Perspex window beckoning me, when chaos breaks loose. Suddenly, without any obvious signal, everybody jumps up and crowds around the window waving pieces of paper and the bloke behind it is calling out names. None of them sound like mine. I turn in blind panic to the guy with the rum bottle who gives me a broad grin and calls to the man behind the counter, 'What about our foreign friend here?'

The lady whose case I looked after joins in, and the *jefe de torno,* almost in embarrassment, feels obliged to assure everybody that I'll get a seat: all in good time. I feel mildly reassured but extremely touched and impressed by the wave of popular concern. In fact the only word I can find for it is one that no longer sounds hollow: solidarity.

The lady with the suitcase asks me where I am headed and when I tell her my next stop is Santa Clara, she insists I visit the Che Guevara mausoleum, which is already on my list. 'Magnificent,' she enthuses, 'absolutely magnificent. But only right for the hero of our revolution.' This with, as far as I can tell, not the slightest trace of irony.

She tells me she is a anaesthetist and a professor at Havana University medical school, and is on her way to the medical school in the city of Sancti Spiritus, the eventual destination of the train we are, hopefully, about to board. She asks me about the *E. coli* outbreak in Europe; she's worried about our hygiene standards.

She tells me she used to work 'in Leningrad' (the change of name back to St Petersburg has not caught on in Cuba). When I tell her I lived in the Soviet Union, she sighs with genuine nostalgia. 'Ah, those were the good old days. Everybody was so friendly. All comrades together.' I ask if she speaks much Russian, but she looks surprised even at the thought, and says, with a broad smile, *'Nyet.'*

Then she nudges me: the *jefe* is beckoning me over. When I get to the window he shakes his head and indicates I should use the door into his office, which he closes firmly behind me. Then he takes out a key and opens a safe in the wall from which he takes a cashbox. He asks for my passport, inspects it, then writes me out a ticket, a few lines in ball point pen on a little white form the size of a post-it note, and says, almost apologetically that'll be seven pesos, '*convertibles*'. I hand over a 10 CUC note and he unlocks the cash box. Now I understand: this is the hard currency till. Hence the security, the locked door, the whole in the wall. He picks out three one CUC notes in change and hands them to me before carefully replacing the cashbox in the safe and locking it. He shakes hands solemnly. I feel oddly honoured. Just for having bought a train ticket.

In the distance I hear what at first sounds like a blast on a jazz horn, a musician warming up. It is followed swiftly by two or three others of various pitches, but much louder, and then I catch on and realize it is a train pulling into the station. Not ours, though, a cargo train heading in the opposite direction.

The minute it passes we are herded onto the platform, scribbled tickets inspected at the door. But it is not as easy as that. The platform, it seems, is only for trains heading towards Havana. To get to trains going in the other direction we have to go to the end of the platform, scramble down some barely usable steps onto the rails and cross the tracks.

Isabel, as I have learned to call the lady with the big suitcase, draws my attention to the veiled full moon and says it looks like it's under water. It does, and any minute now I'm about to feel like being drowned.

A distant roar heralds a blinding light advancing towards us out of the darkness. Slowly like some ancient beast advancing, a great dirty red diesel locomotive bears down upon us. It seems impossibly huge, but I soon realize that this is because there is no platform and we have to clamber up iron ladders into the coaches. The locomotive, I notice, is also Chinese. Cuba may have a hostile superpower on its doorstep, but while the United States has done its best to ignore it, a newly emergent superpower has crept in the back door.

On the train, the feeling of total immersion is instant. I

am thrust into a sea of roiling humanity, except that it feels awe-inspiringly alien. It is not the race or colour of the denizens of this densely packed train, it is as if they belong to another dimension. In the old-fashioned sense: nearly all of them there are twice the size I am.

Admittedly at 5′6″ (1m70) I am on the diminutive side of male humanity. But these guys – and they are nearly all guys – are immense! Not fat. Big. Very big. In the sense that American footballers are big, and even bigger when they put on all that protective armour. These guys wouldn't even find armour big enough. Nearly all of them are dressed in singlets or bare chested, and their chests are twice the size of oil drums while their biceps are bigger than my thighs. Than most rugby players' thighs. And glisten in the moonlight. With sweat. Everybody is sweating. The relatively cool night air has deserted us and the stationary train is like a sauna. A very old, dirty sauna.

So here I am, a middle-aged short white bloke with a shaggy mop of greying blond hair in the middle of a sea of huge young muscular, sweaty black blokes who look like they could pull locomotives with their teeth. I have gay friends who would consider it heaven, but it doesn't feel like it to me. Not least because everybody is staring at me.

Not that I blame them. To their eyes I probably look like a furry albino dwarf, from a planet that isn't Planet Cuba. Not that there's the slightest hint of aggression, just mild amused curiosity. And then a middle-aged black woman with bright orange hair whose profession is immediately recognizable by the dark blue miniskirt and black fishnet tights, – she is the ticket collector – takes pity on me and finds me a seat in one of the few compartments occupied by women. Obviously she thinks I'll feel more at home there. I use the expression 'compartment' in the loosest possible sense. It has no doors or windows.

A few minutes later I'm joined by a familiar face, another male: the bloke from the waiting-room with a bottle of rum in his coat. He takes a long swig, winks at me as if to say, 'see, it all worked out in the end', pulls his baseball cap down over his eyes and is immediately fast asleep. Now I can see the point of the rum.

Managing some sleep on this train is no mean achievement. The compartments have no lighting, which would be a good thing except that the corridor is lit by bright flickering fluorescent tubes and as there are no doors. In any case the corridor seems to be the place to chill for most of the giants who are shouting and calling loudly to one another as we move off and our motion creates a welcome breeze. I wedge my bag under my legs and try to close my eyes, sprawled like everyone else across seats that might once have pulled out to make half-decent sleeping accommodation but are now only loosely connected to the carriagework and slope onto the compartment floor. The air is rich with the sounds and smells of humanity thrown together in much closer proximity than anything I have been used to since I last took part in a scrum on a school rugby pitch. And that wasn't yesterday.

For a few hours of noisy, rocking, bumping, constantly interrupted semi-dozing, I try to dream of anywhere but where I am right now, my mind continuously going back to the neatly groomed Cuban couple in the bar of the Hotel Velasco, who thought it hilarious I was travelling *en tren*. I'm just trying hard to see the funny side.

I'm not sure whether it's a dream or a nightmare when I'm tapped on the shoulder and surface groggily from semi-slumber to be told in a heavily rum-flavoured voice that we're pulling into Santa Clara, the Cradle of the Revolution. I feel exhausted just thinking about it.

CHAPTER SEVEN

Che, Comandante!

In the Royal Navy during the Second World War they used to sleep for just four hours at a time. It's amazing what it can do for you.

By 9 a.m., after yet another glass of thick mango juice, slice of banana bread and a fried egg on a plate, all served up by the genial old gent who opened the door to me in the middle of the night, I'm out on the sunny streets of Santa Clara, strolling down towards the self-same railway tracks I rattled on which into town a few hours earlier.

There are big clouds rolling ominously overhead but the sun is shining and there is a sudden explosion of salsa music from within the whitewashed walls of the house across the road. I'm slowly getting to grips with the Cuban front door system: everyone leaves them wide open for relief from the heat – only the very richest Cubans contribute to global warming by artificially turning the inside of their houses into refrigerators – but in front of every door is a wrought-iron grille which can be separately locked for security. Not that anyone much has anything worth stealing.

A horse-drawn cart with a canopy, of the sort I saw at the station waiting to pick up passengers, trundles by. According to my host they work as a sort of bus service, running services up and down the grid, one lot going north–south, another going east–west. Except that that is only the theory. The drivers aren't employed by any sort of public transport system; they just take passengers and take money so you can never be sure how many are going in which direction or at what time. You just take pot luck. Most of Cuba seems to work on what, if it weren't an apparent contradiction in terms, you'd have to call profit-driven freelance communism.

At the bottom of the hill where the railway tracks cross the road, there's a little shop selling Che souvenirs, opposite a nearly kept children's park with brightly painted swings and roundabouts, artistically ripped up railway sleepers, a bright yellow bulldozer on a pedestal, some concrete sculptural representations of explosive blasts and a train with a 20mm canon on it.

The monument to the *tren blindado*, the armoured train which Fulgencio Batista had sent from Havana to crush the rebellion, is possibly the most singular war memorial I have ever seen. There is not just the fact that it feels like a children's playground, and is all but connected to one on the other side of the tracks, it is at once small-scale and highly dramatic. It feels like a specially constructed downsized theme park exhibit, and yet these aren't mock-ups: these bright red coaches, poised in the moment of derailment, the bazookas inside, the gun on the flat-top carriage, are not reconstructions, but the real items, albeit lovingly restored and preserved.

This was it: the Battle of Santa Clara, the crucial engagement of the Cuban Revolution, involved just a few hundred men and the crucial weapon was a bright yellow Caterpillar bulldozer. It's sitting just over there, looking for all the world like it's waiting for Bob the Builder to take it away. It doesn't look threatening or imposing or anything but comfortingly familiar: if it weren't for the concrete blast spikes and the museum exhibit photograph captions it could be a stylized snapshot of Sunday afternoon 'engineering work' on a British branch line, the picture made perfect by the fact there is nobody working.

So much of the Castro iconography, for us children of the second half of the twentieth century, is imbued with the qualities of both myth and the disconcertingly familiar. I am sure I had a toy bulldozer just like this one when I was a toddler, which, come to think of it, was probably just around the time of the Battle of Santa Clara. Compare it with the other icons of the time: by December 1958, when Che and his fellow revolutionaries got round to attacking their first train, Elvis had already produced his first volume of golden records and people were playing his Christmas album, Buddy Holly was just two months away from his final fatal flight and James Dean had already been dead for two years.

There are enough books on Che Guevara to fill a library, but given that the city of Santa Clara has become a shrine to the most recognized revolutionary on the planet, it is worth taking a minute out to revisit how he got here.

Both men would both have hated the comparison but Ernesto 'Che' Guevara was and is to many Latin Americans what JFK was and is to their fellow continentals up north: the great romantic tragic hero who summed up their ideals and was gunned down in his prime. Guevara didn't even live to see his fortieth birthday.

The young Argentinian was born into a family with Spanish, Basque and Irish roots, impeccably middle-class liberals with vaguely leftist leanings. If they had been English, they would have been *Guardian* readers.

Despite severe asthma, which plagued him all his short life, young 'Ernestitio' became a keen athlete, a football and rugby player and keen cyclist. He played chess and read poetry, particularly Pablo Neruda and Federico García Lorca, but could also quote Kipling's *If* and browsed endlessly among his parents' collection of more than 3,000 books.

His early reading material included Jules Verne and H. G. Wells as well as Karl Marx, Lenin and Friedrich Engels; he studied Bertrand Russell, Aristotle, Nietzsche and Freud, so it was more than mildly patronizing when a CIA report later referred to him as 'fairly intellectual for a Latino'.

It was an instinctive sympathy towards the poor and downtrodden of Latin America that led him to study medicine at the University of Buenos Aires. In 1950, aged twenty-two, he took off on a 4,500-kilometre (2,800-mile) journey around rural northern Argentina on a bicycle which he had fitted with a small motor.

A year later he took time off from his studies to embark on a Latin American odyssey with his friend Alberto Granada, riding a spluttering 1939 500cc Norton motorbike. They travelled through Argentina, Chile, Peru, Ecuador, Colombia, Venezuela, Panama and ended up in Miami before returning home to finish his studies.

On the trip they encountered appalling working conditions at a US-owned copper mine in northern Chile, volunteered for work at a leper colony in the Peruvian rainforest (during which time he swam across the Amazon, a distance of 4 kilometres [2.5 miles]), before ending up working as a barman in Miami to earn the money to fly home.

The trip convinced him that Latin America should be seen as a single entity rather than a collection of disparate countries, but also that the only way to liberate its people from oppressive militaristic regimes was through armed revolution.

The diary he kept was intended to be private, but after his death his family edited the manuscript and it was bought by a Cuban publishing house. Brought out in 1993, the subsequent translation into English publicized as 'Easy Rider meets Das Kapital', it has on several occasions made the *New York Times* bestseller list and became a hit film in 2004.

It was Guevara's second continent-spanning expedition, in 1954, which brought him to Guatemala where he met some Cuban would-be revolutionaries. He ran into them again the following year in Mexico City, including a group who were on the run after carrying out an abortive raid on a military barracks in Cuba. One of them was Raúl Castro, who introduced him to his big brother, a bushy-bearded lawyer-turned-revolutionary called Fidel.

He had found brothers-in-arms; for their part, they had found an earnest young doctor with revolutionary ideals, an odd Argentine accent and funny way of speaking. The best way to explain it is to imagine someone who puts 'man' into every other phrase: 'Y'know, man, there's this thing I want to say, man, and it's like we are so oppressed, man, it's unbe-lievable.' The word Argentinians used in place of 'man', was *che*. A sloppy speech mannerism had given birth to a legend. He had just taken the first step on the road to Santa Clara.

Primarily in the position of medical officer, Che was with Fidel and the 80 others who boarded the leaky old cabin cruiser named after a previous owner's grandmother and set out for Cuba in November 1956. The US-backed Cuban dictator Fulgencio Batista's men found them not long after they had disembarked from *Granma*, and most were either killed or captured. It was during the gunfight that Che put down his medical kit and picked up a box of ammunition. The transition was complete.

The few survivors holed up in the near impenetrable Sierra Maestre mountains in the island's far south-east. Over the hard years of struggling to survive, helped by impover-ished subsistence farmers, Che became a formidable guer-rilla leader. The former doctor also acquired a reputation for ruthlessness, on one occasion summarily executing with a bullet in the head a peasant who had sold information on their whereabouts to government forces.

Despite being given the grand title of *Comandante* by Castro, Che probably was in charge of no more than a couple of hundred men. Encouraged by a botched government campaign to suppress them, they decided to strike back. Santa Clara had a garrison of 2,500 troops but the people were behind the rebels. On the morning of December 28 – while people in the United States were still humming along to Elvis's *Here Comes Santa Claus (Right Down Santa Claus Lane)* – Che and his men took on the troops in a guerrilla attack.

With the help of local townspeople they managed to seize the Caterpillar bulldozer and some tractors from the university's agriculture school and ripped up the railway tracks, right where I am standing now, if the legend is to be believed.

There are, of course, many – particularly among the Cuban exiles in the US – who do not believe the legend, and suggest that there never was a real battle and the train was sold out by officers on board. The official version is that it was derailed, then heroically stormed by the ill-equipped revolutionaries, and townsfolk armed with Molotov cocktails.

Che himself encouraged the most romantic 'triumphant underdogs' version, not least because it was to be a keystone in building his legend. History is always written by the victors. There probably was a battle of some sort, but most of the ordinary troops on board the train and in the barracks had appallingly low morale, harboured sympathy for the rebels and as soon as their officers lost heart, happily gave up the fight, encouraging the wave of defections and surrenders which subsequently swept the country.

Che, ever the propaganda expert, announced the victory over his own pirate radio *Rebelde*, detailing huge amounts of arms and ammunition that had allegedly fallen into his hands. Whether or not the figures were true, the propaganda had the right effect. Within hours of his 'victory' announcement on December 31, Batista fled the country. Castro declared his victory on January 2 in Santiago, scene of his débâcle raid six years earlier, and within the week rode into Havana after a triumphal march the length of the country.

That's the legend. Or the history lesson. I had done the victory monument; now it was time for the shrine.

I had intended to catch an 'uptown' horse and cart bus, but – just like in London – there's never a bus when you want one, no matter what it runs on. So I grab a *bicitaxi* instead, feeling only slightly guilty when I realize it really is an uptown journey; from the *tren blindado* to the Che memorial is a long, slow uphill nearly all the way. I can almost feel the strain in my taxi man's calf muscles as we crawl up to the main square and the blissful relief as we plateau out and freewheel much of the rest of the way to the great grey and rose granite-slabbed parade ground that looks, with its banks of floodlights and towering stone obelisk, like a cross between an American football field and the Nuremberg rally site.

Just to make the kitsch complete there is piped music, playing ethereally from loudspeakers in the floodlights, a mix of revolutionary and Cuban patriotic songs, and of course, inevitably, *that* song, the one that along with *Guantanamera* leaves an indelible impression on anyone who has visited this island: *Hasta siempre, Comandante!*

Written in 1965 by Carlos Puebla to a haunting melody that I have heard done as a romantic song of loss, a martial anthem, and an almost hip-hop version – as with church music in the middle ages, in Cuba if the words are right you can get away with almost any melody – it is ostensibly a reply to his farewell letter when he left Havana for the final time to foment revolution elsewhere. By then his mix of movie-star good looks and revolutionary fervour had made him a global celebrity, feted from Moscow and Beijing to Dar es Salaam, Algiers and Limerick.

After he was captured and brutally executed by Bolivian government troops aided by the CIA in 1967, the song which played on Che's own slogan *Hasta la victoria siempre*, 'Ever onwards to victory', became an anthem, seen as a poignant farewell, a tribute to the legend made all the more power-ful by his martyrdom. Here echoes round the palm-fringed square just as, almost on cue, a couple on a motorbike ride across it. The 'easy rider' thing is no joke: that combination of youthful idealism and footloose romanticism became the distilled essence of the 1960s, and despite the often bit-ter taste of harsh realism that has come to flavour the mod-ern world, it is a mythology that is still remarkably easy to evoke.

The Che memorial complex is an extravagant devotional shrine. Whatever political changes engulf Cuba in the years ahead, it is hard to imagine any future government of what-ever political persuasion demolishing it. Che himself, a giant warrior in bronze, looks out from the top of his granite obelisk, inscribed with his own wishful, visionary, prophetic words:

'I feel myself strongly to be a patriot for Latin America, for any Latin American country, that at this moment if it were necessary I would lay down my life for the liberation of any of the Latin American countries, without asking for anything or expecting anything.'

Before entering the museum housed on one side of the base of the obelisk, I am required to check in my bag and camera. Along with groups of reverent Cuban schoolkids – who have begun every morning of their school life declar-ing 'We will be like Che' – I pass through the great doors to inspect relics, venerated as much as those of any saint. They are curiously touching: a copy of his original registration as a trained nurse, on which he comes across as a better-looking dark-haired Leonardo Di Caprio, a similarity that is even more striking on his name tag as an athlete in the Pan-American games.

This collection of objects brings the man closer. There is the Soviet Zenit camera he used in Mexico in 1955, a set of dental instruments he carried with him and, a testament to his own occasional frailty, an ancient leather and glass asthma inhaler.

Then there are the tools of his other trade, a Colt revolver, a Stevens rifle, a Thompson sub-machine gun, the M1 carbine he used in the Battle of Santa Clara. Next to me a twenty-something Cuban guide it would be easy to take for a California college kid in yellow baseball cap, shorts, sneakers and shades is explaining to his younger compatriots Che's tactics with the bulldozer and farm tractors.

Another glass case holds the 'Transoceanic Wave-Magnet' radio he used to transmit news of the rebels' victory, a cap he wore during voluntary work at wheat mills in 1962, at a time when he was a government minister, his fountain pen and the inkwell he used along with the banknotes bearing his signature from the period 1959–61 when the Marxist revolutionary was Finance Minister and president of Cuba's Central Bank.

It reminds me of the former Bavarian royal residence, now the Münchner Residenz museum in Munich: they have enough pieces of John the Baptist not just to clone him but to rebuild his corpse several times over. We may not have body parts, but these relics are real; the saint died barely half a century ago.

There is even the Guevara universe's equivalent of the crown of thorns: the black beret with the star worn in

Cuban photographer's Alberto Korda's iconic portrait taken of him at a rally in Havana in 1960. Korda entitled the picture *Guerrillero Heroico* (*Heroic Warrior*) and it went on to become a global icon of revolution, for which Korda himself never received a cent, convertible or otherwise, for abuse of his copyright, insisting he favoured anything that would 'propagate his memory and the cause of social justice throughout the world'. He changed his mind on only one occasion, in 2000, suing the vodka firm Smirnoff for using it in an advert, claiming he hadn't intended it to be used to market alcohol. Even then he donated the US$50,000 settlement he received to Cuba's healthcare system.

But there was another incident that helped the Korda image become a global icon. Improbably, but as so often in these things, it concerns an Irishman.

Apocryphally, Jim Fitzpatrick was working as a teenage barman in Kilkee in the south-west of Ireland one evening back in 1963 when who should come in and order a whiskey but Che himself. Guevara was on his way back to Cuba from Moscow and they had touched down to refuel in Shannon airport – where Aeroflot had established a refuelling base – and been stranded by fog. Deciding to make the best of it, the revolutionary had nipped out for a touch of local colour in the form of a drop of the hard stuff.

Stunned by his brief encounter, Fitzpatrick, an art student, followed the great man's career and on his death adapted the Korda photograph into what he himself called a 'psychedelic print', in which Che's 'hair was not hair, it was shapes', 'it looks like he is in seaweed'. Fitzpatrick created the image for a Dutch anarchist magazine, but he also hand-printed thousands and gave them away on the streets of London. He said he wanted them to 'breed like rabbits'. They did, becoming the icon of revolution that has adorned T-shirts and student bedroom walls ever since.

The final case holds mementos of his martyrdom: a copy of the fake Uruguayan passport he used to enter Bolivia, the water bottle and hypodermic syringe he carried, the saddle on which he rode through the Aguarague mountains to Camiri. There is even – the equivalent of the Holy Grail used at Christ's last supper – the plate on which he was served food at a Bolivian school in 1967, just weeks before his capture and execution.

Just across a cool granite-walled hallway from the museum is the holy of holies itself: the mausoleum. Unlike the rubberized embalmed Lenin's grim edifice in Moscow's Red Square or Spanish dictator Franco's grandiose mock medieval tomb carved into the heart of a mountain in the Valley of the Fallen, Che Guevara's last resting place is one of the least intimidating, most curiously relaxing tombs I have ever come across.

For a start the room is gratifyingly cool, with low lighting, with gentle piped music, not religious, martial or mournful, just a cool, laid-back jazz, or gentle Latino folk music, the sort you might put on in the background after a dinner party with friends. The floor is solid wood, the walls made of flat polished granite blocs, thin like Roman bricks, interrupted here and there by a plaque with a bas-relief of the face of one of thirty revolutionary heroes, including the six Bolivians caught and executed along with him. In front of each is a small glass of water with a single flower.

Che's is the same size and shape as all the others, no greater, no more elaborate, at the far end of the room, next to a little tropical garden, not so much a sepulchral shrine as an awe-inspiring fairy grotto. I was prepared for a riot of bad taste, and find instead a symphony of tasteful discretion.

It is also fairly recent, built in 1996 a year after Guevara's bones were found in a mass grave in Bolivia, identified by the missing hands, cut off on the orders of the Bolivian president to be sent to Buenos Aires to identify his finger-prints, and a small pouch of tobacco given him by a helicop-ter pilot which was found next to the body. The remains were 'repatriated' to Cuba – he was bizarrely declared a 'Cuban citizen by birth' after the Battle of Santa Clara – and interred in the mausoleum built in his honour on October 17, 1997. He received a twenty-one-gun salute while a choir of school-children sang – what else? – *Hasta siempre, Comandante*.

'It gets more than a million visitors every year,' my *bici-taxi* man tells me as I climb back on board (the power of the convertible peso is such that he was waiting around for over an hour to be sure to catch me coming out). Conversation lapses though as he pants heavily to get us back up the hill to Santa Clara's main square, stopping only briefly to visit a sort of children's zoo where there is yet another statue of Che. I try to look impressed but I've had about as much hero worship as I can take for one day.

On the way we pass alternative examples of Cuban art-istry: a white wall painted with satirical anti-American cartoons. They are mostly crude propaganda by state-spon-sored artists, but not without humour: a grotesque over-weight marine bristling with weaponry including rockets and machine guns, holds a mobile phone to his ear, saying, 'Sure, Mom, I'll watch out for the terrorists.'

Back in the main square, I climb out and over tip my *bici-taxi* man – with a 5 CUC note, a good week's wages for any-one paid in national pesos. I hate the thought that I might be distorting the market, but he's done me stalwart service and the impulse to put a smile on his face is just too great.

Apart from anything else I realize what I need after my morning of worthy worship at the city shrines is a stiff drink, and the *bicitaxi* man has pointed me in what seems the right direction, a bar called La Marquesina on the corner: 'They have great music there in the evening too.'

Right now what I want is a shot of rum. Straight. I walk into a splendid dark room with a long dark Victorian hardwood bar and a guy in white shirtsleeves and a black waistcoat behind it. 'What's your best rum?' I ask him, and without thinking he brings down a bottle of Havana Club 15 *años*, and pours me a shot, rich, dark and naturally sweet. I raise it only to see staring down at me, the iconic beret-clad face embedded in a Cuban flag, who else but the man himself? I raise my glass silently: Cheers Che!

◆

Supper in Santa Clara is relaxed, the usual home cooking: barely done pork with some oily fried potatoes. But my host Pablo has procured me a bottle of red wine: Spanish *tinto*, absolutely *ordinario* but drinkable. He shares a glass with me (getting wine for his guests, paid in CUCs, is the only way he can afford to drink it) and we discuss the changing world. We are in the open courtyard which, as in Matanzas, here too is at the centre of the house, except that he has made a wet weather cover – of corrugated green plastic. Which turns out to have been a very good idea as the dark clouds above us have opened again and there is now a little line of steady waterfalls pouring onto the concrete floor. Pedro shrugs.

He makes a point of avoiding politics but points out ruefully that a surgeon is Cuba earns just 350 pesos a month (that's about £12), though as he is charging me nearly double that per night (cheap for me, life-changing income for him). He is hardly impoverished. Nor does he need to advertise. My panic about getting a phone to call ahead and book rooms was unnecessary; I am here because he is a friend of the woman in whose house I stayed in Matanzas. And he has already organized my accommodation further down the island. They may have limited access to the internet in Cuba but social (and commercial) networking is doing fine on the telephone.

Like Isabel, the anaesthetist on the train, Pablo belongs to the generation for which communism wasn't an aberration but an alternative global system. He served as a doctor alongside the up to 18,000 Cuban troops sent to Africa during the horribly complicated part-tribal, part-ideological battle for Angolan independence. The Cubans' role was primarily to fight back against South African forces that invaded to set up a regime favourable to Pretoria. They ended up also fighting an invading force from Zaïre in the north and gave support to the SWAPO guerrilla movement fighting for the independence of South African-ruled South West Africa.

Pablo shakes his head when he thinks about it. It was clearly not a particularly happy experience – there were the usual allegations of atrocities all round – although as a doctor, he clearly believes the Cubans did a good humanitarian job. There are also those who believe that without the Cubans' intervention, South Africa would never have allowed South West Africa to become independent as Namibia in 1989[4]. But at least 2,000 Cubans died during the fighting.

Apropos of some comment or other Pablo decides he must look something up on the internet, clearly proud of having access to it. He leads me into an elegant dark-panelled, book-lined study and fires up an ancient-looking PC. I only realize how ancient when the bulky humming CRT screen finally comes to life and reveals it is running Windows 95. But just as he launches Internet Explorer and finds Google to locate the answer to whatever was on his mind, there is a crackle and simultaneously the screen goes black and the lights go out. 'It's a power cut,' he mumbles tetchily. 'It's

---

4. In early November, 1989, I was sent by the *Sunday Times* to Windhoek to report on the elections ahead of Namibian independence, but left early, only just in time to get back to Berlin to witness the fall of the Berlin Wall. See *1989: The Berlin Wall (My part in its Downfall)* also published by Arcadia Books.

because of the rain. It happens,' and then he says the phrase I have been waiting for, '*Cuba e' Cuba*.'

This is where I play my joker. Packed in my rucksack, in an outer pocket so I know how to find it, is a torch. Not just any torch, but a wind-up torch. I had an inkling getting batteries in Cuba might have been a problem. It does the trick and gets a gasp of amazement. He's heard about them but never seen them. That's Cuba, it's me that thinks it this time: the government spends a fortune on importing Chinese energy-saving light bulbs but nobody has wind-up torches.

But within minutes, he and his wife have produced a vast store of candles. Power cuts are clearly a regular occurrence. His daughter-in-law emerges from the kitchen to help light them while keeping in check the excited giggles of two of Pablo's granddaughters. Then without warning the lights come on again. I decide it's time for a nightcap at the Marquesina and head out leaving a scene of blissful domesticity: three generations, the grandparents in rocking chairs, gathered round the television, watching an ancient sitcom.

It could be anywhere, I tell myself.

But in the modern world, could it?

CHAPTER EIGHT

Sun, Sand and Rain

The next morning it is still raining. Santa Clara is a sea of umbrellas, which the locals of course call parasols. They mostly use them '*para sol*', for the sun. Funny then that we in England who have practically adopted this ancient device as national costume call it an umbrella, a 'little shade'. It takes the French to call it what we should: a *parapluie*. For the rain!

And when it rains in Cuba, it rains. It has been raining all night. Constantly. Heavily. Pablo's inside-outside courtyard was on its way to becoming a swimming pool, watered from a green corrugated Niagara.

After a long conversation on the phone with the station Pablo has found what he believes to be the time of my next train connection, leaving at 9.30 in the morning, which would be a relatively civilized time if it weren't that of course they recommend getting there at least two hours early. But Pablo *thinks* they might sell me a ticket any time on the same day, so in theory – a theory he miraculously believes will work – I might be able to pick one up just after midnight.

I walk up into the main square, with the idea of going to the bank to change money. The sign on the door says is open, but it is closed. A man inside shakes his head and points at the unlit fluorescent tube on the ceiling. The peso drops. The power has gone again. And even in Cuba, no power = no tills.

An improvising taxi-driver hustles me while I am gesticulating at the man on the other side of the door. 'Later, it will be open later,' he says. 'You like a nice ride, out to country, see old church.' Normally I would have brushed him away, but he's also rubbing his thumbs and forefingers together, indicating he can change. So with just a little reluctance I climb in the back of his car, a relatively luxurious fifteen-year-old Peugeot.

In theory Cubans are not allowed to deal in foreign currency, even to swap CUCs for national pesos; in practice everybody does it. Anything that brings hard currency into the country is tolerated. It ends up in the government's coffers anyway. Locals are of course allowed to change CUCs into national pesos and vice versa in a bank. One CUC buys you 24 *nacionales* but it costs 25 *pesos nacionales* to buy one CUC. Even under communism, there's always a margin. On the street, Cubans will cut you exactly the same deal. It's just that the government feels it's somehow morally corrupting for its citizens to do what the banks do. Given our recent experience in the capitalist world, they may have a very good point.

For my taxi driver, whose name is Santiago, it's a doubly lucky day: not only does he change some euros into CUC for me, he manages to persuade me to give a large part of them back to him in exchange for a guided tour of the countryside north of the city, including the little town of Remedios famed for its ancient church with thirteen gold altars. Given that the rain still hasn't stopped and the streets are filled with yelping schoolkids splashing in puddles, it seems a better idea than sitting soaking up rum all day in La Marquesina.

Also, Santiago is quite the conversationalist. It turns out he is a trained engineer who has not only been abroad, but has a residence permit for the Canary Islands. But because he is not an EU national, he can't get a work permit which means it is far too expensive for him to live there. Back home in Santa Clara he has a relatively decent car and because his family have a good sized house enabling them to let out a room for foreigners as a *casa*, he makes a reasonable living. Just about, he insists.

That does not make him a fan of the system. There is just one thing wrong with this country, he blurts out, in an admission I have not heard from any other Cuban yet: 'Fidel Castro.' And then, as if an afterthought, he adds: 'And his brother.'

The irony is that Santiago is not necessarily a radical anti-communist, campaigning for the middle class to take back power from the proletariat: in some ways his attitudes are rather the reverse. 'Look at our leaders. They're all city boys. Or were. Lawyers. They make rules but they don't under-stand how stuff works. What you need to make an economy run.'

'Look at those fields,' he cries almost in despair as we drive north from Santa Clara through scrubland where a few scrawny cattle are not so much grazing as mooching about with their mates wondering when the rain will end. 'There are maybe 20 cows there. But it is a big field. Why not 200? We have sun, we have rain. It could grow grass for them to eat. But all the land belongs to the government. Then the government pays farmers just 80 pesos a month to work the land. Why would they bother?'

I take his point; 80 pesos is about £3 (US$5). 'Without the *Libreta*,' Santiago fumes, 'they would starve. Sometimes they do anyway.' The *Libreta* is the Cuban ration card, introduced in 1962, which is intended to ensure everyone gets subsist-ence rations. It guarantees an almost free supply of rice, black beans, sugar and potatoes. If you have a child under seven years of age you also get milk. This is what 90 per cent of Cubans live on. Anything else is literally a luxury.

What annoys Santiago most is not communist ruthlessness, but an impractical romanticism: 'The heroes of the revolution think jungle, savannah is more beautiful than farmland, more authentic. But you can't eat that.'

'Pah!' he says pointing to the propaganda signs every few kilometres. One declares boldly: 'The young are rich with new ideas.' In his early forties, Santiago is young – by the standards of the octogenarians in power in Havana anybody under pensionable age is young – and he has ideas. I just don't think the men in Havana are going to like them.

He complains that the price of fuel no longer makes such a sought-after job as driving a taxi as profitable as it was, even if things are much better than they were in the early 90s after the collapse of the Soviet Union.

Thanks to the 'revolutionary friendship' between the Castros and Hugo Chavez, the late Marxist president of oil-rich Venezuela, Cuba has had an adequate supply of fuel. Cuba trains Venezuelan doctors and dentists and gets oil in exchange. It was only later, after leaving the country, that I discovered Chavez had been in Cuba at the same time as I was, at a top government hospital in Havana receiving treatment for cancer that prolonged his life even if in the end it couldn't save it.

Under Chavez Cuba and Venezuela have had what is widely referred to – in a phrase that has a certain irony to British ears – as a 'special relationship'. But that does not mean that ordinary Cubans get cheap fuel: 'Petrol is 1.30 CUC a litre and diesel 1.10,' Santiago complains. You simply can't buy it for 'national' pesos. It sounds unimaginable to our ears, but then owning a car is unimaginable to the vast majority of Cubans. Those few who have access to a vehicle as part of their job get a free fuel ration, as do farmers and factories. Selling fuel to private individuals is effectively a supertax on people like Santiago effectively running private – theoretically illegal – taxi services. It is unlikely to earn him much sympathy from the masses to whom owning a car is the equivalent of being an investment banker.

'What about sugar?' I ask naïvely, looking for some successful branch of the Cuban economy and vaguely aware that the price has risen on world markets of late.

'Hah! We gave the Russians all the sugar they wanted,' he snorts. 'Everything was devoted to sugar. We produced millions of tonnes. Millions more than we needed. When the Soviet Union collapsed it was all we had to eat. So what did they do? They got rid of all the sugar plantations and refineries. And what did they replace them with?' He points at the scrub landscape. 'Nothing. Maybe a few goats.'

To make the point he swings by what was once a flourishing sugar refinery and is now – poignantly – a museum of the sugar industry. 'Come,' he says, 'I will show you.'

We pull through a wide gateway and the woman in the gatehouse beams when she sees Santiago. This is clearly not the first time he has brought her a customer. I realize I am being strung along a bit here, but in a way that's what I've paid for. I hand over my entrance fee (in CUC) for my guided tour of the demise of Cuba's sugar industry.

Still unable to wipe the smile off her face, the gate lady beckons us over to what looks like an ancient industrial mangle over a water tank. She takes a thick piece of sugar cane about two foot long and feeds it between the rollers squeezing it to produce a greenish-grey juice. It takes three canes before there is enough to fill a glass and I sip it gingerly. Unsurprisingly it is sweet. Very. And a bit warm. Not really my cup of tea.

By now the guide has been summoned, a bright-eyed pale-skinned woman with green eyes, who could almost be

Irish, who is thrilled to have a customer, if a little uncertain about her English. I tell her I can manage a decent bit of Spanish, but she is desperate for the practice. Monica is thirty-five years old and not only has she – understandably – never been abroad, she has never been to Havana; in fact she's never been further than Caibarién, the coastal town at the end of the road.

She's one of the few people to be still working at what was once the province's major industry. The sugar mill here closed more than a decade ago, which she says also proved a kiss of death to Caibarién, which used to be a major seaport.

She shows me into a little room converted into a makeshift cinema while she pushes a button marked 'Inglés' and disappears outside for a smoke. For the next 10 minutes I sit through a dull little documentary on the rise and fall of the sugar industry from its slave trade origins to today's 'modern revitalization', which has little in common with the rusting relics outside.

Then Monica takes me on a tour of various bits of machinery, some of which are obvious antiques brought in to display but most are just left as they were when the mill ceased functioning. It's not so much a working museum as an industrial ghost town. Or perhaps I should say ghost train: she tells me there is normally a little steam train that runs to Remedios. Only not today. When was the last one? She's not too sure about that either.

One day, she says as we leave, she'd like to go to England. Or the United States. She seems a little hazy about the difference. But not today. And not tomorrow either.

Remedios is only a few minutes drive away. One of the oldest little towns in Cuba, it was founded some time between 1513 and 1524. The 1524 date is the first known because that is when a captain in the army of Spanish conquistador Diego

Velázquez de Cuéllar (the conqueror of Cuba and no known relation to the later painter of the same name), married the daughter of a local Taino Indian chief. Allegedly he went on to father 200 children. Presumably not all by her.

With the rain still pouring down, there is little incentive to admire its faded colonial architecture other than from the car window. But the church is another matter. In fact, there are two of them, both several hundred years old, though one is in a serious state of decay, while the other, the *Iglesia Mayor* (main church) has been expensively maintained. Santiago drops me at the door, and says he'll go for a smoke while he waits.

Inside the dark church porch a man in civilian clothes pounces on me almost immediately, describing himself as the priest, even though he is in civvies, and offers me a guided tour. Free? 'Of course, it is the house of the Lord.' I'm sceptical, but accept.

Dominating the interior is the vast golden High Altar which strikes the eye immediately not least because this floor-to-ceiling baroque wonder is covered with gold leaf. For much of its existence the ordinary parishioners would not have known that, because for most of its history Remedios was plagued by real-life pirates of the Caribbean, who turned up to loot and pillage more times than Johnny Depp has reprised Captain Jack Sparrow. To stop said pirates slicing chunks off the altar, it spent several centuries covered in whitewash.

It was only during a 1944 restoration project, financed by a local millionaire philanthropist (in the days when Cuba had such things) primarily intended to preserve the magnificent seventeenth-century mahogany ceiling that the whitewash was chipped and the gold underneath discovered.

The priest leads me around the church pointing out the other altars and their attendant images. The Iglesia Mayor in Remedios is remarkable because there aren't just a few of these. Including the High Altar there 13 in total. The priest is at some pains to point out that each has at least two names. These are not just saints in the orthodox Roman Catholic sense, deceased holy human beings who have influence with God. In the exotic landscape of Cuba's unique contribution to human religions, they are demigods in their own right. Welcome to the wacky world of Santería.

It is a concept I am vaguely familiar with but this is the first time I have heard someone who appears to be a Roman Catholic clergyman discuss it as if it were the most natural thing in the world. An Afro-Caribbean-Latino fusion as exotic, diverse and individual as the music that sprang from the same ethnic roots, Santería is one of the greatest examples of *laissez-faire* pragmatism in religious history.

Basically the slaves imported to Cuba, mostly from the Yoruba tribe of what is now Nigeria, did not want to give up their old gods, but were forced by the Spanish to convert to Christianity. The lucky thing for them was that it was not the Christianity of the puritanical stern and serious Protestants, but the far more colourful Roman Catholic version, with its plethora of saints often worshipped by the devout in their own right. The Yoruba simply grafted their own gods onto them.

'This is Saint Francis of Assisi. But some people prefer to call him Orula,' he says, pointing to a gilt, tonsured figure. In the version I learned at Sunday School, Saint Francis of Assisi was a sort of humble, balding, berobed Doctor Doolittle who could talk to the animals (and favourite of the present pope). In Santería he has a few other things to deal with: for a start, Orula is fond of coconuts and black chickens, his favourite number is sixteen, he is a seeker after knowledge and the patron of all priests (known as *babala-wos*). Is Orula/Francis who knows the future and facilitates communication with the gods. His worshippers wear neck-laces of green and white beads.

'And this,' the priest (though I am beginning to think I should refer to him as a *babalawo*) says reverently pointing to a dark figure on one altar, 'is Babalu-aye'. It is the first time he has not used the Catholic name first. And his other name? 'Saint Lazarus.' My knowledge of Catholic saints is scant, but I assume this is the same Lazarus as Christ raised from the dead. It seems more than probable as he explains to me Babalu-aye is seen as the 'lord of the body', associated with epidemics, including smallpox and AIDS. Scary.

One statuette particularly interests me. Having written a thriller based on the disputed origins of the cult of the Virgin Mary[5] I am fascinated by the little black figure in a gold robe with her own glass-fronted altar and the flag of Cuba behind her. This, the priest tells me, is a representation of the Virgin Mary worshipped as the patron saint of Cuba. But also, he adds as if it were the most natural thing in the world for a practising Roman Catholic to say, as 'Yemaya, goddess of the sea. Her symbol is the star.'

To my own surprise, I give a nod of understanding. Maybe there is something in these parallels after all. A Catholic church near where I once lived in south-east London was dedicated to 'Maria, Stella Maris': the star of the sea. Scholars also believe Yemaya was regarded as the divine incarnation of the river in Nigeria, and may ultimately be linked back to the Egyptian goddess Isis. I could take it even further, but that is literally another book.

The priest is now pointing out yet another Virgin Mary, on a separate altar. Despite the stereotypical snow-white com-plexion of so many European representations of the 'Mother of God', this one is easy to imagine as Yemaya. For a start,

---

5. *The Black Madonna* (2009), by Peter Millar is published by Arcadia Books.

instead of sitting solemnly nursing her special baby, this Virgin is dancing. It is easy to see why: she is clearly pregnant. 'The Immaculate Conception,' the priest says. Quite.

The interesting thing about Santería, and the one that most Roman Catholics from other parts of the world have the greatest problem with, is that it makes no reference to one of the more relatively important figures in Christianity: Jesus Christ. I ask the priest about this, and he just shrugs and smiles. Back in the cab, Santiago tells me it's because in African culture they see it as a bit a weakness having a god who gets killed. Just to confuse me further he says the religion has two other names – Lucumi, which sounds exactly like the Turkish word for Turkish delight – and the Regla de Ocha. Just what the differences are I have no idea. He shrugs and says, 'names'. I tip him a CUC and walk back into the light.

And light there is indeed. The great golden orb has suddenly emerged from behind the swathes of dark clouds. All of a sudden one of the oldest religions of all and appears particularly attractive: sun worship. I may have been sweating and seeking shade on the streets of Havana but I feel like I have spent the last twenty-four hours living under Niagara Falls. And as it turns out there is within close striking distance one of those things most foreign visitors to Cuba come for: a beach.

In fact we are close to some of the finest beaches in the whole of Cuba, the Cayas Santa Maria, a chain of little islands not unlike the Florida Keys (which were originally called *cayas*), linked by a 48-kilometre long causeway stretching out into the Caribbean and already well on the way to being a second Varadero, if not worse. They are almost totally off-limits to native Cubans. There is a checkpoint at the beginning of the causeway which requires a passport and an entrance free, payable of course only in CUCs.

But Santiago knows what he claims is a nice little beach just outside Caibarién. Within minutes I am stripped to my shorts clutching a cold beer and dabbling my feet in water that actually is the pale pastel blue colour of the tourist brochures. The beach is only 100 metres or so long, with a small hotel for Cubans at one end, with a rickety little shack serving food. Santiago proposes fetching something – we are both hungry by now – and I agree but with little expectation that it will be edible. My mistake. I am about to have the best meal I will have in Cuba.

The best, because it's the simplest. Over on some rocks at the end of the beach a couple of lads are fishing. Whenever they catch something they bring it over to the shack and a couple of grinning, broad-shouldered lads gut it, whack it the barbecue, sprinkle it liberally with sea salt and black pepper, and serve it up, fresh as could be, straight from the sea, even if you do have to eat it with a tiny reusable wooden fork off a piece of cardboard ripped from a case of beer. Who needs posh cutlery when you've got fish this good.

I have no idea what it sort of fish it is – it vaguely resembles a sea bass, but I suspect it is some local variety I wouldn't know if I was told it. The Cubans don't seem to know either. '*Pescado*,' the cook says with a shrug: fish. That's good enough for me. It's one of the best fish dishes I've eaten anywhere. Ever. And definitely the cheapest. The lads weighed it first and Santiago offers to pay. I let him, knowing he'll charge me for it later, but it hardly breaks even a Cuban's piggy bank: 9.60 *pesos nacionales*, about £0.40 ($0.60). Santiago orders two. I think he's going to take one back to his wife. But he eats both. There and then. Since the 'Special Period' Cubans have a *carpe diem* attitude towards food: if it's there, eat it.

◆

By the time we roll back into Santa Clara in late afternoon, however, the black clouds have rolled back too. I settle my account with Santiago who has one last pitch to throw at me: do I want some cigars?

This is a hustle that is omnipresent on the streets of Cuba, particularly in Havana, where street vendors will sidle by going, 'Psst Meester, you want seegar,' much in the same way blokes in Brixton with dreadlocks will try to sell you hashish. There is almost inevitably a catch: Cubans cannot afford Cuban cigars. The majority of the population smokes – got a light is one of the most popular pick-up lines, which makes *no fumo*, I don't smoke, almost as good a deterrent as answering in Russian – but they do smoke cigarettes. Not bad cigarettes, mind you, in fact probably far better than most of the 'fine Virginia' sold in the United States and Europe, but far less acceptable to the dwindling number of 'first world' smokers, because they are a lot stronger and unfiltered. In other words they taste like the real thing.

I don't smoke as a rule, and never have done, except for the odd joint at university – my enjoyment of which was much diminished by the presence of tobacco – and when I was sent by the *Sunday Times* to report on the drug trade in Amsterdam and had the immense perverse pleasure of submitting an expense claim for a quarter ounce of cannabis and three ready-rolled joints to Rupert Murdoch (paid without demur). But I have been known to enjoy a fine cigar. And they don't come any finer than Cuban.

Sadly the myth that they are rolled on the thighs of dusky maidens is untrue. I visited the Partagas cigar factory in Havana on my previous visit, and the business is done mostly by middle-aged men – the girls put on the little paper-rings or do the packaging – a sign, even in supposedly egalitarian but really traditionally macho Cuba, that this is serious: 'man's work'.

There is a skill in taking the various grades of tobacco – the main grade used for flavour, the thinner shreds which help keep it burning, and the top quality whole leaf outer wrappers – and blending them into a quality cigar. Most westerners can't easily afford the top quality ones either. A top notch Cohiba, Fidel's favourite back in the days when he was seldom seen without one, named after a Taino Indian chief, costs around £17 (US$25). Each.

So I have a few doubts when Santiago says he can get me a box of 25 Cohibas for 35 CUC. There is obviously a risk that they are not quite the real McCoy – the cigars sold by street vendors in Havana tend to be knocked up from sweepings from a cigar floor factory, with one half-decent leaf wrapped around them to look good. But it is also an open secret that anybody who is anybody in Cuba has a friend in a cigar factory who can 'acquire' the real thing, or near equivalent, as a knockdown price. And Santiago seems to me to be that sort of bloke. In any case, I am not going to smoke more than a few myself, and friends back in England will be delighted, so I agree. He promises to deliver them to my *casa* later that evening.

Right now I have another matter on my mind: keeping dry. The thunderclouds have opened and torrents of water are pouring off badly-tiled roofs, or down the furrows of the corrugated iron, the cobbled streets of the old town centre are awash. Santiago has left me at the corner of a street known simply as Boulevard. This is Santa Clara's equivalent of Bond Street, the pavements made of polished granite with a smart-looking bar called the Europa on one corner and a well-kept national peso shop on the other.

More in an attempt to get out of the rain than anything else I dash inside the peso shop and am immediately plunged into a moment of *déjà vu*. This could be Warsaw or Gdansk circa 1982: the shop is clean and the shelves are well-stocked, as long as you want tricycles or plastic potties. There are dozens of the former and hundreds of the latter, available in different colours. There is precious little of anything else at all. It is the classic problem of the centrally-planned economy: there is a shortage of potties, let's make millions.

When supply and demand is concentrated in the hands of a few individuals the law of market economy nature loses touch with reality. If there is someone deciding what he or she thinks the market needs, rather than someone trying to think on their feet and work out what will sell, what you end up with is a glut of plastic potties.

They are selling though. I see one man leave with two. This is another fact of the centralized economy: if you know someone who could use one, buy two, you never know when they might be available again.

I opt instead for the Europa bar next door and a cold Cristal beer. Despite the torrential rain, it is still over 30°C out there. The bar is heaving, almost exclusively with Cubans, further proof of the emergence of a new, tiny but growing CUC-rich class. The sign on the wall spells it out clearly: *moneda nacional* is not accepted. It is hard not to see this as a slap in the face for the ordinary Cuban to know that the currency in which his wages are paid is all but worthless in bars in his home town.

But, bizarrely, Cubans don't see it like that. They remember the period before the US dollar was made legal tender, and subsequently converted into the CUC. Nobody had anything, and nobody wants to go back there. In this curious state of communism on the potential verge of transition, it has become widely accepted that it is better for some people to have nice things than for nobody to have anything. At least this way there is a chance of trickle down, rather than stagnation and starvation. By accident Cuba has evolved a truly aspirational culture.

It is an attitude that I am about to have explained to me by an earnest young man who unsurprisingly tells me his name is Ernesto. Unsurprisingly not because he is earnest but because this is Santa Clara, shrine to Ernesto 'Che' Guevara. I imagine half the male population is called Ernesto, or at least claims to be; it is not unsurprising for Cubans to invent fictitious names when talking to foreigners.

He is trying to sell me a copy of the party newspaper *Granma*'s edition for young people *Juventud Rebelde* (*Rebel Youth*), which considering that about 70 per cent of its content is identical to *Granma*, is about as unrebellious as you can get. When I decline he tries to tap me for a CUC but I offer to buy him a beer instead.

Which he accepts gratefully and before long we are deep in discussion (or as deep as my relatively shallow command of Spanish will allow) of the Cuban economy. Ernesto is no outspoken critic of his government or the ruling party, but he does have some clear-cut views on what is happening to his country's society.

'They say we are a one-class society. It is not true. Not now. Now we have six classes: the top are people who work in the tourist industry and have easy access to CUCs, the second are people whose business lets them work in both currencies (he means taxi drivers like Santiago), the third are those whose families always had a house big enough to rent rooms (the *casa* owners), fourth are people married to foreigners, fifth are people with relatives abroad who send them money, and last, largest and lowest, are people like me, most people, who work in the state-run economy and get paid in pesos.'

According to Ernesto he is a baker who earns 200 pesos a month, or about eight CUCs, around £6 ($10). We talk prices and he is horrified when I say a beer in London costs the equivalent of five CUCs, and green with envy that the British national minimum hourly wage is the equivalent of his monthly salary. But I burst the bubble when I tell him that the average rent for a one bedroom flat in London is the equivalent of 1,200 CUCs (£800). He pays nothing. The flat comes with the job.

When dealing with economies so radically different in conception, the numbers game doesn't work. Yes, in comparison I am very rich and he is very poor. But only here. If I bumped into an Arab oil sheikh or Russian oligarch in London – and our money-based class system means that is very unlikely although there is no shortage of either – they would make a very similar comparison. The age-old problem of communism is that its apparently moral aim of trying to iron out unjust inequality has had to resort time and again to immoral means: repression and confiscation. And they in turn just build up a different system of inequality. The famed 'middle way' is as elusive to modern politicians and economists as the North-West Passage was to seventeenth-century mariners.

The nautical metaphor seems particularly apt at the moment, as I am beginning to think the only way to leave the cosy confines of the Europa bar – with its images of the Eiffel Tower, Brandenburg Gate and Tower of London on the walls – may be in an inflatable dinghy. Or perhaps padding in an upturned plastic potty from next door. Maybe I should have bought one after all.

But the downpour isn't bothering a couple of teenage lads across the way, who have stripped down to their shorts and are taking advantage of Boulevard's showpiece polished granite pavement for a spot of body surfing. This is as much entertainment as chatting with Ernesto has been enlightening, but by now I have bought him two beers and a burger and if I am not to have him as an accompaniment for life, it is time to go. Especially as a large man with a moustache has now entered the conversation with the clear intent of making sure the foreigner does not take away any unflattering ideas about the Cuban populace's lack of enduring revolutionary fervour.

Back at the *casa*, Pablo has rustled up *gambas al ajillo*, prawns in garlic, hopelessly overcooked so that the prawns are chewy and there is no perceptible taste of garlic. It is a curious fact that among denizens of hot climes in general and the Caribbean in particular, Cubans use almost no spices: tourists from Mexico must find it impossible to taste anything. I was once advised by a bartender in the Yucatán that a glass of Chardonnay tasted better with a dash of Tabasco. He wasn't wholly wrong. But only *in situ*. Don't try it at home.

Pablo clearly believes this is a real gourmet meal and is particularly proud of his starter: asparagus soup. Out of a packet. It's not hard to tell because not only does it taste only very vaguely of asparagus, but it has lots of little lumps of undissolved powder in it. Cuba's gastronomic culture remains that of America circa 1959, when convenience food was considered the height of new age sophistication. I can imagine he fairly danced with joy when he somehow or other got hold of it, and would be horrified if I told him I wished he hadn't.

My last task is to make the long slog in the dark drippy evening, the overcast skies accentuating the lack of street lighting, down to the station to wait for the magical hour of midnight when I might be able to buy my ticket for tomorrow. It is not optimistic. A chalk scrawl on a big blackboard inside announces that because of the heavy rains there will be NO trains to Havana until washed-away track can be replaced. I am travelling in the opposite direction but it is not a good omen.

On the stroke of midnight I knock on the ticket office door and ask for the *jefe al torno* who turns out to be not Cinderella but one of the ugly sisters. A fierce-looking white woman with thick-rimmed glasses, her black hair pulled back tightly into a bun, in blue uniform with the trademark fishnet tights emerges and shouts, '*Qué?*' She is not exactly enamoured at being disturbed. The remarkable thing by our standards of course, is that she is there at all. Cuban stations may have only one or two trains a day, but they are staffed twenty-four hours. Zero unemployment is easy to achieve if government creates non-jobs for workers paid in peanuts. Except that there is a shortage of peanuts.

But I am glad to see her. Or was until she opens her mouth.

'Come back tomorrow,' she says.

'But it is tomorrow, sort of.'

She consults her watch and reluctantly concedes the point.

'There might be no train.'

'But this is where it starts,' I protest.

She shrugs, as if to indicate that has absolutely no relevance to anything and says:

'Can I buy a ticket?'

The look on her faces implies the very idea is impertinent and the concept a huge inconvenience, not least because it is – theoretically – her job to sell me one. She sighs wearily and says, 'If there is no train, you won't get a refund.'

That seems a bit harsh, but as the price is only CUC 9, a fortune to her, but barely the cost of a one-day Travelcard on the London Underground it seems a fair risk to me, set against the alternative of a pre-dawn rise.

Shaking her head at either my insanity or wanton profligacy with hard currency, she examines my passport, takes the money and hands me the ticket.

Her final shot is brusque, if initially reassuring. But with a sting in the tail:

'Be here at 9 o'clock. Sharp. The train leaves at 9.30. If there is one!'

CHAPTER NINE

Railroading in Style

There are many reasons why a city, monument or natural wonder may claim the much-prized right to be placed on UNESCO's list of World Heritage Sites. Not surprisingly, older countries tend to have more than newer ones, and a greater number tend to be human constructions rather than wonders of nature. For example Italy and Spain have the most in Europe with more than 40 each, from the Amalfi Coast and the City of Venice to the Alhambra and Burgos Cathedral.

France boasts 37 led by Versailles and Le Mont St Michel. The United Kingdom has 28 including Westminster Abbey and Edinburgh Old Town. The continental-sized United States by contrast has just 21, over half of which are natural wonders such as the Grand Canyon. Cuba in comparison, with less than five per cent of the land mass, does rather well with nine, nearly all of which are the products of human artifice. Perhaps the most unusual of all is the historic centre of the little inland town of Camagüey, the most recent addition having been put on the list in 2008.

It is that, plus the fact there is a train which goes there and Pablo has already rung ahead to arrange accommodation with a *casa* inevitably run by a friend of his, that makes Camagüey my next destination. Getting there, however, is not as easy as it ought to be.

Pablo blessedly makes the first part easy by giving me a lift to the station in his car, sadly once again not an American classic, but a representative of their relatively new wave successors: a run-down, thirty-year-old Moskvich, with a door panel that has rusted away and been admirably replaced with hardwood. He may be one of the better connected *casa* owners in Santa Clara but he still can't get the cracks in his windscreen fixed or his wipers to work. Blessedly it has stopped raining.

My cigars, reliably delivered by Santiago as promised, are in my backpack. I have no idea if they are the real thing, but they are in a proper Cohiba wooden box with the proper tax-paid customs stickers. Pablo is impressed.

The station is crowded. I can't help being struck by the stylishness of the average Cuban – male and female – despite their relative poverty. It is a style all of its own, of course, helped by the tropical weather requiring only a minimal level of clothing and the fact that food rationing means very few Cubans are fat. Certainly not by US or indeed UK standards. But it's not so much quality and cut of the clothing, it's attitude and the way it's worn.

The default style for young women is an ultra-skimpy version of micro-short shorts, coupled with low-cut tops worn over push-up bras. Overt sexualization is not something Cubans worry about too much. It is, if you'll pardon the expression, *de rigueur*. For blokes too. Most young men favour very tight blue jeans worn with equally tight T-shirts to show off those pectorals, usually sporting the grotesque logo of some heavy metal band. Giant belt buckles are compulsory, the most popular being a vast silver American Eagle. The United States may be the ideological enemy, but it is still the distorting mirror role model.

In theory I have 30 minutes before my train goes, but I've given up hoping it'll leave on time, especially after what the ugly sister told me last night. To kill the time, I actually pick up a copy of *Granma*. The main story is a feature on a new series of agreements signed to further deepen the 'special relationship', with Venezuela. I don't know it at the time but this is hardly a coincidence with Chavez currently in hospital in Havana: 'More painkillers, *presidente*? Certainly, and could you up the oil deliveries please.' I'm being unfair; both the Castros regarded the Venezuelan strongman as their fairy godfather.

There's also what almost amounts to a genuine news story, about more power cuts in Matanzas due to the heavy rain. It's easier to blame forces of nature than human error. The piece talks about a 'cyclonic system' over the whole island but assures us the worst is over. And then to my surprise there's another dinosaur horn blast and through the open doors to the platform I catch a glimpse of a great orange diesel locomotive chugging into the station. A few minutes later we are ordered onto the platform. It is only 9.20. Could it possibly be that the train will leave on time?

Thanks to the daylight I am at least able this time to get a good look at the loco, which seems identical to the one which pulled the 'Spirituario'. It's not exactly cutting edge by European standards but it doesn't look a whole lot more antique or unreliable than the workhorses which pull Amtrak trains across the United States. A quick glance at the writing on the side makes absolutely clear where it comes from, and that it is of substantially more recent construction than I had imagined:

'Manufactured by the 7th February locomotive corporation, Beijing, 2009'. A further sign of the other, still developing special relationship. One that, with my discussion with Pablo still in mind, goes back to the Angolan conflict when one reason South Africa intervened is that it was afraid of the growing number of Chinese advisers across the sea in

Cuba. It is worth remembering that Cuba may still look on China as a 'fellow communist country', even if it no longer meets the old impoverished stereotype.

But if the locomotive is of relatively modern Chinese production, the rolling stock is another matter. So far I have been unable to ascertain accurately where the Cubans have acquired their carriages, although I know that both China and Mexico and the former communist countries of Eastern Europe feature.

There are no tell-tale signs that I can see, but that's hardly surprising since the bodywork has been painted so many times that it's tempting to say you could cut it with a knife, but it would have to be a machete. Inside there are both compartments and open carriages, the windows cracked or missing, the seating faux leather in black or blue patched here, there and everywhere with shiny red vinyl. The interior false ceiling is made of curved hardboard, except where it is missing altogether. Fluorescent tubes dangle down and the electric links between the carriages are stretched alongside the rubber connectors, wires wrapped in insulating tape mostly, but occasionally, seemingly bare. I take extreme care not to touch any, although it must be at best 50-50 that they are actually carrying current.

Middle-aged female inspectors in the by now familiar blue miniskirts and fishnet tights usher us on board, checking both tickets and identity cards, though most of the Cubans' credit-card sized bits of laminated paper – the standard identity card it is compulsory to carry at all times – are so limp and cracked from years of exposure to sweat, rain and 80 per cent humidity that it is a wonder she can recognize photographs. It is more a ritual than anything else.

I find my allocated seat, alongside a group of youngish women in one of the open carriages. I suspect this might be policy for foreigners. They seem well-mannered if a little shy, one of them deeply engrossed in a book of crossword puzzles. There is a communal exhalation of incredulity when, dead on the dot of 9.30 a.m. the locomotive lurches into life and we pull away from the platform. It seems too good to be true.

It is. Barely 60 seconds later we shunt to a stop. I'm wondering if the Cuban railway people have been taking hints from their British counterparts: at least the statistics will show our departure was on time! At 9.34 we set off again. At 9.35 we stop. At 9.36 we're off again. At 9.37 we stop. This is not looking good. At 9.39 we set off once more and this time we're on a roll. Not just that, we're passing the *tren blindado*, scene of Che's finest hour. I stare out the window and can honestly imagine – it's not that hard – our train hitting ripped up rails and teetering off the tracks while desperadoes hiding in the jungle hurl Molotov cocktails at us and pepper the coaches with gunfire. I'm a believer.

Two Ministry of the Interior *Policía Ferroviaria* (Railway Policemen) with serious moustaches walk up and down the carriage self-importantly. We're picking up speed now, which is a blessing, not least because there is a hugely refreshing through draft of air rushing through the carriage. It's only when I watch the retreating backs of the policemen that I realize why it's such a powerful draft. As they jump the six-inch gap between the footplates to pass into the next carriage, I can see beyond them to where the rear door of the train should be. I say 'should be', because it isn't. Instead there's an ever increasing vista of a long line of railway track receding into the distance, and now already, just seconds after we passed over it, repopulated by wandering dogs, a cow and a few motley human beings.

At 9.55 we stop again. One of the girls seated in the row beside me looks up in exasperation from her reading, an agony aunt column for older teenagers in a girls' magazine called aptly enough *Muchacha* (*Girl*). I wonder about its politics, if any, but suspect that apart from a poem on the back cover about the *tren blindado,* it is pretty much like girlie mags anywhere. Without the advertising. Which, come to think of it, makes it completely different.

The pause is an opportunity for the in-train catering to arrive, two men in blue waistcoats doing a push-me, pull-you act to manhandle what would be a supermarket trolley if Cuba had supermarkets over the perilous gap between carriages. Going in the other direction is a man with some loose wires in one hand and a soldering iron in the other. I'm not reassured.

The trolley reaches us and they're selling some orange liquid which is not thick enough to be mango juice and I have yet to see orange juice in an island just south of Florida. In any case it is unimaginable that anyone could drink it with the train rocking and rolling as the men with the trolley bounce up and down like toddlers on a trampoline. They also have what look like sandwiches.

Pablo provided what is so far reliably proving the best meal of the day in Cuba: a decent breakfast, of some fresh mango, pineapple, guava, coffee and a fried egg in a bun. But I'm still tempted. I have no idea how long I'm going to be on this train, especially at our current stop–start rate of progress. The prognosis was six hours, for a distance of barely 300 kilometres (170 miles), but in my opinion it's anybody's guess. The girl beside me doing crosswords has started showing baby pictures around: she's on her way to Santiago de Cuba (at least another six to eight hours' travelling time) for the first glimpse of her nephew. Her brother's first child was born eighteen months ago, but this is the first time she's managed to get a train ticket to visit them. Makes me realize what an exception they make for foreigners, or rather their hard currency.

Before I make my mind up whether or not to buy something from the trolley – what they have is disappearing fast – I decide to check out the on-board toilet facilities. Arguably the best decision of the entire trip. To say Cuban train toilets leave something to be desired would not just be an understatement, it would suggest the person speaking inhabited an altogether alien reality. British train toilets leave something to be desired. American train toilets leave something to be desired. Italian train toilets leave something to be desired. Remarkably perhaps, French ones really aren't bad these days. But Cuban train toilets are the best advertisement yet seen for colostomy bags.

It is not just that what passes for washing facilities is a rusty oblong metal basin not properly fitted but jutting out over its equally rusty pedestal with a hand-painted scrawl on the wall above saying *agua no potable* (not drinking water). Which is a bit of a bad taste joke because there isn't any *agua, potable* or otherwise. Not in the so-called sink, and not in the toilet either, fairly obviously because the foul, blackened, rusted pipe that should connect the toilet bowl to the cistern above, only makes it half way up the wall. Which at least makes it wholly irrelevant that there is no chain, cord or handle of any device attached to the empty cistern.

Then we come to the toilet itself, the sitting accommodation. Or rather we don't. In fact we stay as far away from it as possible. If you're a bloke and have no sense of smell or can hold your nose and your breath and your privates at the same time, you can just about dare to use it although for once, ladies, you'd excuse us for aiming from a distance. But it won't matter to you, because you'd have to be insane to consider using it yourself. Not only is there no seat – I had taken that as read – but the bowl itself is not just filthy, rusty and looks – I assure you I was not going to get close enough to do anything other than catch a glimpse of the sleepers and gravel hurtling by underneath – dangerously sharp edged. Obviously if *in extremis* there was absolutely no alternative you'd be desperately trying to avoid even the slightest contact between your nether regions and this sharp-edged tetanus trap, but giving the constant jolting motion of the train you'd be a braver man – or woman – than I even to consider it.

I have no idea what the women on board this train intend to do, other than cross their legs for hours on end and dash out in a crowd at stations, though I wonder if their facilities are much better. I know what I am going to do, though, and that is not eat or drink another thing on this journey. No input, no output. Better than that, I head back to my seat and open the medical pocket on my rucksack, I am going to take two Imodium. Preventively.

But it is a couple of hours of jolting, sweating journey time later that I encounter the biggest shock. One that, really, I should have anticipated.

I've strolled down to the end of the carriage to stretch my legs and enjoy a view through a different window – yes, I know it isn't going to change much – but I've been on this train for more than four hours now. It's just a few lines, scratched and almost illegible at the bottom of the cracked window frame. To me it's like that scene at the end of the original Planet of the Apes where Charlton Heston and the girl come across the decapitated head of the Statue of Liberty on a beach.

Just seven words, even if it's longer in English: *Türgriff erst bei Stillstand des Zuges betätigen*: do not operate the door handle until the train has come to a complete standstill. It's not the instruction that has knocked me back. It's the language. This train – the rolling stock – isn't Mexican or Chinese. It's German. Almost certainly East German of course, but German all the same. It's only now with that terrible realization planted in my brain, that I begin to recognize it, to see everything with new eyes: the sensible double luggage racks, large one on top to take bags not needed on the journey, the familiar height of the backrests and the squared-off metal brackets that attach them to the bodywork, the few remaining traces of wood veneer below the windows, mostly covered in a thick layer of grime and grey industrial paint.

But above all else it's the empty spaces on the compartment walls above the seats, paler rectangles with screw holes at each corner. Once upon a time, they would have held quaint little black and white photographs of the historical cities of the German Democratic Republic: Dresden, Meissen, Erfurt, Weimar. True, trains in old East Germany were not up to the standard of the high-speed network already being developed in the West, but they were efficient, ran on time (mostly) and, above all else, clean.

These carriages would have been a gesture of solidarity to a fraternal state, from ill old Erich Honecker – the man who boasted he built the Berlin Wall and predicted it would last at least a hundred years – to big bushy-bearded *compañero* Fidel.

Sitting in a café in what had been East Berlin a couple of years after the Wall came down, Markus Wolf, once East Germany's chief spymaster, told me how Fidel came on a state visit once but climbed out the window of his suite in the middle of the night to avoid his official guards and go whoring. Different days, different times.

The landscape is surprisingly constant: palm-fringed savannah dotted here and there with the rusting abandoned ruins of sugar mills. In Ciego de Avila, more vendors line the platform, offering the inevitable plastic bottles of mango juice, polystyrene cups of coconut milk and plastic bags of dry biscuits. One guy in a baseball cap has a different offering: a bubble pack of pills. Testament to the shortage of easily accessible prescription drugs. I ask the girl with cross-word puzzle books if they are headache pills. She looks up and with some embarrassment says that they are 'for the toilet'. Say no more. I understand completely. Local Imodium!

By early afternoon we are getting close to my destination. The last but one stop is called Florida. I have to pinch myself to remember that it just means 'Flowery' in Spanish. It is obviously a popular enough destination: several dozen people are jumping down off the train, throwing bags out to friends or relatives standing in the fields beyond the end of the platform. Almost as many get on trying to sell more edibles. For a country with a supposedly centralized, state-controlled economy, there is a lot of in-your-face private enterprise going on.

Just under an hour later, and an hour late, we pull into Camagüey. I unload myself onto the platform in a vast scrummage of people. There is a group of solders in uniform climbing on board, pushing against the flow of people trying to disembark as if nobody knows just when the train will depart. Which is almost certainly the truth.

I scour the crowded platform in vain for Pablo's pal who was supposed to come and meet me. At last, with the platform almost empty and the big orange locomotive growling sullenly in anticipation of departure, a bloke with a shaven head, blue shorts and a bright yellow Carlos Santana T-shirt comes up to me and says, 'Mister Peter?'

Ten minutes later, after a nerve-wracking ride in a relatively well-kept Lada through what seems like an incomprehensible winding maze of streets (of which more anon), we pull up outside a bungalow: a terraced bungalow: a single storey pastel-blue little modern house with a red-and-white striped awning, wedged between two beautiful but crumbling colonial-style houses at least two centuries older.

I suppose you could call it World Heritage Site View.

CHAPTER TEN

Negotiating the Labyrinth

Within less than two hours however, I am feeling deeply *au fait* with the real reason for Camagüey's World Heritage status: I'm lost.

My intention was merely to take a quick stroll round the city centre to get my bearings in the daylight. I had agreed – more in hope than expectation – to take dinner at the *casa*. Rodrigo, the man in the Santana T-shirt, assured me his mother-in-law was a great cook.

'Take a left at the end of the street, then a right and you're heading for the town centre,' he said. 'We're on Calle Principe in case you need to ask someone the way back.'

Finding my way into the town centre was as easy as he suggested, past the birthplace of Ignacio Agramonte, another hero of Cuba's nineteenth-century independence struggle. The main square is named after him too, and as I entered it there was a quaint little flag-raising ceremony going on. A teenage boy in vintage military uniform and a girl in a flouncy frock carrying a bouquet of flowers came out and stood to attention while a little band played the national anthem. It was quite touching in a mildly kitsch sort of way.

Beyond the square was Maceo, a neat little parade of shops, not unlike the Boulevard in Santa Clara, a scrubbed and polished showcase for the tourists, with granite pavements and windows apparently full of goods. It was only when I took a closer look that I remembered where I was. The shops were open, but there were no lights on inside while the goods on display in one window were repeated in the next. There were probably more Che T-shirts than the better-dressed Cuban – who on the evidence preferred to advertise Metallica or Motörhead – might need. There was also a lot of plastic buckets. In different colours.

It reminds me of Weimar or Erfurt in the 1980s, little East German towns whose ancient heritage was slowly crumbling into the cobbles but each had a 'modern' show street like a layer of thin sugar icing over a cardboard façade. Back there and then as here and now, the shop windows displayed more goods than were usually available inside. There were always items in the window that could not be sold because they were 'for display only'.

Reality comes up to me in the form of a street sweeper in a pristine white and yellow uniform who nudges me with his elbow, covertly inviting me to inspect the piece of contraband in his hand: it is a 25 centavo coin, a quarter of one national peso, worth approximately 1p. 'Only one CUC.' he hisses. I look at him in genuine amazement. 'Che Guevara, Che Guevara,' for it is indeed the great man's head that graces it. I wonder briefly if the government deliberately doesn't feature the great global image on any of its hard currency just so locals can hope to fleece the tourists by selling them a coin in common circulation at 100 times its face value.

By now I'm at the top end of Maceo in a square called Plaza de los Trabajadores (Workers' Square), which thinking back over the route I've taken I rashly decide must be only a stone's throw from Calle Principe. Just over there, a left and a right and . . . I'm somewhere I haven't been before with not the faintest idea in which direction I should be heading.

I have a simple map, but none of the streets around me

are on it. It turns out there is a reason for this, although not a very good one. Camagüey, it appears, is a critical case of a phenomenon that afflicts a lot of Cuban towns; most streets have two names: an old pre-revolutionary one, often religious, and a newer one, usually named after one of Castro's heroes or cronies. And you never know who is going to use which.

Camagüey has a tradition of conservatism and Catholicism – Pope John Paul II delivered a homily here on a visit in 1998 – so here most people prefer the old names, but maps tend to use only the new ones. That means that what people call San Fernando is marked as Bartolomé Masó, while San Esteban is Oscar Primelles and Santa Rita is El Solitario. To make matters even worse, you cannot be sure which will be on the street sign, if there is one. So for a map to be any use at all, you have to know not just where you are to start with, but possibly also both names of the street in case the sign on the wall has the other one.

All that, however, is just extra complication to the main problem which is that Camagüey is a city deliberately designed to get people lost. That, rather than its pretty colonial architecture, is its chief claim for inclusion on the UNESCO World Heritage Site.

Whereas every other colonial city founded by the Spanish in the New World was laid out formally – Madrid even passed legislation, the Laws of the Indies 1573, requiring colonial towns to be built to a grid around a central plaza – Camagüey is a maze of oblique angles, retreating curves, U-bends and dead ends. Without even the organic growth pattern that marks many mediaeval European cities, Camagüey is a city planner's schizophrenic homage to irregular geometry.

A few joysuckers claim its chaotic development was haphazard but most natives and historians believe this inhabited maze which could swallow a small army was designed deliberately to do just that. Because its rich cattle market made it even more of a target for pirates than little Remedios, the inhabitants of what was then called Santa Maria del Puerto Principe6* (it was renamed Camagüey for an old Taino Indian chief after independence) moved further inland and redid the street plan.

It didn't necessarily help a great deal. One of the more famed visitors was Henry Morgan, who built a reputation as one of the more ferocious pirates of the Caribbean, despite the fact that he held the title of Vice Admiral in the Royal Navy at the time. He dropped by in 1668 with some 500 freelance villains, looted the cathedral and tortured what few citizens he could find. It would be nice to think his ghost is still trapped in some Camagüey blind alley, but he went on to infamously burn Panama City to the ground before falling out of favour with King Charles II and drinking himself to death in Jamaica.

I'm feeling in need of a stiff tot of rum myself by the time I finally get back to Calle Principe, thanks only to kindly meant imprecise directions and eventually running across the landmark birthplace of good old Ignacio Agramonte again.

Dinner is on the table. Or rather covering it. I know that what I'm paying in CUCs is the equivalent in national pesos of a month's salary for most people, but I wasn't expecting a month's supply of food. Especially as the standard of cooking is what you might expect from somebody who's asked their mother-in-law to come round and lend a hand. It's not

6. Coincidentally the same name was given to the capital city of the neighbouring island, Haïti. When the French captured it in the seventeenth century they changed the spelling to Port au Prince, but couldn't alter the way the natives' referred to it, which is why today it is properly pronounced 'Prince' after the almost identical English and Spanish fashion rather than the nasal French 'Pr-AH-ns'.

awful; it's just not very good. Or rather, what she's done with most expensive ingredient isn't very good. It's fish. What sort of fish I have no idea. And I expect she didn't either. I'm wondering if even the fish did. However it started out, it has ended up as a great grey overcooked pile of vaguely fishy protein with a texture like a load of tissues left out in the rain.

It comes served with a few basic ingredients for a salad: some grated carrot, a bit of shredded lettuce, one small tomato and some dried-up cucumber. Not assembled, you see, but just set out, separately on a plate, with a lot of cooking oil and vinegar slopped over them. It's well meant, but not exactly thought through.

The one thing that really does work, however, is the one she probably makes every day and has just knocked up here as an extra filler, as if one were needed with half a steamed shark or whatever it is on offer: black beans and rice. These *frijoles*, the Cuban staple, have been boiled up until tender in a deliciously tasty onion broth and come with the rice served on the side to add at will. It would have been a good, if unadventurous, nourishing and tasty meal on its own. My biggest problem, however, is feeling obliged to choke down a quantity of the expensive fish.

With the television on in the background and two young children running round and arguing, that feeling of 'living alongside a local family' is definitely overdone. Especially as my meal is laid out as something special, separate; the family have either already eaten or will eat later. I am beginning to understand that meals in Cuba are seen as necessity rather than occasion. People eat food because they have to and do it when they can. The concept of *cuisine* in everyday life is about as absent as it was in ration-book Britain in the 1950s.

I am secretly desperate to face down their obvious disappointment that I haven't cleaned my plate and escape this haven of chintzy domesticity that has a little too much about it of a 1960s American soap opera. The family are rich as Croesus by Cuban standards, which means they can afford to live in the materialist comfort of US suburbia a generation ago, and with all the lack of roots and tradition that go with it. For them, the revolution might never have happened.

Wandering back into town feels like a different world. I am careful to note landmarks along the way not just to avoid getting lost again but to feel back in a less candied Cuban reality. Passing each open window is like watching a series of cameo tableaux behind wrought iron grilles: a *bicitaxi* in the middle of a living-room, an old couple on an ancient *chaise-longue* watching a sitcom on television, a Baptist church on the corner with girls in red skirts and white shirts standing up to 'give testimony' at the Saturday night service. A sign on the wall says: 'Home is home, prayer is all'. Next door is the district headquarters of the Communist party. Their signs says, 'We face a war of ideology. Let us fight a battle of ideas to win it.' Beneath it two old blokes with baseball caps pulled won over their eyes are dozing peacefully.

The real party is going on in Agramonte Square, outside the Café Ciudad. A lively, busty young woman in tight jeans and a skimpy white halter top with stiletto heels and a Panama hat tipped racily over one eye is shaking her maracas and singing her soul out in front of a four-man band on guitar, saxophone, congas and trumpet.

After a time chilling in warm moonlight and salsa sounds, that tot of rum definitively beckons. The place to have it is El Cambio, a surprisingly hip-looking bar on the corner of the square, with paint-streaked walls covered with deliberate graffiti and adorned with a few carved heads like totem poles. I order a *Siete Años* shot and a can of Naranja to wash it down.

El Cambio is the epitome of Camagüey cool. Hemingway

might not have drunk here but you could imagine Hunter S. Thompson would have. There is a whole mid-70s vibe to the place: some cool jazz playing on the stereo and a tall black girl in ripped blue jean shorts with a handbag slung over her shoulder trying to make a call from the payphone on the wall in one corner. A glance at the cooler cabinet soon makes it obvious though that this is a joint aimed almost exclusively at the foreign tourist trade: there's not just Bucanero in there, but Becks too. And Red Bull. And, most remarkably at all – given that this is Cuba and there's supposed to be a 100 per cent trade embargo with the United States – the ultimate symbol of American global hegemony: Coca-Cola. Can Coke have engaged in illegal sanctions-busting?

The barman sees me stare, smiles and says, 'Imported from Canada.'

Meanwhile, across the room a guy at a table on his own is fiddling with some wooden figure or other. I try to guess how long it's likely to be before he tries to sell it to me. And underestimate by approximately 30 seconds. I've been waiting for this. Camagüey has a reputation for being particularly plagued by *jineteros*, the ubiquitous touts who live off tourists, though so far apart from the street cleaner trying to sell his 'Che' coin, I've had no bother. Eventually though – after maybe about five whole minutes – he sidles up to the bar, pulls up a stool, takes a sip of his drink, which looks like neat dark rum, and introduces himself:

'*Hola*, my name is Steve.' He gives me a beaming smile displaying a mouthful of ivory white teeth, save for one that looks filled with either silver or tin, and holds out a hand. I know what's coming but I smile back and take his hand: Cuba is a friendly country. Even the rip-off merchants have a laid-back charm.

We sit there for a moment or two like a couple on a blind

date stuck for conversation, Steve – and it has to be highly improbable that is his real name – beaming at me as if tongue-tied but probably just trying to muster his English. For a bizarre moment I realize what it must be like to be a girl at a bar being picked up without wanting to be. But I know that's not what this is about.

And, sure enough, after a few more minutes of mildly uncomfortable silence marked only by a half-effort of a laugh and a matey punch on the arm and the clinking of glasses to consummate our wonderful new friendship, he gets down to business as he pulls the wooden figure out of his bag and set to polishing it.

This is the bit where I'm supposed to respond by showing the merest modicum of polite interest that will allow him to launch his sales pitch. I stare straight in front of me, over the bar, and concentrate on sipping my rum. I can almost feel the frustration next to me, growing as he pays ever more exaggerated attention to his polishing. It's not fair, I'm not playing by the rules. But then it's his game, not mine. For the moment. Eventually, and without any more effort at seductive small talk, he cracks and says, in not too badly broken English, 'What do you think of this? Do you like it?'

It's my turn to relent. I take a look at the thing which is some sort of crude totem pole thingie with what appear to be flowers and animals carved on it. It reminds me vaguely of something my well-travelled American uncle used to bring back from Africa, things that looked a bit like ancient ritual tribal carvings but were really mass-manufactured in sweatshops in Mombasa. The main difference is the wood is dark brown, not black.

'Very nice,' I tell him, doing my very best to convey that I am merely being polite and not a potential customer, and turn pointedly back to my drink. He does at bit more rubbing at it and then says, 'You know how long it's taken me to make this?'

I shake my head in a desultory sort of way, still trying to indicate that I'm really more interested in my rum than small talk, and a lot more than shopping for second-rate statuettes.

'Fifty hours, man. Can you imagine?'

Frankly, looking at the thing, no, I can't. He gives a deep, theatrical sigh, then says, 'But times are hard, y'know. I'm thinking of selling it.' He makes a good fist of looking sheepish, shy, awkward and desperate at the same time and says, 'Would you like to buy?'

I give him a broad smile, which is cruel because I'm getting his hopes up. 'Funny you should say that,' I tell him as I reach into my own little shoulder bag, 'Because I'm in the same business, sort of.'

That gets an odd look, which gets odder still when I add, 'My speciality though is metal toys'.

I've been waiting for this moment, just a little wickedly, almost from the moment I landed in Havana. From the depths of my bag I bring out a little red model of a London double-decker bus. Obviously made in China. My wife had bought me a handful of these from one of the tourist trap junk sellers on Oxford Street, with the idea – gleaned from years living in the Soviet Union, and a visit to Egypt where a policeman once asked me if I had a pen, then said thank you and walked off with it – that in semi-third-world countries a bag of little goodies to give out was one way of making useful friends. I had considered giving one to old Pablo's granddaughter, but discovered that the wheels came off almost as soon as you touched the thing, and, coming from health-and-safety addicted Britain, was painfully aware that to a small child they could be almost as lethal as the pin-sharp little metal rod that served as an axle. I had considered simply chucking them in the nearest bin, but at the back of my mind a wicked little alternative scenario had taken route. And now it had materialized.

'It took me two months to make,' I say.

'Steve' peers at the little red bus, then gives me a look, for just a second, as if to say, 'You're having me on, aren't you?' And then he glanced back at the statue and the bus and gave me another look that said, 'Of course, you bloody are!' and we both burst into simultaneous laughter.

I try to keep a straight face while he looks me in the eye for a long moment, then shakes his head and gives a deep belly laugh, sticks his hand in the air and high-fives me, following up with a bit of genuine global English: 'Fuck you, man. Fuck you!' There are some American imports that even the trade embargo can't ban.

We chink glasses again, only this time I offer to buy him a shot of rum. He accepts avidly. Then, thinking that maybe I've softened up, takes out the totem pole again and says, 'Are you sure you wouldn't . . . ?'

In response I hold up the little bus and say, 'Just five pesos to you.' Then adds, 'Convertibles. CUC.' He creases up, shaking his head. But the smile, when it comes back, is genuine. I've made him laugh. All of a sudden he reckons I might just speak his language, one way or another.

All of a sudden it is if we have both crashed through an invisible wall: he is no longer just another hustler, I am no longer just another mark. We shake hands again, not a high-five, just a shake. 'My real name is Juanito,' he says. I do my best in Spanish which is about as good as his English and for the next half hour or so we exchange life stories, or a sort – I suspect both of us are making stuff up (I certainly am) – and swop drinks.

There is a reason for this. Juanito, it turns out, isn't drinking local rum at all. Or rather he is, and I'm not. I'm on

Havana Club, which most locals can't afford; he's on local hooch distilled by a mate of his and turned brown not by ageing but by a bit of burnt molasses. He only tells me that after I've tried a swig.

The barman is already laughing. It's part of the deal, the pact, the great Cuban conspiracy. In any bar in a capitalist society – try it in your local – a punter who brought in his own hooch and sat there drinking it while trying to pester (relatively) wealthy real customers would be tossed out on his ear. But here our barman is not the owner, and not on a share of the profits, or a performance-related wage, nor does he feel beholden to his employer: he's just a civil servant, like everybody else from the farmer to the factory worker, holding down a job like any other poor schmuck who works for the government. Albeit one where he can expect to get tips in the all-important CUCs.

And that's the point, of course. He also charges in CUCs and there's no way in a million years Steve, or Juanito, or whoever, can afford to pay. But because this is a CUCs only bar, he can't buy anything else in there either. So the barman lets him come in and drink his homemade hooch while trying to con whatever cash he can from the tourists. In our economies you'd automatically assume the barman would be asking in return for a share of any profits, but here I genuinely don't think he is. He gets hard currency tips – which he definitely doesn't share – and in return he's willing to let a fellow comrade try his own hand on the market economy.

It's not exploitation, it's not communism, it's not even capitalism, it's just a way of life. It might even be a curious form of Christian ethics: 'Do unto others as you would have done unto yourself.' Live and let live. Not so much dog eat dog as share a spot in the shade on a sunny day.

The hooch, by the way, is horrible. Probably not

poisonous, but with at best the delicate flavour you might get from adding a spoonful of honey to half a pint of white spirit. I do my best not to retch. Then order another Naranja to wash it down. Juanito looks envious so I buy him one too. He cracks open the can and gulps at it as if it were nectar. Naranja too is available only for CUCs. Emboldened by my seemingly lavish hospitality, he glances at his bag again, clearly wondering if it might be worth one more go at flogging the wooden totem pole. I shake my head, making clear a dead horse would be a better bet.

He smiles, shakes his head, and before I know it we are into a discussion of life in Cuba and life in what he likes, somewhat wistfully, to call 'the real world'. He's as keen to learn colloquial English as I am to get a handle on the Cuban dialect, and delighted to hear I can help him with a few phrases of German too: 'German tourists have much money.' I nod. These days, that's a given.

'No "s",' he tells me. '*Qué?*' I reply, à la Manuel in Fawlty Towers. What do you mean, no 's'? It turns out he means Cubans don't pronounce it. Two months, in Spanish '*dos meses*', in Cuba sounds like '*doh meh*', instead of *dos mayses*. They aren't very big on 'b' either, which is why the ubiquitous phrase that accompanies every shoulder-shrugging explanation of the way things are sound like 'Cu-a e' Cu-a'. In fact, Juanito makes clear, Cubans aren't keen on overprecise pronunciation at all. Not only is the Castilian lisping 'th' sound for 'c' or 'z' unknown, given half a chance most Cubans will elide any consonant they can get away with.

'Particularly where you are going – *el oriente,*' he tells me. It would appear, to my surprise, that Cuba has an east–west divide much the same way England has a north–south divide. Camagüey is pretty much the middle market. *Los Habaneros*, he explains, look on people further east pretty much the way Londoners look at anyone who lives north of the Watford Gap, while the inhabitants of Santiago de Cuba, which was the first major Spanish settlement and is still revered as the birthplace of Castro's revolution, regard the capital's pretensions with the same disdain British Geordies heap on 'soft southerners'.

The accent, he tells me, is also more pronounced in the east, with a greater historical influence from neighbouring French-speaking Haïti. There is no doubt where Juanito's sympathies lie: people from Havana, he tells me, call easterners *Palestinos*. I'm not sure what sort of statement – if any – that might be on global geopolitics but then Cuba is pretty much in a bubble of its own these days.

It's just occurred to me that this is a pretty serious esoteric little conversation I'm having with a bloke who's basically a hustler. Daringly I take it just a little bit farther and ask him if he doesn't have a regular job. He gives me a look of extreme disdain. 'For pesos? There's no job in this country that's worth doing for money. Money that's worth shit, and you don't even get much of that!'

Not exactly what I had been expecting to hear. But doesn't everybody have to have a job? I mean, the state boasts zero unemployment, apart from deadbeat dossers like Miguel back in Matanzas, or wherever he might be crawled under a bush now.

Juanito gives me a sideways look and touches his nose. 'It depends who you are,' he says enigmatically, then adds, 'I have connections.' He's unwilling – fairly understandably – to be pushed into revealing more detail, even taking an oblique glance at the barman who's doing his best not to appear to be listening to our linguistic mishmash of a conversation. But from Juanito's facial expression and body language it's fairly plain he means his family have enough 'pull' that nobody asks any questions. It's the supreme irony:

in this communist system you have to be hard wired into the system in order to opt out of it.

I try to pussyfoot around the subject for a few minutes, looking for any reaction to mentions of communism in general, the state of the economy, even Fidel's health, all of which gets little more than sceptical looks from my conversation partner. Until, that is, I mention Cuba's great global icon, the hero of a million student bedroom posters: Ernesto 'Che' Guevara himself. That gets me a reaction, even if it's not remotely what I had been expecting. Juanito throws back his head and roars with laughter. 'Che Guevara?' he says, and then in loud and perfect English: 'That man was a fucking lunatic!'

I immediately notice the expression on the barman's face, but even that isn't quite what I expected. Not exactly shock, or offence, or terror, more a sort of highly surprised, hard to suppress amusement. He quickly turns to face the wall studiously polishing a glass.

I've obviously touched a nerve here. Within minutes Juanito is giving me a tirade, not against Che or communism but against foreign tourists. 'You know what I hate? I hate the rich bastards from Spain or Germany or wherever who come here and tell the likes of me, I live in a paradise after they've spent a week lying on their arses in some all-inclusive hotel in Caya Coco that's off-limits to most ordinary Cubans.'

A bit like this bar, I suggest warily, though of course it's not off limits, just out of the ordinary local's price range. He gives me a wicked smile of acknowledgement. He offers me another shot of hooch. I take it, and in return buy him a packet of 20 local cigarettes, made from the sort of black shredded tobacco that never gets near a Cohiba or Romeo and Juliet but is all most Cubans can afford, it they are lucky. They cost me 0.60 CUC, barely 60 US cents, but enough to put a smile on Juanito's face. We've done a deal, of sorts. We are equals. Even though I'm still not going to buy his totem pole. Nor, frankly, finish his hooch.

'Hey,' he says, 'do you want to help me?' I nod, politely, though at this stage non-committally. 'Tomorrow,' he says, eyes bright now as if he's just thought of a world's best wheeze, 'I could sit out there, on the square, with my figurines, and you could come over and look impressed, and if some foreigner comes up, you can tell them how good my stuff is, and how you've watched me work. You could even buy one. Or pretend to.' He adds the last phrase with a roll of his eyes in response to the sceptical expression on my face. 'Why not?'

I'm laughing. And then I think about it. Why not, indeed? What do I care if some tourist on a day-trip from the all-inclusive zone can be persuaded to part with a few CUCs to make Juanito's day a bit better? I shrug and say, 'Sure', and he high-fives me again. I've just signed up to be a hustler's apprentice.

So, I say, thinking the best way to get the measure of my new business partner is to ask him the age-old interview question, 'Where do you see yourself in five years' time?' It may seem silly but it's a pretty loaded question in a country where the law – and almost every aspect of society – has been laid down by one man, now in his mid-eighties, and his brother still in power and only a year or two younger.

His eyes fall. Like so many of his compatriots, old and young, Juanito just can't imagine life without the Castros. Then he lifts his head again and looks me in the eyes and I know that what he is about to say is the complete and utter truth. 'What I would really like,' he says, 'is to go to Bangkok and fuck girls the way the Italians do in Cuba.'

I'm tempted to burst into laughter, but I don't, because I realize he means it.

And as if on cue, we are suddenly joined by a bouncy young black woman in a flouncy skirt who kisses Juanito on both cheeks and, having had a rapid fire shake down on the state of his newly acquired friendship with *un extranjero,* and apprised of my linguistic skills, leaps into the conversation with a question of her own:

'How do you say in German, "I want to make love with you",?' she asks with alarming directness. I'm about to ask why she wants to know, when I realize just what a stupid question that might be. 'To say nicely,' she adds, almost primly, before spoiling it just a little by the clarification, 'Not fucky, fucky, I won't want to be crude.'

I help her with the correct pronunciation of *'Ich will mit dir schlafen,'* which is still the rather quaint euphemism that the majority of German tourists will probably want to hear, even though it would be obvious that neither she nor they would be intent on doing too much sleeping.

Under the circumstances maybe there is some excuse for me being just a tiny bit surprised when a few minutes later she mentions the fact that she is married. I know Cuban men can be remarkably broad-minded but I doubt that they are wholly immune to jealousy. 'Is okay,' Juanito smiles and says, 'He is Canadian. Lives in Canada.' And his lady friend beams too, as if that explains everything. Married to a foreigner, she can get an exit visa whenever she wants, – which is what most Cuban women want from foreign men – but she couldn't find a job in Canada and chooses to come back to Cuba often. I don't like to ask if it's for the work!

'Come,' she says to Juanito, grabbing him by the arm. 'It's time to party, have a real drink.' He shrugs and beckons me to join them. I want to know where we might be going, but he just says, 'Come on, you'll see.'

About five minutes later we have wandered through the dark streets of Camagüey's labyrinth to a rather dingy bar on the edge of what looks like a small park behind railings. This, it turns out, is an outdoors peso bar, a place Cubans can actually buy cheap rum or expensive beer in their own currency, although even here some things have to be paid for in CUC. This is where the hustlers hang out with after hours hotel bar staff, paid 'dancers' in hard currency bars, anybody loosely connected to the parasite industry that lives on the back of the mainstream tourist economy.

Juanito is clearly amused at having brought me here – to the slightly scandalized reaction of the others, until it kicks in that even if I have got beneath the surface of their society, I'm still fair game. Maybe even more so, I realize as I get pinched on the bottom and turn round only to discover that it's a tubby little lady in her 60s bursting out of an over-tight dress and smiling in a manner she can only assume to be winsome. Behind her I see Juanito roaring with laughter, his hand round the married Cuban-Canadian's increasingly revealing décolleté. 'I tell her you need dancing lessons,' he shouts. I smile daggers back. The dumpy granny in front of me is rubbing my leg and suggesting she could be 'my friend'. I make my excuses and run. For the bar.

There's no safety to be had there either. I order a beer, only to find that the barman is adamant I should pay CUC. It's not absurd – he isn't trying to cheat me on price, just make sure there's more 'convertible' around (nobody really puts any value on pesos at all, it seems). I hand him a CUC 5 note. He charges me CUC 1, the going rate in cheaper provincial towns, but gives me change in 'national' pesos, with a mock apologetic smile. The sight of the money, however, has already brought me company, although I suspect the giggling Juanito across the room generously handing out the cigarettes I bought him may have played a hand in it. Not least because one of the two blokes so eager to make my acquaintance is barely five foot tall, has no eyebrows, dyed platinum blond hair, and a wasp waist clad in silver micro-mini shorts.

Just in case I'm in any doubt, he manages to lisp – the first time in Cuba I've heard what is a typical trait of Castilian Spanish even in the most macho men – and pout simultaneously. He may not be the only gay in Camagüey, but he is the first ostentatiously camp man I've come across.

Homosexuality is not illegal in Cuba. This genuinely is, after all, a supposedly liberal, 'progressive' – to use that horrible word beloved of English *Guardian*-readers and Labour Party luvvies – society. But there is a feeling that Fidel, the ultimate big bearded macho man famed for his big cigars, and wielding AK47s and baseball bats with equanimity, somehow doesn't quite believe it exists. And whether for that reason or not, it's not much in evidence.

That doesn't mean that 'Xavi', as he introduces himself, isn't glad to be gay, and pretty self-confident with it. As is his 'partner' – my command of the language here doesn't quite let me know in what, or how many, senses he means that – who happens to be a rather large, slightly tubby, balding, bespectacled guy in a faded brown suit. We chat nonchalantly enough for a few minutes, long enough for me to buy them both a beer, and to give me an excuse to leave. It's one thing to get under the skin of a society, but another altogether to get stuck there.

There's no getting away, however, before Juanito has dragged me on to the dance floor – actually a square area of dusty tiles set into the ground between the trees – first for a samba of sorts with his dark-eyed improbably Canadian housewife, then – inevitably – with my dumpy little would-be pension age dance teacher. Determined to strut what remains of her stuff – which is actually quite a lot – she proceeds to display her proficiency at what most Cuban dances invariably default to: a sort of vertical lap-dancing where the female grinds her posterior against her partner's crotch. And in this case there is an awful lot of posterior, even if thankfully it is closer to my knees.

After that, there's no stopping me heading for the door, but Juanito is there, with me, an arm round my shoulder, determined, he says, to make sure I get home, but also, I somehow feel, to make sure I am actually staying in a *casa particular,* in other words that I am what I say I am. Actually, I'm glad, not so much for his company by this stage, but because I genuinely was getting worried about finding my way back to the *casa,* because I can no longer remember precisely in which direction it is from here, nor how to get back to where we started.

It turns out to be a lot closer than I had feared, something I realize when we pass the first building I recognize, the local office of the CDR, *Comités de Defensa de la Revolución,* with its ever-vigilant doorman, dozed off in a shabby armchair. I notice Juanito takes care not to wake him. These offices, one to be found in every district of every town, are the often dozy but nonetheless omnipresent eyes and ears of the party, political patriots, the ones with most to lose if ever the revolution should be reversed.

Juanito leaves me at the door of my little bungalow with a *ciao, compañero, hasta mañana.* We agree to meet at 3 p.m. on the square.

Somehow I just know he isn't going to show.

CHAPTER ELEVEN

Cu'a e' Cu'a

Juanito's unsolicited saloon bar language tuition has been little short of a miracle. All of sudden I've started to understand a bit more, And be a bit more understood. The explanation of the missing 's' is a revelation. When I ask the girl behind the Plexiglas the time of today's train eastwards, she looks blank for a moment and then says something that sounds like, 'Ahhh latoona', I can now nod enthusiastically. Yep, a Las Tunas, that's where I want to go. The bad news is that it was at 4 a.m. this morning. The worse news is that it was indeed the only one and the next is tomorrow at 'ochi-maya' – las ocho y media – 8.30, which means of course that I need to be there at 6.30.

This is not good news, but *Cu'a e' Cu'a*, as they say. There is nothing to do beyond chilling my heels for another eighteen hours and, more immediately pressing, chilling my parched throat and resting my sore feet. This turns out to be surprisingly easy and pleasant, because against all common sense, logic and anticipation, at the other end of the station, abutting the near derelict puce semi-ruins, there is an open-air bar, with high stools, electric fans and cold beer.

I perch myself there with a cold can and, for lack of anything better, a view of the television which is playing that most riveting of programmes, the Cuban review of international news. The big item, probably not playing high on many other news editors' agendas right now – except possibly, just possibly, and even then I wouldn't bet on it, in Caracas – is a meeting of the Cuban–Venezuelan Intergovernmental Commission, which has 'concluded with the signing of important contracts'.

Just what those 'contracts' might be is obviously not mentioned. This is government business. All the average Cuban citizen needs to know, in the eyes of the national news media, is that his government is doing good stuff for him. Precisely what that 'good stuff' might be, or who is paying for it, is no business of the common man. That does not mean it is all bullshit. The Cuban–Venezuelan 'oil for doctors' deal also happens to fit pretty precisely with the old mantra of communist economics: 'from each according to his ability, to each according to his need'.

There is also the fact, unknown to me at the time sitting by the bar in Camagüey, that Chavez was just about willing to sign anything in return for treatment by Cuban doctors for a cancer which he at one stage alleged might have been deliberately caused by United States secret services.

That may sound ridiculous – and I am fairly certain it is, but only fairly, because I have to remember that when I lived in Moscow as a British reporter, the US embassy solemnly informed us its intelligence assets had proof the KGB had treated the steering wheels of certain westerners' vehicles with chemicals that would allow them to trace our movements, and which incidentally happened to be carcinogenic. These were the same guys who had put metal grids on the street-facing windows of their apartments because they believed that the KGB was beaming carcinogenic rays into their kitchens. The same guys who had planted an explosive charge in a cigar in an attempt to kill Castro. The same guys who, after spending a fortune on Soviet workers to build them a new embassy in Moscow, allegedly discovered that the concrete walls were riddled with electronic listening devices. Just because you're paranoid doesn't mean somebody isn't out to get you. Like being schizophrenic doesn't mean there aren't two sides to every story.

The secondary item on Cuban news on this bright sunny June morning is a meeting of the 'International Campaign of Solidarity with the Five'. The 'Cuban Five' are a big issue in Cuba, and despite the so-called 'international campaign of solidarity', pretty much a non-issue anywhere else in the world, not least because of the confused and complex nature of US–Cuban relations. You may not have heard of them, but it is hard to travel anywhere on Cuba without seeing posters dedicated to the five men jailed in Miami in 2001.

Here, for example, from the official posters displayed at Havana airport is a 'question and answer' on 'the five'.

'Who are the five Cuban heroes jailed in the USA?'

'Five young professionals who decided to devote their lives away from their homeland, to fight against terrorism in the city of Miami, the hub of most aggressions against Cuba. The five men were put on a manipulated trial in Miami, a completely hostile city dominated by a Cuban-origin mafia, where no fair and impartial trial was possible in keeping with US and international laws.'

On the other hand, here is the version on Wikipedia (http://en.wikipedia.org/wiki/Cuban_Five):

> 'The Cuban Five, also known as the Miami Five (Gerardo Hernández, Antonio Guerrero, Ramón Labañino, Fernando González, and René González) are five Cuban intelligence officers convicted in Miami of conspiracy to commit espionage, conspiracy to commit murder, and other illegal activities in the United States. The Five were in the United States to observe and infiltrate the US Southern Command and the Cuban–American groups Alpha 66, the F4 Commandos, the Cuban American National Foundation, and Brothers to the Rescue.'

Wikipedia is of course, the online encyclopaedia anyone can edit and many people do, often to make the 'facts' fit their own interpretation. As of January 2012, its editors added the note that 'The neutrality of this article is disputed' and redirects the reader to the 'talk page', where it becomes obvious that 'disputed is an understatement. (http://en.wikipedia. org/wiki/Talk:Cuban_Five)

Personally I have no idea of the truth of this case: their appeals against conviction were overturned by a US court in Atlanta in 2005 but a subsequent court decision reinstated them. I hold it up as yet one more proof that what most people consider to be historical truth depends on who wrote the history they read.

René González was released on parole a few months after this on condition that he spend the next three years in the United States, despite claims from his supporters that his life is in danger there from anti-Castro exiles. At the time of writing however (March 2012) he has just been granted permission for a limited two-week visit to his sick brother back home. Watch this space.

Meanwhile back in Camagüey, Ramón somebody or other, another member of the Cuban politburo whom nobody knows, is delivering a lecture to a regional party congress in Las Tunas. One day, maybe soon, he or one another of the relative nonentities chosen by the Castro brothers over the past half century may take over, but until they do, nobody much, even in Cuba, pays much attention to their personalities. My only interest is that this is happening in Las Tunas where I am hoping to put my head down tomorrow night. Even with my Spanish, newly tuned to Cuban rhythm and pronunciation, working on overload attention, I soon start to nod off over my beer, partly of course because my metabolism is still working equally hard on last night's alcohol intake, but also because there's only so much party political

Orwellian newspeak gobbledygook anybody can cope with in any language.

The bar staff are clearly immune. I slide off my stool and slope back townwards. Half-way along Calle República, the city's main drag, I encounter the best reason I could have imagined for another rest stop, the Hotel Colón, named for Christopher Columbus (*Colón* in Spanish) with cool colonnades, pastel-painted pillars and ancient leather furniture, I commit the heresy of wishing I had eschewed my incongruous middle class *casa* bungalow for a bit of communist-preserved old colonial style, even if the air-conditioning isn't working.

That is getting to be a problem. It's hot. Very hot. And so am I. Not least because I'm wearing heavy denim jeans, and it's 35°C out there with a humidity factor of close on 70 per cent. The sweat – as my Northern Irish father would have said if he ever experienced such temperatures (and he did in India during the Second World War) – is dripping off me. The simple solution is to slip into something more comfortable, except that I haven't got anything more comfortable; the only pair of long cotton shorts I brought with me didn't survive being soaked through in Santa Clara and then drying out stuck to my steamy body. So there's nothing for it but to go shopping. Except that it's Sunday. And I'm in Cuba.

The former isn't necessarily a problem, as the shops are all open to midday. The latter is. And one I'm already anticipating, despite the fact that in Camagüey's meagre couple of shopping streets, there is no apparent shortage of lightweight summer apparel in the window displays. But then I've lived in Communist countries before. On a journalistic trip back to Moscow in the late Eighties – a year or two after I left – Virgin Atlantic managed to lose my suitcase, with the result that for two days I had to borrow the *Sunday Times* foreign editor's underpants, because in the current phase of whatever five-year plan was then in operation, underpants were 'off'.

And so it proves. Yep, there are cotton shorts in the window. No, there aren't any on the rails inside. And no, of course the ones in the window aren't on sale: 'They're in the window'. 'We have lots of swimming shorts?' And they do, but lime-green above the knee with a netting gusset wasn't exactly what I had in mind. The only other choice is the same in purple. Does anybody know where I might find ordinary cotton shorts? Or even lightweight summer trousers? Sorry, sir, this is all there is.

Eventually the doorman at a peso shop on República tells me to try a CUC shop on Maceo, the polished granite paved pedestrian street that is obviously intended to be the show-piece for foreign tourists. Bizarrely it's called Futurama, although Bender and Leela are reassuringly absent. And yes, they have shorts: 12 pairs. All different. One fits. Which means that if I don't want to spend the next few days in my sweaty heavy denim jeans (I know, I should pack better) then it's a pair of heavier than I would like blue knee-length heavy cotton shorts with a disconcerting elasticated waist-band. Imported from Italy no less!!! Not exactly the cheap, locally-made cut-offs I had been hoping for. The one conso-lation, not least in a country where you're carrying two cur-rencies, as well as ID, phone card, and nigh on useless credit cards, is that they have lots of pockets. They cost me CUC 31.75, just over £20 ($30), which is rather more than I would have paid in Debenhams, but then there isn't a Debenhams in Camagüey.

Changed and feeling mildly cooler, or at least better ven-tilated, I head for the main square and my rendezvous with Juanito. But 1 p.m. comes and goes and no Juanito. I wonder if he's slept in; it wasn't entirely clear when we parted in the early hours of the morning that he was heading home. There was more than a touch of the all-night party person to his demeanour. But somehow I know that's not it either. I find myself unconsciously hoping he's maybe decided he was a bit too free in his conversation with a foreigner and decided to lie low. I'm hoping it's that. And not that someone else thought the same, someone else who was listening. Someone who might have done themselves a service by doing the state a service and Juanito a disservice. Part of me doesn't believe it – not least because none of me wants to – but there is also a part that isn't sure. Because even as the tourists start to turn up, Juanito doesn't.

I can't help having a bad feeling about this. My subconscious is reminding me that Camagüey has a reputation. It has been a pirates' target and a den of pirates in succession, but more recently – and more relevantly – it was the last place where one of the heroes of the revolution was seen alive. Camilo Cienfuegos was a dashing, bearded revolutionary and one of Castro's intimates. He came back from exile with him onboard the *Granma* and was a charismatic, extreme left-wing leader whose style and zeal could have made him a rival to both Fidel and Che Guevara. But on the night of October 28, 1959, just 10 months after the revolutionaries' victory, he boarded a Cessna 310 for Havana and was never seen again.

Despite an intense land-sea search no trace of the Cessna or Cienfuegos' body was ever found. The revolution had a martyr and Fidel and Che lost a close colleague, who might also have been a close rival. On that basis there have been persistent rumours ever since – largely stoked by anti-Castro exiles in Miami – that Cienfuegos was killed on Castro's orders. There has never been any proof, nor any real reason other than the joys of conspiracy theory, to believe it. Castro not only tolerated his biggest rival, Guevara, but put him on a pedestal as a national icon. Cienfuegos' face is on the 20 peso note, while Che named his own son Camilo after Cienfuegos.

An alternative theory which might go a long way to explaining the hero's disappearance and the absence of any explanation is that Cienfeugos' light aircraft was mistaken for a hostile spy plane by the revolutionary Cuban air force, who accidentally shot it down, and the embarrassment then and since was simply too great to admit it. There is of course also the possibility that it really was just lost because of an air accident. But as a firm believer in the cock-up theory of history, I like the second explanation not least because amongst the acts for which the Order of Cienfuegos, a medal instituted in the dead hero's memory, can be awarded is shooting down an aircraft. There's a sense of irony about it which I'd like to think was conscious.

Either way, I try to put Juanito's no-show down to tropical torpor rather than imagine him languishing in a cell for fraternization with a foreigner, and head off through the sleepy, sun-drenched streets of Camagüey in search of shade and a spot of lunch. It's a Sunday afternoon and the heat seems to have sapped the very life and soul from the scorched streets of the city. I am noticeably flagging, keeping in the few shadows cast by low houses from a sun almost directly overhead. A bicycle bell makes me jump and I turn and see in the lee of the overhanging gable of an old colonial house a grinning brown face on a *bicitaxi*. '*Hola*,' he says. '*Hola*,' I reply. And then, implausibly, he recognizes me. '*Hé, tu es un amigo de Juanito.*' Hey, you're a friend of Juanito. It comes out, of course, as: '*tu e' un ami'o*,' but I've learned to look out for the missing consonants. He spotted us in the bar last night. I ask him where out mutual friend might be, but he just shrugs. Any minute now he's going to tell me, '*Cu'a e' Cu'a*'. Instead, he offers me a lift.

I'm getting short on CUCs though – having blown the

budget more than intended on my Italian shorts – and the *casa* still has to be paid in the morning plus there is the difficulty that this being Sunday the banks aren't open and Camagüey doesn't boast an ATM. All I can offer, I make clear in advance, is a few national pesos he seems happy enough. A completely free ride was never in question. I am a foreigner and that means I have more money than him. A lot more. In any currency. I manage to make him understand that a restaurant with a bit of shade would be nice, and a few bumpy minutes bouncing on an unpadded wooden seat later I am on San Juan de Dios, the most colourful and atmospheric, ancient square in Camagüey, in the corner of which, within a bright blue painted colonial era building just across from the pastel yellow eighteenth-century church is the Campana de Toledo, probably one of the smartest looking restaurants in town. Empty.

There is a reason for this, as I discover shortly after 'tipping' Juanito's *ami'o* 20 pesos, less than one CUC, about half the normal rate, but about four times what he would have charged a native. Fair enough really. The Campana de Toledo looks as if it has everything a hungry, hot pedestrian could desire: the delightfully cooling ceiling fan and shady terraced courtyard are extremely welcoming. Certainly a lot more welcoming than the staff. It takes more than twenty minutes before anybody turns up. And when they do, in the face of a dour-faced middle-aged waiter in a starched collar that must be hell to wear in this temperature it is only to tell me that I can have a beer but no food. Food, it would appear, is 'off'.

Surely they have something, I ask, pointing out that the kitchen is supposed to be open and they charge in CUCs. He looks a bit grumpy, and I realize that this is a state restaurant and although they may charge in CUCs, the staff get paid in pesos. About five minutes later, he comes back with the beer

– a Bucanero of course – and tells me they can rustle up a little snack of *moros y cristianos*, the black beans and white rice that is the Cuban staple, its 'Moors and Christians' an unusually racist hangover from Spanish colonial days.

I agree, because I'm hungry, and it is always possible that a smart place like this might just about manage to do humble food well. Except that, of course, they don't. An hour later, having drunk one more beer than I intended and spent as much time as I can be bothered pushing overcooked soggy rice and undercooked hard beans around on a plate, I pay – to my horror, rather more than I would have for a decent meal in an English gastro pub, and this out of my dwindling supply of CUCs – and leave without tipping. I get a surly grimace from the waiter, but then I didn't exactly get a service with a smile.

The heat has abated slightly and there are faint life signs in the seemingly comatose body of Camagüey, or '*Cama'way*,' as I am learning to say. I wander back into the main part of town – San Juan de Dios is visited mainly by tourists – to find doors and windows behind wrought iron grilles open now revealing scenes of domestic bliss, or at any rate domesticity: a bloke in his vest watching baseball on a tiny CRT telly, a woman in a shawl (can she be cold?) darning a shirt, a bloke tinkering with what looks like a motorbike engine on the floor of his living-room. Here and there even the wrought iron grilles are open and kids pile out onto the street, girls skip and run along the cobbles or sit gossiping on the steps like miniature versions of the mothers they will soon become, boys throw things at one another or playing tag, the lucky one or two struggle with a toy scooter on cobbles.

It is a good half hour's walk back to the main square, at least by the route I take which seems to be a lot longer than the journey on the *bicitaxi*. I realize I am hungry again. Or rather that I never really stopped being hungry. Luckily there is a restaurant on the corner opposite the Cambio bar, open and serving actual food. For national pesos. In the evenings. At lunchtime – when the tourist coaches from the beach resorts are expected to be in town – they only take CUCs.

There is an interesting sort of price relationship: prices in pesos are twice what they would have been at lunchtime in CUCs, which means everything is approximately 90 per cent cheaper. I opt for the chicken, which I am gradually coming to realize is the safest bet, only to find that the foreigners have had it all. Chicken is off. In fact, everything is off except for *biftek de jamón,* which might be a piece of gammon but could also be a pork burger. I decide to pass and numb the hunger pangs for a bit with a can of Cacique beer, which at least is devoid of Bucanero's cloying sweetness.

By 8.30 p.m. República is heaving. It is promenade hour, the epitome of Mediterranean culture transported to the Caribbean. This could be Spain, Turkey, Italy or Greece, everyone out in their Sunday best doing a spot of window shopping. Camagüey isn't short on window dressing. There is a women's fashion store that could hold its own with Swedish chain H&M, except that in Cuban terms the prices are pure Bond Street. The Panamericana chain – prices in pesos, but also astronomical – looks almost as good as BHS (which is fairly faint praise), but I know from experience too that much of what is on display is just window dressing. Items in the windows aren't necessarily for sale inside. And even if some of them are, it would be a miracle if they had your size.

All of which fills me with wonder at how well the average Cuban turns out for the evening promenade, in chic tight, tight, low-cut jeans, with big silver belts and figure hugging T-shirts. And that's just the blokes. Not that the girls dress much differently, apart from a commendably socialist, economically efficient use of much less material, particularly in the jeans, which I suspect go through several lifetimes, starting out as ultra-tight denim leggings and ending up as little more than denim knickers.

Blokes my age of course are mostly dressed in sensible slacks with polished shoes and open-necked white shirts, as opposed to my grubby polo shirt, sandals and heavy Italian shorts with an elasticated waist. And I'm supposed to be the one from a sophisticated European nation visiting a down-and-out third world country.

The biggest queue in town is for the ice-cream parlour. There is something of a 1950s American feel-good film about the scene of all these fresh-faced teenage kids giggling and jiving as they queue for wholesome, old-fashioned refreshment with nothing ahead of them but an evening strolling around town or heading for a dance hall with little likelihood of alcohol (unaffordable) or narcotics (unavailable). You can almost imagine an old-fashioned Georgia or Alabama Republican right-wing congressman from that era nodding approvingly, except of course that absolutely nobody here is even aware of skin colour, not least because there are so many variations.

The other advantage – and I do hope the Cuban kids too regard it as an advantage – is that when they go dancing, 90 per cent of the time it is still to their own music rather than cultural colonial imports from the United States. Cuba is one of the few places in the world where you won't hear John Denver's *Country Roads* telling you West Virginia is 'almost heaven'. Here country roads are still *carreterras rurales* and if they bring tears to the eyes, it's because they're absolute shit to drive on. Or would be, if you had a car.

Back in the Cambio, still vainly in the hope of bumping into Juanito. The barman gives a shrug of shoulders with a smile that, having lived in East Germany where the Stasi had informers everywhere, I can't regard as wholly innocent. Instead of Juanito, the man dominating the bar tonight is the sort of Cuban who definitely does have a car. Probably a big one. It would have to be. The man himself is big, brimming with muscle and if I had to stage a wild guess at his family history I would suggest his ancestors might have been the biggest tribesman any pirate could drag out of central Africa onto a slave ship only to find him seizing control of the ship in mid-ocean and feeding Bluebeard to the fishes. It is hard to resist the analogy: for a start he is wearing a blue and white spotted bandana. And puffing a big fat cigar. And showing off his mobile phone.

With good reason. In a land where only a few years ago mobiles were not only scarce and horribly expensive, but also illegal, he has a brand new state-of-the-art Blackberry on which he is playing aloud a video version of the latest Floridian badass Black-Hispanic rap hit, a clear suggestion that the immunity to cultural colonialism might not survive a transition to capitalism.

As a foreigner, with a third-rate, non-3G mobile in my pocket, I am an obvious target to which to display his technological up-do-dateness. When, on repeated urging and his determination not to believe I don't have one, I finally succumb to the 'I've shown you mine, now show me yours' line, the look on his face is pure ecstatic one-upmanship delight. Beaming all over his face and puffing smoke from his thick cigar in mine, he tells me in a language that I can only describe as Black-Hispanic-Floridian-Cuban-English, *'You have phone, you wan' proper phone, no un telefono miki mau.'* Yep, some smart ass Cuban wannabe gangsta has just told me I am a loser because I have a Mickey Mouse phone!

The fact that he is smoking a cigar also shows what a big timer he is in local terms. Cigars may be the national pride and joy but these days they are strictly for the tourist market. Even Fidel, for whom a big cigar was once as much of a personality statement as it was for Winston Churchill, has given them up. For health reasons. The Cambio does sell cigars, notably the top brand Cohiba, the same as I got at black market rates from my driver in Santa Clara. These, however, are undoubtedly genuine and cost a fairly eye-watering CUC 19.80 each, which is actually not that bad consider you would pay nearly £25 in Britain. They are, of course, unavailable in the United States, except for Arnie Schwarzenegger[7] who famously smoked them in a tent adjoined to his office when he was governor of California – they are as beyond the grasp of most ordinary Cubans as a day-trip to Miami. That is not to say most Cubans don't smoke. They do. But they smoke cigarettes, which are substantially cheaper and ironically boast US-themed names such as Hollywood and Vegas, though there is one which has distinctly more politically correct branding and an advertising slogan to match. Popular. *Yo soy Cubano, yo soy popular!* I'm Cuban, I'm popular, but the Spanish also suggests 'one of the people'. Not exactly Mad Men, but not too bad for a country where everything is run by the government.

This particular cigar smoker is keen to treat me to his life history. Or a version of it. He's keen to make clear that despite his obvious affluence he is a man of the people too, even though he's not exactly preaching communism. What I'm getting is an old-fashioned rags-to-riches story, the sort you might hear in a bar in Chicago, even if it does have a particularly Cuban flavour: 'Man, I not know who ma daddy was. Mi mama, she *una puta,* a whore, ma daddy prob some fuckin' turista.' I sympathize but it's not as if he's listening. Apart from the usual obligatory, *'Daydon?',* the standard

---

7. See *All Gone to Look for America*, by Peter Millar, Arcadia Books 2009.

abbreviation of '*Dedonde vienes?*' – where do you come from – he's not interested in anything but himself.

Unlike my conversation with Juanito the previous night this is not so much an exchange as a tirade. This guy may have a traumatic family history but the sad truth is he's a first-rate example of a human archetype common to both capitalism and communism: the pub bore. I make my excuses and leave. The night may be young, but I'm not.

In the morning I have a train to catch. And in Cuba that means you've got to be on your toes.

CHAPTER TWELVE

Changing Carriages

Camagüey's near derelict station at 7.15 in the morning is implausibly busy. There are actually two trains doing a fairly passable impression of coming or going, even though the one I am here to get – the only one I had been told was scheduled for today – is not due for another two hours.

At least one of the two locomotives belching smoke, oil and diesel fumes next to the platform is certainly being used to take passengers, although I'm not absolutely certain it ought to be, seeing as the vehicles lined up behind it bear a closer resemblance to cattle trucks than anything designed for human conveyance.

Nonetheless humans are piling out of them. Little humans: scores of kids with skin colours every hue of the human rainbow but every uniform a pristine brown with white shirts, indicating they are middle-schoolers, aged roughly between eight and ten. This heap of rusting cattle cars, is, it would seem, the equivalent of the school bus and has trundled into Camagüey from the little villages between here and the coast.

The other doesn't exactly look fit for human conveyance either, certainly not humane conveyance. The carriages are marked clearly *Ferrocarriles de Cuba* (Cuban Railways) in yellow paint, clearly done by hand and quite probably by someone still suffering under the effects of a few too many tots of rum. Apart from that – and the fact that most of them actually have windows with at least a few panes of glass in them – these carriages look like they were not so much bought off the shelf from a railway supply company as put together by someone with a load of scrap metal and a welding gun.

Up front, leaning out of the window of a red and yellow locomotive belching steam into the palm trees, a big black man is doing a remarkable impression of a Caribbean Casey Jones wondering whatever happened to the Cannonball Express – because there is absolutely no danger of the locomotive he is in charge of ever acquiring that nickname.

For much of the next hour he shunts his ramshackle collection of carriages one way and the other for no purpose obvious to me and without anyone making any attempt to board them. At least it is something to watch as the minutes turn into hours for the hordes of us gathered on cracked black plastic seats loosely anchored to iron struts laid out across the floor of what passes for a waiting-room in the creeping dereliction of Camagüey station.

There is something almost hypnotic about watching this facsimile of railroad activity and it is with a shock that I look at my watch as yet another train pants into the station and I realize it is exactly 9.20 a.m., the hour my train is due to arrive. And here it is! Two trains in a row approximately on time! The *jefe de torno* unties one end of the piece of rope that was the demarcation line between waiting area and platform proper and we're off, storming the carriages, pushing pieces of improvised luggage through open windows and clambering up the treacherous rusty iron steps onto the train.

Inside it's actually not that bad. Probably also East German in origin from the familiar look of the luggage racks, many of which are still functional. I notice this quite quickly because the middle-aged, well-dressed man who is one of the five other passenger sharing my compartment is taking great care in placing a rather rickety looking cardboard box with holes in it, which seems to comprise the whole of his luggage, at the end near the door.

My other fellow travellers are a young couple – she in cut-off jeans and silver-embroidered bikini top, he in cotton slacks but bare-chested – the middle-aged man who could have bought his stripy polo shirt and grey chinos in Marks & Spencer's – and a couple of older women, both wearing tight jeans and black halter tops, possibly at an age when they ought not to be.

The corridor is still chaos. Passengers are piling onto the train at the nearest open door, wisely not wanting to take any chances on how soon a train that actually arrived on time might decide to depart. Those already on board are bustling past one another in opposite directions as they hunt for their reserved seat. Meanwhile, hordes of vendors – quite happy to take the risk of being carried off in a country where trains regularly slow down to walking pace – hawk half-litre bottles of home-brewed *aguardiente* hooch, unappealingly grey wafer biscuits, greasy-looking pork fritters, boiled sweets and the inevitable plastic bottles of mango juice. I'm only taking a relatively short ride but most people on board are in for the long haul, all the way to Santiago.

It's not just people selling stuff though, there are would-be buyers too, sticking their head through doors looking for goods (I use the word 'doors' loosely: it's a long time since any train compartment I have yet seen in Cuba was acquainted with a physical door).

The doorway to our compartment is now being graced by a very plump apparition from an over-the-top Gothic comedy show. Dressed in micro-mini denim hotpants above fishnet tights, head wrapped in a multicoloured scarf and wearing a fluorescent pink camisole under what appears to be a string vest, the one thing that leaps instantly to my mind is Matt Lucas playing the 'only gay in the village' in Little Britain.

I'm trying my best not to giggle, but my amusement turns to revulsion (and pity!) as she – it is a she – hauls up string vest and camisole to reveal a protuberant brown tummy covered in pink bumps. Self-preservation has me panicking about unknown tropical diseases. She tells us it just appeared overnight and thinks it has to be a rash or insect bites. It's still not exactly the sort of thing British railway passengers routinely reveal to one another. But then nor do they lack basic drugs such as antihistamines which by common agreement is what this woman needs. Cuba has universal free healthcare but a lack of funds and the US embargo means even the most basic medicaments can be hard to come by.

My own luggage contains sticking plasters, blister plasters, the essential Imodium and copious quantities of sunscreen and insect repellent, but not much else. Like most 'first world' travellers, I had just assumed – in this case rashly – that if I need something fairly basic I can pick it up wherever I am. Not in Cuba. The other side of the coin is that people routinely keep whatever medical supplies they might have on them, especially when travelling. Within minutes the others in my compartment have produced an extraordinary array of half-full bubble packs, tablets packed in silver or orange foil, all of them unbranded generics. How they know which is which is beyond me until I realize that they probably never have a choice. The same drug isn't sold under a multiplicity of brand names. If you can get it at all, you know what it is.

One of the bubble packs I recognize as what the bloke on the train from Santa Clara was selling. What it is I have no idea, but the woman with the ailment reckons it is what she needs. It is immediately, unquestioningly handed over. No money asked for and none offered. It's the old communist mantra, although the first time I have observed it actually working: to each according to her need, from each according to her ability (in this case, to provide). Or you could just call it common humanity. Either way I am impressed.

Not so with the punctuality, though. The train may have pulled in dead on time, and been boarded – in almost pirate fashion – instantly. Forty-five minutes later, timetable notwithstanding, we still haven't moved. On the platform there is an announcement to passengers behind the piece of rope that has been restrung to mark the separation between platform and waiting-room that Train 5 to Havana via Santa Clara will be delayed owing to a problem with the locomotive. There is a general groan on board our train too, even though it is going in the opposite direction. There has been no hint from the loudspeaker as to how long either delay could be despite the fact we are now already nearly an hour late leaving. It could be hours. Even days.

Inside the compartment it's hot and, given the relatively relaxed standards of dress, the smell of sweat is rising. I'm almost refreshed when a few drips of what seems like relatively cool water land on my head, until I start wondering where they could have come from. Then a loud cheeping follows and the man in the 'smart casual' collection leaps to his feet and takes down the box with holes in it from the luggage rack above my head. I've just been peed on by a chicken.

He is profuse with apologies. I'm too amused to be angry. He explains he is a chicken farmer in Las Tunas, and this is a prize bird. It turns out to be an excuse for almost everybody to introduce themselves. The young man with the bare torso is called Dario and is a nurse, which explains why he had the right bubble-pack, his girlfriend is a teacher, the younger of the two older women a university lecturer in Spanish and history. She is immediately fascinated by the fact that I am a foreign writer and tries at length to engage me in a bookish conversation that stretches my linguistic skills, not to mention extremely limited knowledge of recent left-wing Latin American literature. Happily there is a sudden jerk that throws all of us into or out of our seats. We're moving. 10.50 a.m., only ninety minutes later. We wave sympathetic farewells to those on the platform still waiting resignedly for news of the locomotive for Train 5 to Havana.

The university lady wants to know where I am headed and just nods when I say Guantánamo. I am beginning to realize that it doesn't quite have the same resonance for Cubans; first and foremost it refers to the town, one of the oldest in the country, only secondly does it refer to the bay which ought to be that town's outlet to the sea but is blocked by the foreign base squatting astride it. She insists Santiago is much nicer. She lives in Siboney, she says proudly, then has to explain that it is a seaside town not far outside Santiago and is both very pretty and very famous because that is where Fidel (nobody needs to add the surname) holed up to hide after his first abortive attempt at revolution. She tells me I will understand when I visit the museum dedicated to the birth of the revolution in Santiago.

I am more surprised to hear that Siboney's best beach is called Daiquirí, which up until now I had only known as a cocktail. That gets a laugh all round. You get good daiquiris in Cuba; Hemingway, inevitably, is amongst those credited with inventing them. It turns out that Daiquirí as a place name goes back to the long vanished indigenous Taino people, but that its global fame was established early in the twentieth century when an American mining engineer working in the area ran out of gin for his G and T, and made the best he could with what was available, pouring white rum over the locally plentiful staples of limes and sugar.

I manage to entertain them with news that this wasn't very different in fact from 'grog', the standard Royal Navy tipple for sailors in the Caribbean. If necessity is the mother of invention, locality provides the raw materials. The supposed 'Hemingway' variation, also claimed by the El Floridita bar in Havana, added a few drops of maraschino liqueur and was served frozen (as are most in American bars today, although to purists you ought to ask for that version specifically).

Neither is on offer in our cramped train compartment, but we do have the next best thing, in the sense of 'the only thing' available: Dario hands me a bottle of dark ruby red liquor labelled *Tradición 16%*, and urges me to take a glug. It tastes strong, but most of all it tastes like warm, sweet cough medicine. I pull a face and his girlfriend hands me a plastic cup of hot sweet coffee, to wash it down with. Actually the two go quite well together and my reaction wins a round of applause, and a round of *Tradición* for everybody too.

The result is that we are all quite merry when, sooner than expected, though more than an hour and half later than it should have done, our train pulls slowly into Las Tunas and it is time for me to say goodbye.

'Try the local wine,' says the university lady. 'You will like it.' I smile politely, but I think she is having me on. Cuban wine? I don't think so.

CHAPTER THIRTEEN

Tuna Fishing in Cuba

There have to be more enticing, certainly more prepossessing names for a city than Las Tunas, especially one not situated anywhere near the sea. Something fishy here, you might suspect. Being told that its full name – rarely used – is Victoria de las Tunas doesn't help. Victory of the red-fleshed, blue-fin sushi favourite over the evil porpoises or bottlenose dolphins perhaps?

Ironically, the 'Victoria' bit was bestowed by the Spanish in 1869 after winning a battle here in the islanders' first war of independence, which goes a long way to explaining why nowadays it isn't often used and this town of some 150,000 people is usually simply called Tunas: pronounced the same way US Americans say the name of the fish *tuna*.

But the *tuna* in Las Tunas has never had anything to do with fish. *Tuna* is a native form of tropical cactus, a species of prickly pear which can be peeled and eaten or its juice extracted to make a wide variety of non-alcoholic drinks. Allegedly the town got its name because they grow freely in the area and became a nickname used by the hordes of merchants who came to the area to buy its main product: beef from cattle ranches. There aren't many of either any more as far as I can see.

But there is an endless array of the usual run-down *bici-taxis* to get me to next *casa*. My driver is a jovial, elderly bloke, a good decade older than I am, with a thick pair of glasses, full head of grey hair and scrawny, hard-pedalling thighs desperate to convince me that, instead of the *casa particular* I have already booked, I should stay at his place instead, or his cousin's place. His cousin can even throw in a *chica* for free, he says, turning round to leer at me lasciviously – and dangerously, as we narrowly avoid another pothole. I decide to decline the offer.

Las Tunas has been dubbed Cuba's most boring town, but in the afternoon sunshine it seems rather pleasant, the houses neither collapsing tenements nor seventeenth-century relics, but fairly modern, relatively well-kept little two-storey provincial homes, most pre-revolutionary and in the late colonial style, painted in an array of bright pastel colours, like those where I saw the kids playing baseball in Matanzas. Not too many rusty tin roofs. Always a plus in Cuba.

The landlady of my *casa* is waiting for me. I'm her only guest, but the accommodation is more than suitable: more or less a studio flat with cooking facilities and large, if basic, bathroom on the ground floor of a pleasant two-storey stone-built townhouse at the far end of the main road in from the station.

Strolling into the main square, I see banners to remind me that Las Tunas is currently hosting the regional assembly of the Communist Party of Cuba, under the slogan MORE EFFICIENCY AND PRODUCTIVITY. Maybe that's why the town looks like it has all been given a fresh lick of paint. Most strikingly of all is a splendid symmetrical, neo-classical two-storey building with a clock in the centre painted a shocking bright blue. This is the town hall, dominating – not least by its alarming colour – the main square named after Vicente García, a local lad who, the inscription on the statue of a stern, sword-wielding gentleman tells me, was a Major General and hero of the first Cuban war of independence.

This was the abortive war fought against Spain from 1868 to 1878 which bizarrely ended in a stalemate, the result being an end to slavery (the slaves had been freed and joined the rebels), but the continuation of occupation. García was the last of six 'presidents of Cuba' declared during the war. Afterwards, he emigrated to Venezuela only to be poisoned by the Spaniards putting ground glass in his favourite dish, a pork, plantain and okra stew, an assassination almost as bizarre – if more successful – than the CIA's attempt to kill Castro with exploding cigars (they never actually got them to him).

The memorial relates how García famously captured the town from the Spanish in 1876, thereby turning on its head the name Victoria de las Tunas they had given it for an earlier battle. I suppose that explains why the full name has survived.

For a town famously supposed to be boring, the main square is delightfully quixotic. Apart from the bright blue *ayuntamiento*, and Señor García, there is a sweet little whitewashed church which looks like it dates back to the 1600s, the art deco pink and white Hotel Cadillac, a cinema with what looks like a giant red and white radio mast towering above it, several random pieces of municipal concrete work that look a bit like bus shelters (except that there are no buses) and, dotted at regular spaces along the edge of the square, tall palms waving gently in a warm late afternoon breeze.

There is also a pleasant café with outside tables, serving hot coffee and cold beer, inevitably for CUCs only, which is why the only Cubans in it are those working at the bar and a very young girl flirting with a group of three middle-aged Italian men. The words of my *bicitaxi* man come disconcertingly to mind. Is this the end-product of a decade of Berlusconi? Or is it a more local endemic epidemic?

The Cuban exile community in Miami try to make out that prostitution in Cuba is the result of poverty, a corrupt moral climate and an uncaring communist government. Some of that is certainly be true, but as an umbrella explanation nothing could be further from reality. It was the communists who banned the prostitution that under the Batista US-funded dictatorship had been one of the island's economic mainstays. The moralists in the United States tutted, but still came here for their holidays, filling the casinos and bordellos they banned back home. The reality was that they simply exported to a convenient offshore *oubliette* vices they pretended to abhor at home – out of sight, out of mind – a bit like they still do with Guantánamo Bay today.

There is no doubt that the Castro government turns a blind eye to the local womenfolk turning tricks for tourists willing to pay them in CUCs, but those who do are, on the evidence – like the fat old lady who propositioned me in the bar in Havana – mostly freelances, rather than in hock to some pimp. People trafficking in Cuba is all the other way.

Nor is their any official laxity about foreigners propositioning underage girls. The age of consent in Cuba is sixteen, as it is in most of western Europe. I am not making any national judgements here, but it is a fact that in Cuba Italians in particular have a bad reputation. In 2010 three Italian men were jailed in Bayamo, not far from Las Tunas, after the body of a young girl was found following a sex and drugs escapade at a hotel. But any suggestion that Havana is the Bangkok of the west is far from the mark.

There is at least one aspect of Italian culture, however, that has found mammoth favour amongst ordinary Cubans: ice-cream. Just as in Camagüey, there are crowds here queuing for the stuff, this time on the steps of a puce-pink colonnaded building on the main street. The sign above the door says it is called Yumurí, presumably after the river, and the crowds are patiently waiting to be served by a man dispensing ice-cream.

Yumurí certainly justifies the 'yum'. On offer are six exotic flavours, all of which look remarkably good. I join the queue and plump for mango. They have surely enough of the damn things without having to add any artificial flavouring, I hope. It's a good bet. The ice-cream is delicious, cold, refreshing and a perfect mix of fruitiness and creaminess. But then I'm not really surprised. It has been my experience over the decades that communist economies are absolutely crap at providing almost any of the normal consumer pleasures of life. But they can do ice-cream. Even the Russians could. And in a curious twist of economic history Italianstyle ice-cream ended up in Cuba after a lengthy journey via New York and Moscow.

Way back in the 1930s Stalin's Internal and External Trade supremo Anastas Mikoyan tasted what was to most Russians a little-known delicacy on a trade visit to New York. Mikoyan was hugely impressed and off his own bat imported American machinery to make it in Moscow. Whereas shortages and incompetence blighted much of Soviet manufacturing, Mikoyan kept standards in the ice-cream industry rigorously high and under his own personal control. Stalin allegedly joked to him, 'Anastas, you like ice-cream better than communism.' Not a bad choice, but deciding whether or not to laugh at Stalin's 'jokes' was never an easy call. The call came for Mikoyan shortly thereafter in the Great Purge of 1937 but it may say something that all he faced was dismissal; most of his colleagues were executed. He would later get his own back by helping write Nikita Khrushchev's 'secret speech', denouncing Stalin after his death.

It was Mikoyan who was chosen by Khrushchev sent as the first top Soviet official to visit Cuba after the revolution and it may well have been he who persuaded Fidel to get into ice-cream. The result was Coppelia, Cuba's state-run ice-cream business, of which Yumurí is the Las Tunas incarnation. There is no doubt that Mikoyan was considered a linchpin in the Soviet–Cuban relationship. He was deputy prime minister at the time of the 1962 Cuban Missile Crisis which ended with withdrawal of Soviet missiles in return for guarantees that the US would neither invade Cuba nor assist any future Cuban exile invasion such as had occurred at the Bay of Pigs the previous years. Mikoyan was given the tricky job of telling Castro – who had urged a nuclear strike against the US if an invasion were threatened – that they would also be removing smaller weapons not included in the deal.

If Coppelia is Russia's sole long-term legacy to Cuba, it has been a huge success, offering a vast array of often unusual flavours and every town in the country has its ice-cream parlour or street vendor.

For me, however, the highlight of Las Tunas main street is the shop a few doors down from the open-air ice-cream trolley. If I hadn't stopped for my little tub of mango delight and retreated into the shady colonnade to eat it before the sun turned it to liquid, I might otherwise not have noticed this extraordinary emporium with orange foil coating its windows and the usual Cuban lack of interior lighting. But standing in the shade of its doorway my eyes wander over El Telégrafo's window display. And boggle. It's not particularly striking at first glance. It's dark and it takes a few seconds for the eyes to adjust before I realize I am staring into the display case of the most remarkably exotic inventory of any shop in Cuba, and possibly the world.

First glance is deceptive: here are a few women's dresses and T-shirts hung on white plastic hangers, some shoes beneath them, a plastic shopping bag in front, also for sale, as is the bright orange bubble wrap next to it. But let the glance wander and there are also some men's trousers, a pile of baseballs, a domino set, some plastic toy lorries, two ladles and three green buckets, a garden fork, an industrial-looking spade, a milk churn and an oil pump. And in the next window? A coil of barbed wire, an elegantly displayed 18-inch machete, some energy-saving light bulbs and a few pickaxe heads. The next? A few plastic plumbing joints, a handful of bottles of washing-up liquid, a solitary tin of furniture polish and two pots of paint, some elegantly-arranged blue plastic cutlery, a thick-rimmed set of coffee cups, and lying up on its side against an internal pillar, yep! a kitchen sink.

Tearing myself way from the Harrods of Las Tunas I wander down past the end of the main street where the town gradually seems to fizzle out into a sprawl of dusty suburbia, where tin roofs begin to appear. On my right is a small house with what at first look appears to be a bit of particularly *avant-garde* sculpture displayed on a concrete slab outside. It is a long tangled piece of metal shaped in a rough curve. It looks angry, post-modern, deliberately distressed. Arresting. Only on closer examination I discover – with a bit of a shock – that it is indeed angry, and distressed. With good reason.

It is the small plaque on the wall of this simple wooden house that alerts me. It reads simply 'Here lived Carlos M. Leyva González, Martyr of Barbados'. Barbados is somewhere I associate with sandy beaches, rum cocktails and a thriving upmarket tourist industry, not martyrs. But then that's because I learned my history in another world.

The piece of ironwork in the garden is indeed a sculpture, by Juan Heznart Hedrich from Matanzas, created in 1978, and the reason it looks like nothing so much as a piece of aircraft wreckage is because that is precisely what it is supposed to represent.

The aircraft in question was a Douglas DC-8 belonging to Cubana airlines and this modest little monument in a garden of a small house in one of Cuba's least visited towns is a poignant evocation of what many natives still consider their country's darkest hour. It is a monument to an incident that, for reasons which will become clear, few foreigners have heard about. Or if they have, they have forgotten, or worse still, dismissed it.

Amongst global sporting events there are many which attract a lot more attention than the Central American Fencing Championships. Nonetheless, for Cuba back in October 1976 it was a big thing. That year's event was being held in Caracas, Venezuela, and the Cuban team included Carlos Leyva González, the twenty-nine-year-old young man with wavy hair in shirt and tie whose face is depicted on the metal plaque attached to the wooden wall of his former home. The big thing for Cubans was that their team had had a good competition: the best imaginable, in fact. They had taken a clean sweep of gold medals. They were therefore in party mood on the way home, flying on Cubana de Aviación's Flight 455 from Guyana via Trinidad, Barbados and Kingston, Jamaica, back to Havana. When they landed in Trinidad they found two Venezuelan men looking for a flight to Barbados (despite having signally declined to take an earlier British West Indian Airlines flight). The team were in such high spirits that one of them helped the pair change their tickets to fly with Cubana.

In Barbados the pair left the plane, but unknown to the team, did not quite take all their baggage with them. Eleven minutes after CU455 took off from the island's Seawell Airport (now Grantley Adams International) the plane reached an altitude of 18,000 feet when two bombs, one in the rear lavatory, one in the central section of the plane, exploded, one destroying the control cables, the other blasting a hole in the fuselage and starting a fire.

The Cuban captain radioed back to the Seawell control

tower: 'We have an explosion aboard. We are descending immediately! We have fire on board! We are requesting immediate landing! We have a total emergency.'

A few minutes later, still eight kilometres short of the runway, the aircraft plunged into the sea killing all 73 passengers on board, including 11 Guyanese, five North Koreans and 57 Cubans including several government officials and all 24 members of the gold medal-winning fencing team, several of whom were still in their teens. It was, at the time, the worst ever terrorist attack on a civilian aircraft in the western hemisphere. It was later discovered that the bombs had been detonated by a pencil-shaped detonator concealed in a tube of Colgate toothpaste.

The two bombers were subsequently arrested in Venezuela and jailed and the plot traced back to anti-Castro Cuban exiles Orlando Bosch and Luis Posada Carriles, both of whom belonged to organizations linked to the CIA. They too were arrested but all four were acquitted by a Venezuelan military court. The prosecutor appealed and they were retried by a civilian court. All spent various terms in jail. Bosch was released in 1987 and moved to Miami where he died in 2011.

Carriles, believed to have been the prime mover in the attack, escaped jail in Venezuela, fleeing to El Salvador where he became involved with CIA operations there. He was also implicated in a bombing campaign in Havana in the mid-1990s intended to cripple the country's growing tourist trade. Eventually, he made his way to the United States, where he was arrested on for nothing more serious than immigration irregularities and soon released. The CIA denies involvement in the bombing of CU455 but documents since released prove that it had at least advance warning of an attack against a Cuban civilian airliner.

There is no doubt that Posada Carriles has blood on his

hands, just as there is no doubt that today (as of 2013) he still lives happy and unrepentant in Miami with an American wife and two children. His nickname is 'Bambi'. Anti-Castro exiles see him as a hero. In Cuba he is considered as bad as Osama bin Laden. At eighty-four, Carriles is two years younger than Castro. It remains to be seen which will laugh last. Or if anyone will see the joke.

Sitting there in the shade of an unkempt palm tree in the garden of this little wooden house, I found it worth reflecting on the fallibility of 'history', and the cold cynicism of the old maxim that one man's terrorist is another's freedom fighter. And that soundbites such as the 'War on Terror' do not necessarily define what terror is and when those who declare themselves to be fighting terrorism on behalf of civilization can in their own ends turn a blind eye to acts of terror. Or even tacitly condone them.

But *Cuba e' Cuba* (I'm at it now) and despair never quite overcomes *joie de vivre*. Almost directly opposite this poignant little monument is a bar with salsa music pouring out. I climb the stairs to the first floor of Las Antillas to find a group of young twenty-something Cubans drinking beer and laughing. Cubans with CUCs, obviously: the beer is Bucanero, and they are ordering it in copious quantities. In the garden below there is a statue of naked girls and dolphins cavorting over a concrete pool conspicuously devoid of water. It's supposed to be a fountain. Then the music starts up again and the locals have taken to their feet doing that curiously Cuban dance that anywhere else in the world might be taken for lap-dancing: the girls grinding their posteriors into the crotches of their male partners.

There's a funny thing about dancing in Cuba. It is sexy, in the sense that all the rhythms and motions are inspired by sex, but it isn't erotic. It's not intended to evoke desire; more to celebrate the act, rather than lead to it. It's intended to be joyous, but not necessarily flirtatious, unless you obviously want it to be. And then you won't be on the floor long. At least not standing on it.

But before I've had any more time to philosophize about a way of life expressed on the dance floor, the couples have split and the dance turns into a conga and before I know it I am dragged to my feet and thrust into it. I do my best for a few minutes but can't quite keep up with their youthful enthusiasm, and respectfully slump back into my plastic chair. Eventually they too give up and go back to their beer and light up cigarettes. It's been a happy reminder that for most Cubans – both those with and those without the luxury of access to CUCs – life is about living it, about every day experiences and relations with other people. *Carpe diem* could be the national slogan. Eat, drink and be merry while you can, just in case tomorrow we're hungry, thirsty and the merriment will be harder to come by.

Things, as such, don't matter for most people, largely because most people don't own many things. True, that is changing, as marked by the enthusiasm to possess the latest mobile phone. But for the moment at least, the slogan of Wall Street's former (and future?) Masters of the Universe is irrelevant. Here it isn't a case of 'He who dies with the most toys wins,' but rather, 'He who manages to have a good time without any toys at all.' It may not be a great blueprint for capitalist entrepreneurialism but it's a hell of a recipe for a life of hedonism. The guys give me a high-five as I get up to go. *Hasta la vista.*

On the road back into town, though, I catch a glimpse of one of those leitmotifs of Cuba's potential future, a refugee from another society which not so long ago was in the throes of arguably worse poverty than the Castros' Cuba today, and is now well on its way to being a global superpower, and perhaps – frighteningly – even the model for global civilization despite still pretending to espouse a communism that is now little more than totalitarianism: China.

The sight itself is nothing more scary than a bus. But it is a Chinese bus. What is most disconcerting about it is that it still appears to think it is in China. The lettering on the front and along the sides is in Chinese, as is the roller sign in a window above the driver. I have no idea where this bus is headed, but I am pretty certain it is not where the sign indicates. Helpfully transliterated into English, it says: Handang Hospital Shuttle Bus. Clearly nobody here thought it worth changing the sign. In a town like Last Tunas if there is an actual bus, everybody will know where it is going.

This only slightly surreal vision trundling by along the dusty, steamy streets draws my attention to the other sparse traffic and the fact that even here the old 1950s rusting American limousines which for so long have been an accidental romantic icon of communist Cuba are now increasingly few and far between. The only romantic relic I can see is not American but German, an ancient Opel Rekord, dating from perhaps the mid-1960s. Apart from that, here as in Havana, the echoes are of a more recent past, though one that is equally drifting into the realm of memory: Russian Ladas and Moskviches, cars designed for bad roads and worse drivers, but for long seen only in the land of ice and snow, and now translated here to the tropics to rust away their days as a memory of another outdated empire.

I wonder idly why they don't seem to have any Trabants, the iconic little East German runabout which became a global symbol when they poured west in their thousands after the fall of the Berlin Wall. With their 'Duraplast' composite bodywork – a material related to both Bakelite and Formica reinforced with cotton fibres used as a cheap and lightweight alternative to steel – they would at least have had the advantage of standing up better to the tropical damp. Perhaps they would melt? Or maybe Trabbies were just too crap even for Cubans.

I arrive back in the main square just in time for the evening opening of a hostelry I hadn't noticed earlier in the day, when it would have looked like just another shuttered dilapidated building. It turns out to be another of supposedly boring Las Tunas's peculiarities: Don Juan's wine room. So the woman on the train wasn't having me on after all. It seems unlikely. Impossible even. I haven't seen a vine anywhere in this land-scape of savannah scrub and jungle. The only wine anywhere on display has been Spanish. But there is not doubting the physical presence of Don Juan's wine bar.

The room is light and airy, whitewashed walls with a big, dark hardwood bar, and two waitresses in the obligatory short skirts and black fishnet tights. One is smoking a ciga-rette and looks mildly annoyed by my presence. The other, however, a tall dyed blonde with longer legs than her skirt was intended for, could not be more charming. Especially when I tell her I'd like a glass of wine. Wine, it seems, is not something the Don Juan wine bar has much call for. But they do have some. In fact they have lots of it. There isn't much call for wine.

I ask her what wines they have, and which she would rec-ommend, which causes a bit of embarrassment. Most cus-tomers drink beer or rum. Tentatively, I ask her for a wine list. This causes a puzzled look for a moment. *Carta de vinos*, I repeat, wondering if I've got something wrong. I have. It's the word *carta*.

'Ah,' she replies, getting the gist and adds, 'Soroa.' It's my turn to take a minute to catch on, until she indicates the bot-tles behind the bar and in the glass-fronted fridge standing next to it. Don Juan's has lots of wine, but it doesn't really need a list. There are only two: red and white. Soroa, it turns out, is a brand. For both red and white.

'It is actually Cuban wine?' I ask doubtfully.

She seems surprised, but nonetheless thinks for a moment before saying, '*Sí*,' as if it was the most obvious thing in the world. Whereabouts does it come from, I venture, not exactly expecting a detailed French style monologue on the virtues of *terroir*, chalky soil and south-facing slopes. Which is just as well, because I'm not going to get one. But she does know where the wine comes from. Extremely exactly.

'*Finca Chirigota*, km 79 on the *Autopista Nacional. Provinca Pinar del Río.*'

The other end of the island, west of Havana, which might explain why I haven't exactly seen row after row of vineyards in the island's dusty interior. Pinar del Río, I am aware, is the country's least sweltering province, more mountainous, good for tobacco growing and, I dare say, wine. But then as according to the waitress the vineyard is the only one in Cuba, there's no point being picky.

'I'll have a Soroa, then.'

'Which colour, Red or white?'

'Which is better?'

She has a think about that, shrugs and says 'White.'

'I'll have a white, then.'

'Dry or sweet?'

That's a no-brainer. If they make both, I can bet my last CUC that the 'sweet' is going to seriously sweet.

'Dry, please.'

Within seconds she is back at my table with a bottle straight from the fridge, dripping beads of condensation, held forth for my appreciation with all the attentiveness of a trained sommelier.

'Ah, just one glass,' I say.

She looks suddenly crestfallen.

'There isn't a bottle open.'

This actually sounds good news, given that most customers

don't drink wine, the last bottle might have been opened by Che.

'Can't I just have one glass from this bottle.'

I should have known the answer before I asked the question, and a pang of guilt washes briefly over me as I see the moral conflict fighting on her face.

'Sorry,' she says. 'No. You have to buy the bottle.'

It is gone 7 p.m. but I have already had a couple of beers and was looking forward to a couple later rather than downing an entire bottle of wine on my own.

'How much does it cost?' I ask nonetheless.

'2.40,' she says, quickly adding, 'CUC', thereby sending the price up 25 times. But at £1.99 ($2.40) it's less than half what I'd pay for a glass of bargain basement Chardonnay back in Europe. On the other hand, with even bargain basement Chardonnay, you know what you're getting. Usually. This is unexplored territory.

'If you don't want to drink it all now, we can put it back in the fridge and keep it for you,' she adds.

Done deal. I nod. She smiles and disappears, bringing a glass and then disappearing with the bottle, to open it for me.

The minutes pass. Quite slowly. More than a few of them. The waitress has left the room, leaving the bottle on the bar, where it stands alone, losing its cool (in a manner of speaking) wholly disregarded by the other waitress who has lit up another cigarette. After a good ten minutes, by which time the bottle sitting patiently on the bar in the early evening tropical heat must be well on the way to lukewarm, my friendly waitress reappears and engages her grumpy colleague in heated *sotto voce* conversation. There is obviously a problem.

And her colleague is obviously not going to help her solve it.

After a few moments she comes over to my table, biting

her lower lip and reveals the source of her embarrassment. It's not an unknown problem, just not one I've never before encountered in a wine bar: they don't have a corkscrew.

I resist the temptation to break into laughter, if only to spare her all too obvious embarrassment, and suggest we do what I have done too many times before, from student parties to ill-equipped hitchhiking trips: use the handle of a fork to push the cork into the bottle. The waitress looks a bit doubtful so I take the fork and do it myself, shrugging to make clear it's really not an issue. *Cu'a e' Cu'a*. She is almost tearfully happy as she pours me a glass. I offer her one for herself – I'm seriously not intending to drink the whole bottle – but she backs off waving her hands, leaving me to wonder if the wine is really that bad.

It's not. It's actually rather nice. Dry, not too acidic, with just a hint of flint over an underlying fruitiness. Not exactly a Sancerre or a Chablis, but a perfectly acceptable everyday bottle of plonk on a par with anything you'd pick up in the supermarket without paying too much attention. I wonder if I should look out for Soroa next time I'm in Tesco? Probably not. I have enough random bottles in lurking in dark corners of kitchen cabinets – from Bulgarian Rakia to Croatian Maraschino – to know that there are some drinks which taste better *in situ* than they do when you get them home.

By now it's gone 8 p.m. and time for food. The waitress promises solemnly to keep the rest of my wine, putting it back in the fridge open. I ask if she has any suggestions where I might get dinner and she immediately says El Baturro which I had spotted a little earlier not far away. She smilingly informs me that it does the best food in town. The trouble is that in Cuba that sometimes means the only food in town.

Happily on this occasion that turns out not to be the case. Not least because El Baturro is closed. The sign on the door says open, and there is an *orario* next to the menu that plainly says it is open daily from 6 p.m. to 10 p.m. But it is definitely closed. The door is locked and the interior is in darkness. Fortuitously at just that moment – although it could apply to just about any moment in most Cuban towns – a *bicitaxi* man is passing, and realizing I might otherwise be heading for bed on an empty tum, save for my two glasses of Soroa, I ask him if he can take me to a restaurant. Adding, just to be sure, 'an open one'.

Five extraordinary minutes later we have done what seems like a little circuit of the town centre and I am standing in front of a rather dull but unquestionably open little restaurant called La Bodeguita. I say extraordinary minutes because this particular *bicitaxi* man happens to own what has to be the Rolls-Royce of *bicitaxis*. Not only does it have a proper bicycle seat – rather than the usual variation on leather belts, bungee cables or bundles of rags – it also has, a PSP.

And in this case PSP does not mean *Partido Socialisto Pedalo* or anything similar that you might expect in Cuba, it actually means just what PSP means anywhere else in the world (and if you don't know, ask any kid), just not something I expected to find in the Socialist Republic of Cuba, least of all strapped beneath the seat of a *bicitaxi*: a PlayStation Portable. Complete with games for the pedal-pushing cabbie to amuse himself when without a fare and with a large library of digitally downloaded music to entertain his customers – whether they like it or not – when he is on the go. It is obviously his pride and joy and when he notices me staring at it, albeit in amazement rather than in the outright envy I imagine he gets from most local Las Tunas customers, he cannot resist showing off its features.

Which is all very well, but I've actually seen a PlayStation Portable before and I didn't come here to be impressed by the multiple games software available from Japan's most famous multinational. I came here to eat. With some difficulty I make my excuses but not without, under entreaty, agreeing that he can pick me up from the *casa* tomorrow morning to go to the station to catch my onward train. In fact, it didn't take much to persuade me. If I am to be certain of catching my train, I need to be at the station shortly after 6 a.m. If he is really willing – and he assures me, crossing his heart several times – that he is, to turn up at 5.45 for a 2-CUC fare, then good luck to him.

The menu at La Bodeguita is limited, but then it is a long time since I have looked for anything remotely resembling a gourmet experience. In Cuba, particularly in the provinces – and Las Tunas is about as provincial as you can get – all a restaurant dish has to be is edible. And luckily this menu boasts the one thing that I am increasingly finding to be a reliable fallback: roast chicken.

Unfortunately, the waitress says, with a smile uncannily resembling Sybil Fawlty's, chicken's off. I glance grumpily across the room at the only other two diners, a middle-aged couple, possibly German, tucking into their drumsticks. But all I get from my waitress is the same unnerving smile and the information that that was the last. Instead, however, she is proud to offer me beef fillet. The most expensive thing on the menu, I notice, but then that's only about 10 CUC – double the price of the chicken and a month's salary for the average native – but well under the price of standard pub grub in England. And after all Las Tunas is supposed to be the centre of Cuban cattle country.

'*Muy bien*,' I tell her, very good, which may have been a mistake.

A mistake only because maybe she misunderstood my 'very well' for the instruction as to how I would like it cooked. I would like to give her the benefit of the doubt and blame my Spanish, but I don't quite believe it, because we did actually have that conversation. She asked me how I would like my expensive bit of beef fillet cooked and I replied '*poco hecho*', which I had learned deliberately and I have since checked and know that 'cooked just a little' is indeed the correct way to order a rare steak in Spanish. What emerges from the kitchen, nearly half an hour later, bears the same resemblance to a cow as the preserved saddle from José Martí's unintentionally suicidal charge against the Spanish back in 1895. With half a bottle of Chilean red for lubrication (Soroa was 'off'!) I chew as much of it as I can. It'll keep me from getting long in the tooth. This, remember, from a country that serves pork rare!

In comparison it is a real pleasure to see the genuine delight on the face of the waitress back at Don Juan's as I collect the remnants of my Soroa white (more for form's sake than from a genuine desire to finish it) and head for bed. Except that bed's a bit further than I remembered. And for once there isn't a bloody *bicitaxi* in sight. Probably because the man picking me up before dawn has gone to get an early night. Making him a lot more sensible than me.

But, thanking God for the grid system – and the fact that this isn't Camagüey – I wander back towards my *casa*, a route that coincidentally takes me past the Parque Maceo, where there just happens to be a bar still open, with a few locals shooting the late night breeze. Inevitably, I join them. But there's a problem when I come to pay: this is a peso bar and I've run out of pesos. All I have in my pockets are CUCs.

No problem, you might think: pay in one and get the change in the other. Except that it doesn't work like that. There's bookkeeping. This bar isn't licensed to accept CUCs. And it's illegal for Cubans to exchange them other than at a branch of the state bank. That, of course, is a rule more honoured in the breach than the observance. But there is another problem, which is that there are only four of us in the bar, of which two are local lads, barely capable of standing and stoney broke, having blown their last pesos on beers they probably couldn't afford. The other is the forty-something waitress, who might or might not have been willing to change money for me, but doesn't actually have any. At least not enough to change a 10 CUC note which represents as much money as she makes in a month, not exactly what most women carry round in their handbags, even if it is only £8 ($10) for me.

Under other circumstances I might have cut my losses, but there is another factor. There are two beers on sale: not just Cacique, the fairly common, hoppy peso lager, but also something called Rubia, which I have never heard of before. It turns out to be a slightly stronger lager served in smaller brown bottles. I know this because I am drinking one, by the neck, from the bottle (they have no glasses). The waitress, who tells me her name is Judith, which for some reason she thinks is Russian – it isn't but then it isn't Spanish either – has worked out that as I have a 2 CUC coin in my pocket (the only one I have), if she buys a couple of beers 'for friends' and I have no more than three, but leave the coin on the counter, then it will all have worked out.

'Rubia is a real local beer,' she tells me. 'Made near Las Tunas. There are other beers from small breweries based in Cuba's smaller towns, she says: 'Tinima – strong beer, six per cent. And Latina – from Guantánamo.' They are all cheaper – and a lot more interesting – than the big brands punted at the CUC-carrying foreign tourist market. A bottle of Rubia costs 8 pesos here, which means I could drink six of them before my 2 CUC coin was used up. I only want the one. But I accept her offer of another, for the road, and wander off happily into the humid night. I have to get up in five hours' time.

CHAPTER FOURTEEN

This Train Doesn't Go There

There's a surreal moment just as dawn is breaking over Las Tunas when the bleary-eyed landlady of the *casa* stumbles into my room in her nightdress and announces abruptly and rather rudely that my 'taxi' is here.

I stumble, equally bleary, out of bed, pull on some clothes, grab my rucksack and lurch out the door to the *cocorico* sound of cockerels crowing in next door's garden to find my beaming *bicitaxi* man in cool shades with some Miami rapper blasting away from the PlayStation Portable under his bottom.

'*Buena*,' he says, which I gather is Cuban hip short for '*Buenas dias*'. Apparently he's been waiting 15 minutes already – it's only 5.45 a.m. – and announced himself to my landlady when he arrived, which might very well account for her less than congenial attitude. Clearly fares paid in CUCs are few and far between in tourist-deprived Las Tunas.

Any vestige of a hangover fades as he pedals us up a street of pastel houses, low palms and wandering dogs all seemingly oblivious to the cacophony we're inflicting on them from the PSP. One or two people standing at bus stops even smile and wave and jiggle a foot in time. In a sane country you'd question their sanity but then *Cu'a e Cu'a*.

The station ahead is all but deserted. There is a signal absence of people not just on the street outside but also inside the relatively clean and tidy pastel-blue painted waiting-room. Obviously there is no timetable posted and no indication of what time a train might depart – in any direction – except for the less than reassuring absence of any other potential passengers. Until I discover a pudgy woman with a scowl on her face reclining on an uncomfortable looking chair behind the Plexiglas ticket office window. She is decidedly unimpressed by – and uninterested in – my arrival. One look at the expression on the face of the woman behind the counter, whose eyelids have drooped again, suggests it might not be a good idea to ask her about train times. I do what by now I know any Cuban would do in my situation: sit down and wait – on the floor, given the absence of seats.

Shortly after 6.15 a.m. a more cheerful-looking bloke comes in through the door on the other side of the counter, looks around and then waves an arm at me, not calling me over but nonetheless clearly trying to tell me something. I haven't a clue what he wants but he's looking a bit agitated. Then he smiles, realizing he's got a stupid gringo on his hands, points to the fluorescent light tubes above my head and the switch by the door. I get the message, get up, go over and click it. Nothing happens. I shrug and look back at him. He shrugs and looks back at me and says '*otra vez*': do it again. I can't quite see how that's going to work as the switch was up to start with but then I realize he means flick it up and down. I do, and there is a worrying hum, followed by a lightning flash, then nothing, then a brief flicker, and suddenly the strip light bursts reluctantly into life. He smiles, gives me a thumbs up, shrugs and says, '*La capacidad.*' I'm not sure if he means 'capacitor' (which in Madrid Spanish is *condensador*), but I don't care much as the one thing I am absolutely certain of is that I am never going to dabble in amateur electrics in Cuba.

The grumpy woman behind the ticket counter inevitably is not happy to have the lights turned on and glares at me as if it's my fault, before reluctantly pulling herself upright in the chair where, now I come to think of it, she's obviously spent the night sleeping, and starts fiddling with hair clips.

The bloke who got me to turn the lights on has pulled out a ledger of some sort and begun to go through what looks like an exhaustive wedge of paperwork, with endless tallies scribbled in blue ballpoint marked against piles of paper slips which may or may not be tickets.

His female colleague has gone into a coughing fit, which only ends when she manages to find the remote control for the television hanging over my head, pull a cigarette from some pocket and light up. Immediately there is the raucous squawking of Latino females arguing, but not in real life, from the television above my head. I look up and recognize another episode of *Mujeres de Nadie*, this time with the amethyst-eyed blonde woman in the doctor's white coat screaming at a sultry dark haired woman in a low-cut dress who's fondling the bald head of a little fat bloke that I can hardly imagine either of them fighting over. I begin to suspect this is a soap opera for women written more in wistful hope than expectation by men. I'm almost surprised it isn't a Cuban co-production, for it certainly meets the PC qualifications when the sultry dark-haired woman turns on a look of the utmost scorn and screams back: '*Usted e' una capitalista*', almost as grave an insult as a US politician calling someone a 'socialist'.

More in my own version of hope rather than expectation I glance around the station for some indication that there might be a train expected at some stage. Eventually I pluck up my courage and go over to the counter to timidly ask the woman behind it, cigarette in hand, if she is the *jefe del torno*. She nods, a mite imperiously. But when I ask her about trains, she shakes her head and tells me to wait.

The reason becomes clear when, only a few seconds later, another woman arrives looking altogether fresher, brighter and more efficient – not least perhaps because she's had a proper night's sleep – and abruptly dismisses her relieved colleague. Another man has arrived too and taken over the bulky ledger. It occurs to me, though I have seen zero evidence of racism in any way in Cuba, that the two people on the day shift are white while the two on the night shift were black. I am going to assume it is coincidence but I am not one hundred per cent certain. It may be or may not be more reflective of the society in place when the revolutionaries came to power but it is hard to ignore the fact that in the largely geriatric politburo there is still only one male black and only one woman of any colour!

The new woman at the Last Tunas ticket office, however, smiles genially at me over her gold-rimmed glasses, and tells me as kindly as she possibly can that she is unable to sell me a ticket for my onward journey until she has received word that the train has actually left Camagüey.

'Is there a reason for that?' I ask stupidly.

'Of course,' she says still smiling as if talking to a child with learning difficulties. 'It might not.'

Ah, of course. 'When is it expected to leave?' She glances at her watch and says: 'In an hour. Or so.'

An hour later she beckons me over. Hey presto. It's 7.30 a.m. and at least I have a ticket. In celebration I break open the bottle of Rubia saved from last night. The now-warm wine I left for my landlady.

Some forty minutes later, the Rubia has gone and taken my enthusiasm with it. The lack of sleep is beginning to tell, but I don't want to doze off and miss the train. I ask the woman with the gold-rimmed glasses what the latest estimate of its arrival might be. She gives me that special smile again (the one reserved for idiots) and says maybe a bit after 9.30. This is the train I was told just 48 hours ago, in Camagüey, would get in at 6.35. Maybe they meant get into Camagüey. Even then it's late.

Meanwhile the woman at the ticket counter has started taking what appear to be bunches of used tickets and begun sorting them. Into what inconceivable order, I have no idea. All I can see and hear is the constant staccato as she lifts a rubber stamp, dabs it on an ink pad twice, and then thumps it down on the ticket. I'm not sure if it's manifestation of obsessive compulsive behaviour or just that she takes satisfaction from the rhythmic tic-tic-TAC, tic-tic-TAC. Actually, after a while it's curiously comforting, like a jazz metronome. Maybe she plays part-time in a rumba band. By my count she's gone through the sequence at least 200 times by now.

By 9.01 we're finally on the move, in a Cuban manner of speaking. The new *jefe de torno* has called up all those who have already booked tickets and is shouting out a list of names even though all of them have already gathered in a scrum around the ticket window. I'm trying hard to be relaxed, which is not bad given that I got out of bed nearly three and a half hours ago in a house little more than a kilometre away and am still waiting to be given the opportunity to buy a ticket for a train that hasn't arrived but should have been and gone hours ago.

I take the opportunity provided by the scrum to buy something to eat from a vendor who was overwhelmed with would-be customers until just a second ago. All he has for sale is a roll filled with fatty spam. The spam is unsurprisingly disgusting, but at least the bread is good. Cost 5 pesos, about fourpence ($0.6). Finally, last but not least, madam summons up the one hard-currency paying would-be passenger: me. A single to Santiago, I say. She looks up, surprised.

'This train doesn't go to Santiago.'

I look back at her, open mouthed in horror.

'But I was told that this was the train to Guantánamo via Santiago.'

She looks as if I've just said Fidel Castro is a moron.

'No! This is the train to Guantánamo. If you want to go to Santiago, you have to get off at San Luis.'

'Where is that?'

'Outside Santiago.'

This seems obvious. I meant how far outside Santiago, but never mind.

'When is the connection?'

She looks back as if I've just asked if there's a Father Christmas.

'The connection?'

'To Santiago'

'The next train to Santiago is tomorrow.'

'And the train from Santiago to Guantánamo?'

Same look.

'There isn't a train from Santiago to Guantánamo. Trains from Santiago go to Havana.'

'Could I change at San Luis?'

This is obviously an option that's never occurred to her.

'When is the next train to Guantánamo that stops at San Luis?' I venture, to help her with the general concept.

'Trains go to Guantánamo every three days,' she says, adding the disconcerting rider: 'Usually.'

I opt on the spot for a ticket to Guantánamo. But she's not sure now she wants to sell me one.

'This train is not going to Santiago. You should get the next train. Tomorrow.'

I assure her rapidly I want a ticket to Guantánamo – right now I'd take a ticket to anywhere – and with a frown that suggests she suspects I am trying to buy a ticket under false pretences to somewhere I don't want to go to, she reluctantly hands it over, counting out my CUCs to the last hard currency centavo. And then smiles.

Not a moment too soon. Suddenly things start to happen with remarkable alacrity. At precisely 9.20 we're all ushered out onto the platform. Amongst my fellow passengers is a man in his sixties whose only luggage, tucked under his arm, is a car tyre with so little tread remaining that in Europe it wouldn't be remotely legal and probably wouldn't have enough substance to it to be used for a retread.

The other factor which strikes me for the first time amongst this bunch is that for an island which, despite the serious lack of prescription medicines, boasts an excellent free health service, the same obviously doesn't apply to dentistry. Almost everybody over 30 is missing a few prominent teeth. That is yet another contrast to the old Soviet Union where dentistry was not exactly brilliant but not only did few people actually lack teeth, amongst the wilier peasantry it was quite the thing to have one or two made of gold. Silver teeth were also not uncommon. It was one of those examples, in a country where freedom of speech was non-existent, of people physically putting their money where their mouth was. The difference with Cuba, I suspect, may have been that during the 'special period' after the Soviet collapse, all they may have had to eat was surplus sugar.

The carriages on this train are unquestioningly Chinese, to match the locomotive, with bright red plastic seats. But this is a train clearly more suited to crossing the dusty plains of Tibet or northern China than dealing with the tropical humidity of Cuba. For a start, this is the first train – the first vehicle of any sort – I have been on which has windows that don't open. Several of the others – trains, cars, buses – didn't necessarily have windows at all, but this has a full set. And, apart from a few small vents on every other row of seats, they don't open.

They aren't supposed to, because from the roof of each carriage a bulky air conditioning unit is suspended. Which would be all well and good if any of them actually worked. They don't. The result is an atmosphere more akin to a sauna than a train carriage and an ever more exotic, not to say *risqué*, attitude towards clothing. Almost everyone on the train under forty – and quite a few above – are dressed in a style I can only describe as rainbow-metal-punk. T-shirts are bright red, bright yellow or purple, invariably printed with some outlandish usually motorbike or rock band-branded logo, often, particularly but not exclusively on the girls, picked out in silver glitter. Jeans, whole or cut-off, are skin-tight – it is one of those accidental blessings that rationing and the Cuban inattention to food means there aren't many fat people, though those there are wear the same stuff – while belts, particularly the blokes', are big, brash metal-buckled affairs with the more studs the better.

But without air conditioning or open windows, absolutely every one of us is bathed in sweat. So when we come to a halt at a village of sorts and vendors with iced mango juice and cold water come on board, they are stormed and sold out within seconds. I opt for the water. I'm not sure that thick mango juice, however cold, would make its way down my throat. I could do with something to eat too, but all there is on offer is thick slabs of something vaguely green and definitely gelatinous which I'm told is guava jam. I decide to pass.

The village where we have stopped – little more than a few tin-roofed shacks – is called Mir, which has to be another of those throwbacks to the old alliance with Moscow. *Mir* is Russian for both 'the world' and 'peace' – a dual meaning which is based deep in the roots of Orthodox theology – but was mostly used during the Soviet period in the expression *'mir y druzhba'* – peace and friendship – the all but ubiquitous politically correct toast when representatives of different nationalities gathered together.

There is then a 20 minute delay because the unimaginable has happened: a group of ticket inspectors has joined the train. This ought to seem reasonable enough, although in most other countries they would travel with the train for a stop or two rather than halt it to carry out their checks. But somehow here it seems peculiarly pointless; apart from me, almost everybody on the train has paid virtually nothing for their tickets. I have to pinch myself to remember that it is not actually nothing, and that Cuban wages are extremely low. But even in that scheme of things the ordinary Cuban – if he or she can get a ticket at all, which is mostly down to the incompetency of the bureaucracy – can travel the entire 1200-kilometre (750 miles) length of the island for little more than the price of a can of beer. It is one more example of how an economy in the absence of market forces totally loses track of its own purpose and effectively ceases to be an economy at all in any meaningful sense of the word. There is no way in which these ticket collectors can be earning the cost of their salary, which is any case paid by the government, which not only pays to run the railway but pays the salaries of everybody (except me!) travelling on it. The whole thing is one never-ending circle which serves only to achieve a semblance of full employment. It reminds me of the little old ladies who used to sit at the bottom of every escalator on the Moscow metro for no other purpose than, in the event of an escalator failing, to tell people they would have to walk.

The only obvious purpose the ticket collectors are serving is to delay our journey. In fact, they have delayed it so much that we now have to back into a siding in order to let a goods train pass. The heat is rising and so is the volume of chatter, a now incessant cacophony of gesticulating, improvised fan waving, chaos. For a country with one of the highest literacy rates not just in the Caribbean but the entire world (98 per cent), almost nobody has brought a book or newspaper to read. It's shocking but not really surprising. Before the revolution in 1959 some 22 per cent of Cubans were illiterate, and 60 per cent (the rural population) only semi-literate. Cuba's communist regime has seen to it that virtually every man, woman and child can read and write, but it has also seen to it that there are limitations on what people dare write and even stricter limitations on what there is available to read. The result that there is almost nothing published that anybody wants to read.

Eventually we start moving again, after a fashion: stopping, starting, stopping. Sometimes violently. It feels like being trapped in a wheelie case being dragged upstairs. At one stage nearly everyone facing forwards is shunted to the edge of their seats. Then we stop again, for good, it seems. A glance out the window reveals that this is one of the few sections of the line where the track is double. We are almost certainly waiting for another freight train to pass. People are hot, tired. Some of them have come non-stop, if you can use that word in Cuba, from Havana and been on this train for more than 18 hours already.

Suddenly a more than lively discussion breaks out between two young men in the centre aisle. An earnest-looking young man with short curly hair and glasses is arguing loudly with a guy in baseball cap and sleeveless vest across from him. Bizarrely it seems the argument grew out of a discussion about blood transfusions, but has developed into a wider debate about religion and even politics, about the poor state of services generally, about how people have a right to expect more. The earnest young man is running down the list of things that people in capitalist countries can do that are illegal in Cuba, from buying and selling houses[8] to employing staff, things that would stimulate the economy, make things work properly. And the argument is spreading, taking in the whole carriage. This is genuine popular, political debate: if anyone in office was listening to them (in the sense of paying attention rather than identifying dissent) it would be democracy. Far from everyone is for change, but the remarkable thing is that this sort of debate happening at all, and nobody seems to be scared of the consequences. Not one person is looking around in terror for the Stasi or KGB man. Cuba may have its share of jailed political dissidents but it has no secret police in the same sense as the old East European communist states. The government relies on the local Committees for the Defence of the Revolution to report any persistent dissent in a neighbourhood, while it is the responsibility of the Interior Ministry to prevent political assemblies – which is precisely what this almost looks like turning into.

Almost. Then there is a loud rumble as indeed a freight train passes us and we start moving again and people quieten down. It occurs to me that this is why dictatorships so famously pay attention to getting the trains to run on time. There is no greater way to start a revolution than by massing a load of people together for hours on end and then deliberately frustrating them.

Slowly, excruciatingly, we inch our way along towards a stop labelled, improbably, Costa Rica. I notice a strange, sweet, almost putrid smell in the air and put it down to the presence outside of some rubbish tip until I notice with a shock that the woman two seats away is changing a baby's nappy on her lap. She finishes and flings the dirty nappy out the window. Nice.

---

8. Cubans were finally given the right to by and sell property for the first time since the revolution early in 2012.

On an island where almost every modern convenience is scarce, everybody uses disposable nappies. It is one of those quirks of what passes for Cuba's economy. A bit like the glut of eco-friendly light bulbs. But then even in the old Soviet empire the availability of everyday commodities under communism lurched between feast or famine. And you never knew which was coming next.

Costa Rica is the end of the line for the earnest young man in glasses, who is getting up and struggling with a mountain of luggage. I notice one large item is wrapped in the bright orange bubble wrap I spotted in the window of El Telégrafo, the Harrods of Las Tunas. I wonder which of the exotic items offered he might have bought: a shovel perhaps, or the crockery, maybe a machete or two to arm the intellectual shock troops of the new revolution. But no, and I can hardly suppress a giggle as, sweating and panting, he manoeuvres his purchase towards the door and I realize that it is, with the inevitability of divine intervention, the kitchen sink.

As the train pulls out of Costa Rica there is a collective sigh of relief mingled with despair: we're on our way again, but for how long? In the sweltering sauna of this train carriage designed for the Chinese steppes, necessity has become the mother of invention with bits of cardboard to the rescue, mostly to be used as makeshift fans. Those lucky enough to be seated near the small vents have wedged strips of cardboard into them to deflect as much air as possible into the train. Which might work better if we were moving at any speed.

On the other hand too much speed might not be advisable as the train is now canting at perilous angles as we round bends. Guantánamo really is the end of the line. At San Luis, I firmly decide not to get off the train and change for Santiago. It looks like little more than a truck stop with an industrial plant in the background and an endless train of rusting oil tankers parked in a siding. Given that waiting for the next train could be a matter of days if not hours, I stick with the one I'm on. At least this way I can be sure of getting to Guantánamo. I'm still not sure about getting back (though that's more than some residents of Guantánamo can say – the ones that live in the camp on the bay, beyond Cuban jurisdiction).

By now it is 4.30 in the afternoon and I have been on this hot, sticky Chinese train with its red plastic seats for more than seven hours, in which time we have covered a distance of just over 250 kilometres (150 miles). The Flying Scotsman it is not. Then suddenly there is a screech of brakes and we crunch to a halt, half-way over a mainly wooden bridge. It sounds as if we have run over an animal, a goat maybe or a dog, though I can hardly imagine an animal stupid enough or indeed slow enough not to have got out of the way.

Nobody on board looks very happy, least of all those whose part of the carriage is still on the rickety-looking bridge. Rather than try to get the whole of the train across, we stay stopped. In fact, a number of people including what looks like the driver have climbed down to the tracks. A man in combat trousers and a navy vest is staring disconsolately under the train from where there are sporadic gushes of steam. I join most of the other passengers – very noticeably *all* of those whose part of the carriage is still on the bridge – by clambering down onto the grass and wandering around aimlessly looking for some sign of a squashed animal. But there is nothing to be seen. No blood on the tracks nor maimed carcass on the wooden struts of the bridge or in the fast flowing white water gushing by below.

It is quite clear from the expression on the face of the man in the navy vest and from the piece of perished rubber he his holding in his hand that some form of piping has either failed or been broken. There's a lot of head-scratching going on. A bloke in overalls appears to be the engineer, but he doesn't exactly have much in the way of tools: just a spanner and some rope. What exactly it is that has broken and how important it is to our chances of continuing to Guantánamo, which can scarcely be more than a few dozen kilometres away, I have no idea. Eventually, however, people are urged to get back on board. After a lot of spanner clanging and some general bodging it would appear the mechanic has done something – possibly used the bit of rope to tie things back together – to let us limp on far enough to get the rear of the train clear of the bridge.

Ahead on the left is what appears to be a dilapidated barracks with a dirty white colonnade, pale green walls and a rusted tin roof. Closer inspection reveals it to be *Empresa Comercial Mixta El Salvador 117 Carretera Larga*, in other words the local excuse for a supermarket situated at the village of El Salvador at kilometre 117 mark on the main road. We stop for a while, presumably while the engineer nips in to see if they have any stocks of rubber ducting which, based on the window display of El Telégrafo back in in Las Tunas, has to be at best an outside possibility.

One way or another 15 minutes later we are off again at a – relatively – cracking pace, hitting at least 50 k.p.h. (30 m.p.h.) to gain momentum to crawl up the sides of the lush green hills and down the other side into a countryside far more benevolent than the harsh dry savannah. We pass a village with a team of teenage lads kicking a football around between two sets of rusty goal posts (at least here it is the global rather than US version of the game), with a pair of oxen freely grazing in what ought to be the pitch and a man in full gaucho-style equestrian rig galloping to keep pace with the train, waving a lasso in the air. He's applauded by a farmer sat atop an ancient tractor with a big straw hat to shade his eyes, a few kids about seven or eight years old in crimson school uniforms wandering home and a young woman in cut-off jeans and a black satin bikini top, not exactly the typical country girl, the *guajira Guantanamera*.

But all of a sudden the train whistles, as if to express the relief and exuberance of its passengers. As far as I am concerned Santiago will have to wait. For the moment I've got here, to the end of the line. Guantánamo. And a pretty grim place it looks, too.

CHAPTER FIFTEEN

The City (not quite) by the Bay

My first sight of a town that became famous around the world for a song about a pretty girl before it became synonymous with a prison camp is of something rare in Cuba: a traffic jam.

There are road works outside the station and a vast array of taxis, private cars acting as taxis, hustlers offering rooms, people come to meet people and *bicitaxis* circling in their hundreds getting in everybody's way and shouting at passengers, looking for fares. The arrival of the train from Havana, it would seem, is something of a big event: hardly surprising, as there is only one every third day. More or less. Usually less, I suspect.

I wouldn't mind so much if the *bicitaxi* men actually knew their way around their own city. The one I light on has no idea how to find the *casa particular* I've booked even though I have the address and know it's little more than a kilometre from the station. Forty minutes after clambering into his rear seat – at least there is one – he's still pedalling round in circles. At first I think it must be my pronunciation of the address, but even when I show it to him written down, we spend so long circling that eventually I work out where it has to be and direct him there. I suspect he's done it just to push the fare up, but there isn't a meter on a *bicitaxi* and when he charges me 2 CUC I can hardly blow a fuse, even though I know that its probably four times what he'd have got from a local paying in pesos. I'm just glad to get out of the heat, noise and dirt.

The *casa* itself is more like a full-time boarding house than any of the others I've stayed at. There are a varied and random selection of thickset black guys who look like they might be retired or aspiring boxers lounging around on chairs by the usual wrought iron gate. One of them lets me in, takes me upstairs to a sitting-room with more boxing types on the sofa watching television and shows me my room – improbably lacy and oddly reminiscent of a bedroom from a 1960s American television programme (remember *I Love Lucy*?). He tells me Lissett, the landlady, will be back later and suggests I check out the roof garden, which turns out to be a few plastic chairs with the landlady's washing hanging on a line above them.

I could do with falling flat out on the bed but there's a problem: I'm starving. I wish I'd had some of the guava jam stuff on the train. Luckily – I think – I'm fairly close to the town centre. Not that it's particularly impressive. Guantánamo itself is a rather dull provincial town, not even as pretty as the supposedly unloved Las Tunas.

Despite being – for all the wrong reasons, and none of them to do with the current Cuban regime – one of the most notorious names in the world, Guantánamo's history is relatively brief, even in New World terms. Christopher Columbus himself sailed into the now infamous bay in on one of his follow-up voyages to the New World in 1494 but decided not to hang about. The British stuck their noses in during the mid-eighteenth century Anglo–Spanish War of Jenkins's Ear – so charmingly named because a Spanish customs vessel intercepted a British merchant ship and cut off the ear of its captain Robert Jenkins to teach the British a lesson. The British changed the original Taino Indian name of

Guantánamo to Cumberland Bay. But by the 1790s, a second garrison had succumbed to yellow fever, and they decided it just wasn't worth the human cost and abandoned it.

Stuck at the far end of the island – the only settlement beyond is beautiful, exotic Baracoa and that wasn't accessible at all by land until Castro blasted a motorway through the mountains in 1964 – Guantánamo wasn't founded until 1819. Even then it wasn't Cubans who settled here. The original founding fathers were French plantation owners evicted from neighbouring Haïti, which is one of the explanations for the local accent which even more than in the rest of Cuba ignores the letter 's' at the end of words, and rises with a French lilt towards the end of sentences. The original name was Santa Catalina del Saltadero del Guaso. It soon began to expand – the present population sprawled along the three rivers, the Guaso, Jaibo and Bano is a quarter of a million – and in 1843 changed its name to the one known worldwide today. But we will get to that shortly.

My first priority is to find a bank and change some more of the euros I have secreted in a money belt. By the time I find one it is, of course, closed, but as usual there's a character loitering by the corner who's more than willing to change a couple of €10 notes into pesos. Pesos, not CUCs. At least he is changing them at the going rate of 25 to 1 and not trying the scam of foisting *nacional* pesos on me at the CUC rate. Guantánamo town is not exactly on the main tourist trail. Down here, at the end of the line, CUCs, so familiar on the streets of Havana, are a relative rarity, and I reckon I can live on the same currency most natives have to make do with.

As if he's reading my mind, my moneychanger – his eyes continually flicking one way and the other to be sure our transaction hasn't been observed – tells me, as if it is a great secret, that there is a *paladar* just a few streets away. I shrug.

Okay, so the privately-run *paladar* restaurants tend to be grouped mainly in the big tourist towns but there is no reason why Guantánamo shouldn't have one. Then he taps the side of his nose and reveals the big secret: '*Un peso paladar.*' A private restaurant where you can pay in pesos? This is a real rarity. I'm not even sure it's legal. From the government's point of view the whole point about legalizing private restaurants was for them to provide a service that the state couldn't – cooking half-decent food – and sell it to foreign tourists in exchange for their sorely needed hard currency, a goodly proportion of which has to be paid to the state.

The idea, as with *casas particulares*, was to get ordinary Cuban citizens to act rather like licensed collectors of tax from tourists, while providing said tourists with a useful service as an accidental, if useful, by-product. The idea of providing a service for Cubans in their own currency would make no sense at all to the communists: the only obvious point of buying things at one price, adding value and selling them to your fellow citizens is surely to make a personal profit. And that sounds dangerously like capitalism! Which is against the law.

However dubious I may be about what I'm going to find, my moneychanger's directions are good. When I find the place it looks like somebody's home, which of course is exactly what it is. There is no sign outside but the lights are on and the door is open and sticking my head round it, ready to apologize and retreat if I find I really am peering into somebody's parlour, I find half a dozen tables with green plastic tablecloths, three of them occupied, and on a stand by the door half a dozen typed sheets of paper which on closer inspection are menus.

'*Hola,*' a smiling man in his early 40s, comes forward to shake my hand and usher me to a table. '*Para comer?*' he says. Something to eat? Yes please.

The menu is not exactly extensive. In fact apart from the offer of a cheese salad – my memories of rubber cheese in Havana are still disturbingly fresh – there is only one dish: pork fricassee. I'm dubious about the pork, but at least having only one option makes choosing what to have easy.

When it comes it is surprisingly good. Possibly not quite as hot as I might have liked but when the ambient temperature – in the room – is 32°C, it doesn't seem to matter all that much. What was advertised as a 'fricassee' is in fact little pork kebabs fried in oil, served with some crunchy fried plantain chips and a side salad of coleslaw and a bit of cucumber. For which the more than acceptable price is 40 pesos (about $1.50, less than one British pound!). But adding a couple of beers from the fridge – Mayabe or Cacique, the two mainstream peso beers which in any case I prefer to the CUC alternatives, more than doubles it.

Bodily needs satisfied, it's time to head back into town to pick up on the nightlife, not that I'm actually expecting there to be any. The reason I am here is not the city itself but the barbed wire fence down the road. But I haven't got there yet, and I am not really sure whether or not I am going to be able to. The Castro government has never been happy with Uncle Sam squatting on a corner of its coastline, and in the circumstances one would imagine they ought to be wryly amused at being able to point the finger so close to hand at Washington's biggest international embarrassment. Oddly, the reverse seems to be true.

The best view to be had of the US base from Cuban territory used to be the scenic viewpoint of Mirador de Malones, set on a hilltop to the west of the bay looking down on it. For a long time, the Cuban army used it as an observation post to keep an eye on the goings-on beyond the barbed wire, primarily because they have always feared the base could be used to prepare some new Bay of Pigs-style intervention.

The army would, for a few CUCs and after extensive security clearance, allow foreign tourists to share their view of the 'imperialist enemy' and even offer them a cocktail while they borrowed the telescope.

But for several years now, curiously sensitive that Guantánamo Bay has become notorious in its own right, rather than revel in offering a bird's-eye view of the world's most controversial concentration camp for unconvicted prisoners, perhaps for fear of being accused of deliberate provocation, the viewpoint has been closed to foreigners. The closest it is now possible to come to the base – though it is in fact very close indeed, much closer than the Mirador but without the raised viewpoint – is the sleepy little port of Caimanera, several kilometres beyond Guantánamo town. But even that requires an escort and official clearance and I am not going to get any further down that road tonight.

The walk back into town from the *paladar* is an object lesson in the eccentricity of Cuban urban architecture, though that is hardly the right word to describe buildings usually more in a state of dilapidation than construction. Here there is what might be an extravagant hotel from some grand Spanish imperial fantasy: high-ceilinged with tall windows, the outside a riot of pastel blue-painted colonial pillars, both Doric and Corinthian, supporting a flat roof upon which as ambitions grew and then dwindled an equally grand second storey has been added, then a jerry-built third. Its next-door neighbour could be something straight out of a spaghetti Western, low-slung with swing doors. And then another riotous palace of pillars and mirrored walls with a second storey utterly decrepit, windowless, with peeling green paint on the walls and a single flickering strip light on the ceiling illuminating a bare-chested fat man in knee-length shorts sitting on a rocking chair as if on the porch of his home, which this probably is. He looks like some tenth-century

Bedouin who has set up tent in some deserted Pharaonic necropolis.

In front of it, squat and stubby next to the kerb, stands one of those iconic items that screams out twentieth-century urban America in the same way a red telephone box once did for England; a fire hydrant.

The next street is pure 1930s art deco, all Odeon lines and curves and the same peeling paintwork, until I come to a bar that could be a subtropical incarnation of some New York or London epitome of urban cool: a great three-storey, barred-window, base-thumping beast of a building covered in creeping vines and largely without a roof. It is called, without the slightest streak of street-savvy urban irony, La Ruina.

I stroll in and settle down with a beer only to be almost immediately plagued by hustlers, trying to sell me 'Che' three-peso notes, yesterday's edition of Granma and in some cases, themselves. 'You want *chica, chica*?' asks one young woman of around thirty, all but thrusting her bosom in my face. '*Spasibo, nyet,*' I reply, reverting to my old pre-1990 stand-by for avoiding unwanted hagglers, and speak Russian at her. It works here too. 'Humph,' she flounces off, 'People say I pretty.'

To my surprise, however, the Russian has encouraged one older man to come over and talk to me. He has passable Russian, about as good as my Spanish, and for a few minutes we get along swimmingly until it becomes clear he too wants to sell me something: old Cuban postage stamps. And he is determined to haggle for them, even when I make clear I have absolutely no interest. He only gets the message when I pull out a handful of pesos, rather than CUCs. He jerks his thumb in the direction of a back room with a separate street entrance, as if to say, that's the place for the likes of you.

Maybe it is too. On the assumption that if it operates in

pesos rather than CUCs there will be fewer hustlers in there, I give it a go. There are four staff but only two customers, sharing a coffee. In the other, hard currency side there were more than half a dozen, but as far as I could see they were all hustlers rather than customers. I order a Mayabe and drink it slowly, relieved by the lack of hassle until, somewhat nervously, the barman plucks up the courage to ask me for something. I sigh and try to work out how to tell him I'm not buying, but when he opens his mouth all he says is, 'Please, would it be possible for you to buy us a soft drink?' By 'us' he means himself and his optimistically smiling female colleague.

It is such a small request that for once I agree. He is as good as his word taking one can of Naranja, the local fizzy orange, and pouring it not just into two glasses but four, handing one to the table waiter, who currently has no tables to wait, and the man by the door who might be described as security if there were ever any people trying to come in. I am so touched that I decide there and then on an act of spontaneous generosity: Naranjas all round. Hey big spender! It's cost me less than the price of a pint of real ale in London, yet it's hard to believe the little ray of sunshine it's brought into these people's lives. Or the torrent of conversation it unleashes. It had not occurred to me that none of the staff waiting in a bar like this, a peso bar, earns enough to buy a can of the cheapest drink they sell in their own currency.

The smiling barmaid Maria is the most forthcoming. My brief question about how they get by leads to hearing half her life story: she is thirty-four and has a four-year-old child but hasn't seen the father for three years. She lives with Marco, the barman who asked for the drink, and earns 250 pesos a month. That is approximately $10, about £7.50. A can of Naranja costs 20 pesos, more than two days' wages. The economics of course are not quite ours, to say the least: the state ration of basic rice, beans, sugar and bread is free as is cooking oil. She also gets a free milk ration because she has a child under six. Although she says she lives with Marco, she basically means she sleeps with him, because she still actually lives with her mother. The flat costs next to nothing while electricity and water costs are minimal, not that the electricity works all the time. She gets a state ration of toothpaste and soap too, but the stuff we take for granted: meat, fresh veg, fizzy drinks and alcohol are all luxury items to be savoured rarely if at all. Like my hustler back in Camagüey, most people make their own sugar-based hooch.

So how late do they work, I ask? Bar closing times in Cuba seem to me extraordinarily liberal. I have never heard anyone ring a bell or call 'last orders'.

Marco looks amazed: 'Twenty-four hours, of course, what else?'

I hadn't thought about it, but the only bars I have seen closed looked closed for good. Possibly decades ago, though given the general state of dilapidation of Cuba's built environment it can be hard to tell. Ruina's back bar, for example, where we are now standing, has no roof and only ivy climbing the walls for decoration, apart from the fridges of cold drinks.

'How can we close? If we went away, people would come in and steal everything,' says Maria, as if it was the most obvious statement in the world and the idea of a bar having a closing time the absurdity.

But then putting a roof on the bar would probably cost more than the government pays the staff. A roof would require real materials. The staff just get pieces of paper that are literally barely worth the paper they are printed on. And not enough of those.

I refer to the hustlers in the CUC bar next door, and my new peso bar friends are sympathetic, but to both parties.

'People have to sell something else to get by,' says Marco. 'Including the girls selling themselves?' He shrugs. 'Are you sure they are all girls?' I give him a sceptical look. I know about the ladyboy phenomenon in Thailand, but in Cuba? 'Oh, yes, there are many *travestidos*. Often you can tell because they have pet dogs. It is a thing for some of them. But they have to have money to afford them. How do you think they earn it?'

I feel more than glad I gave short shrift to the buxom lady trying to press herself on me, although if she was really a bloke what my old editor at the *Sunday Telegraph* used to call 'her embonpoint' was remarkably impressive.

Bang on topic Marco says; '*Cuanto cuesta una chica en Londres*?' How much is a girl in London? It's one of those questions that throws you, not so much because he is enquiring about the going rates of sleazy escort agencies, of which London has as many as any big capital city, but because that's not really what he means at all. He might as well be asking how much an orange costs, or a bar of chocolate. Maria is looking at us attentively, not because she's shocked by his question or my reaction, but out of casual interest, as if she'd also like to know the going rate too.

'It's not like that,' I try to tell him, then add: 'Probably a couple of hundred pounds an hour or a lifetime of bondage.' I'm joking but I'm not sure he gets it.

Bill Clinton's election campaign team coined the phrase, 'It's the economy, stupid.' They should have come to Cuba. They had no idea!

CHAPTER SIXTEEN

Hotel GTMO

Lissett, owner of my Guantánamo *casa*, which seems to double as home from home from a variety of almost exclusively beefy-looking black local lads who spend much of the day lounging on her floral chintz sofa watching soap operas (including the inevitable *Mujeres de Nadie*) and baseball, tells me the only way I am going to get to Caimanera, the closest point to the US base, is with an official pass, a taxi and a 'licensed guide'. I assume that means one guaranteed to toe the official government line on the base and relations with the United States. And the only place I am going to put all that together, it appears, is on the outskirts of town at the government-run Viazul hotel.

A *bicitaxi* pedalled by someone who actually knows his way round town gets me there in barely 15 minutes. And there is no mistaking where you are. On the approach road is a big blue roadside sign that uses language which would be ironically familiar to the US forces on the other side of the wire: HOTEL GTMO. I hear The Eagles in my head reworking Hotel California: Welcome to the Hotel Guantánamo. You can check in any time you like, but you can never leave.

The hotel itself, is a nondescript 1970s box behind railings. The road sign may label it HOTEL GTMO but the malfunctioning neon sign outside has a version of its own: Hotel *uan**namo.

We are clearly in a suburb at least partly reserved for the party élite. On the right is a slab-like concrete building which at first glance, misreading the sign as *policlinico*, I take to be the local hospital, which makes the slogan on the banner above the door somewhat worrying: 'Socialism or death'. It turns out to be *politic* and this is the headquarters of the local communist party. Which I suppose makes it okay. Sort of.

Opposite is a big green expanse of parkland, dominated by some colossal statuary in pink granite, reached by a flight of steps. At first sight it is mind-bending. Think Stonehenge reinterpreted by Salvador Dalí: an arrangement of huge great vertical stone obelisks that then suddenly bend and intertwine with one another, here and there sprouting heads and bodies. Into the columns are carved the names to go with some of them: Mariana Grajales Coello[9] (after whom the square is named), as well as Antonio Maceo Grajales and Máximo Gómez, and of course, José Martí, all heroes of the late nineteenth-century conflict which eventually led to independence from Spain. It is a stunning piece of architectural sculpture, bold, modern, similar in size and dramatic effect to some of the more grandiose pieces of Soviet statuary, yet at once strikingly different, unmistakably Latin.

And just to reassure us that all is for the best in the best of all possible worlds, next to the hotel is a huge billboard poster of Castro. Not Fidel but Raúl, looking for all the world like your favourite bespectacled smiling uncle playing soldier with, in giant letters below, the most audacious slogan I have yet seen in Cuba: 'EN GUANTÁNAMO, SI SE PUEDE!'

---

9. Marianna Grajales Coello was Cuba's Florence Nightingale, running a field hospital during the conflict. She gave birth to thirteen children, nearly all of whom served in the rebel army, two of them as generals. She was famed for her courage under fire and even before the communist revolution was fêted as the 'Mother of Cuba'. Fidel Castro created a 'women's platoon' named after her. Like José Martí, she too is now an airport, serving Guantánamo.

'In Guantánamo, Yes We Can!' I can't not love the fact that here in this Bizarro World, Latin mirror-image of the US, Barack Obama's slogan has found a second home. Or the irony that one of the first things that President Yes-We-Can said he was going to do was close down the detention camp at Guantánamo. And so far, already in his second presidential term, no, he hasn't.

No doubt Raúl has taken the same comfort as Obama did from the slogan's magnificent vagueness.

At the hotel reception desk I'm told the man I need to talk to is called Yanossi and he isn't there. But if I wait he might turn up. In fact he does, in little more than a quarter of an hour, and puts on a grave face when I tell him what I want.

'Yes, it is possible,' he says at length, not looking like he means it. 'Maybe.'

'Maybe. Or yes?'

'Maybe yes. I will have to ask.'

'When?'

'Maybe tomorrow.'

I have a horrible premonition of *mañana* sickness coming on.

'Please,' he adds. 'I need your passport number. Then I will ask and I will call you. This evening.'

I supply what he needs and the phone number of Lissett's *casa*. 'But when,' I ask, 'might I be able to go?'

'If yes, then tomorrow.'

'Really?'

'Maybe. Maybe yes.' He smiles.

It seems about as optimistic an answer as I'm going to get as I head back into town with 'Guantana-mayra' running through my brain, though it occurs to me that this is the first place I haven't actually heard it being played.

In the mean time I may as well take in the sights

Guantánamo has to offer, chief among them the city museum, which allegedly offers an unusual view of the US base. The museum is congenial quaint little colonial building with a courtyard fringed with palm trees at its heart. As in Matanzas, I am the only visitor and the attendant feels obliged to follow me round each room, not so much to be sure I don't steal or damage anything, nor to offer any supplementary information on the exhibits, but simply because it's marginally less boring than sitting by the desk which is what she does for most of most days.

There are some interesting enough exhibits about the history of slavery in '*oriente*' – eastern Cuba – and the usual collection of machetes and blunderbusses plus a few ancient photographs of landlords and revolutionaries from the turn of the last century. But when I ask her about the 'other' photographs, the more recent ones, she pretends not to know what I am talking about.

'The ones with *los Americanos*,' I say, then correct myself, remembering Cubans are proud to be *Americanos* too – '*los gringos?*'

'Ah,' she says eventually with a knowing smile. 'Not here. Gone.'

I give her a sceptical look but she just smiles back and shrugs.

I find it hard to hide my disappointment. This has to be all part of some strange new attitude to the Obama administration. The pictures I had hoped to see were of rows of naked US marine buttocks. Not for any lascivious gratification, I hasten to add, but because they represented one of those hilarious moments of Cold War culture clash. Back sometime in the 1970s the marines stationed at Guantánamo Bay thought the most hilarious thing they could do to show how they felt about communism was to demonstrate one of the latest capitalist crazes: mooning. An entire platoon of them had, for a laugh, turned their back on the watching Cuban guards, bent down and dropped their trousers.

But rather than take offence at being faced with such a gesture of imperialist disdain the Cubans apparently thought it hilarious and took photographs which they then for several decades hung on the walls of this very museum. If you want to see what capitalism looks like, the message was, here you go. If US citizens had been allowed to visit Cuba, I always wondered if they would have been proud of their armed forces. Or if the servicemen themselves, had they been allowed to visit, might not have regretted 'posing' for Cuban cameras in quite that position. Sadly, it seems, now that a few US citizens are finally being allowed to visit, we may never know.

That leaves the main attraction in Guantánamo museum as a very different if rather more salubrious exhibit, and one that commemorates a more daring feat. One with a room all to itself. At first glance it looks like the rusting hulk of some antique diving bell, a great lump of grey metal about three metres high with a porthole, a hatch and a bright orange bottom, on which are stencilled the letters that give it all away: CCCP.

This primitive-looking chunk of heavy-duty ironwork is the grim reality of the Soviet version of that supposed ultimate example of twentieth-century futuristic technology: a spacecraft. To be more precise this is the re-entry module from a Soyuz spacecraft in which on September 18, 1980, along with a Russian colleague, Guantánamo-born thirty-eight-year-old Arnaldo Tamayo Mendez became simultaneously the first Latin American, and first person of African ethnic origin to go into space. He and colleague Yuri Romanenko spent just over a week on board the Salyut 6 space station before returning to earth in this diabolically unsafe looking spherical iron lung, landing in the dark somewhere in the desert of what is now Kazakhstan. Rather him than me.

Back out in the baking heat of Guantánamo town I try to go to the bank again only to find this time it's closed because, as in Santa Clara, there's a power cut and the tills have closed. I exclaim in despair to the man blocking the door, '*La economía de Cuba es muerta!*' This country's economy is dead. He shrugs his shoulders and says, '*Si, Señor,*' as if I'm an idiot for only just noticing it.

As chance would have it however, stomping away angrily from the bank, I come across an aspect of Cuba's economy that is doing rather nicely indeed, and may even offer a ray of light in the darkness: Guantánamo's main Mercado Agropecuario, still a relative novelty in Cuba: a farmers' market.

Introduced in the mid-1990s to supplement the meagre state rations by allowing co-operative farmers to sell supposedly surplus production, these markets have now become a vital part of the still severely strapped supply chain for the ordinary Cuban family. As well as being an example of just how fertile this country could be and how its farmers could probably end the supply-side crisis overnight if only they were allowed to. When Marco and Maria manage to save a few pesos from their meagre salaries, this where they come to splash out on such luxuries as a few eggs, or a chicken they will make last a week.

In a semi-derelict concrete hall with a roof over only half of it, makeshift stalls on rickety wooden tables are piled high with produce: oranges, bananas, little yellow mangoes and big red-green ones, pineapples, dried beans, cabbages, onions, limes, cucumbers, garlic, tomatoes. The prices are in pesos, *moneda nacional*, not CUCs, and they are ridiculously cheap. Six pesos (no more than a few pence) will buy you a pound of oranges. I do a double take. Yep, a *pound* of oranges: 1 lb. In a country where everything else is metric, as throughout the rest of Latin America, prices in the free market are given per lb, as if somehow an Anglo-Saxon ghost lives on in the spirit of free enterprise.

The tomatoes, rich, ripe, red and reassuringly irregular in shape and size look too tempting to resist. I ask the dealer for four.

'Four pounds?'

'Er, no. Just four tomatoes.'

He gives me a sour look, which is a chilling experience now that I come to notice he is the size of a small volcano and has only one ear, which seems more likely to be the result of some form or urban or other warfare rather than a Vincent Van Gogh artistic temperament. But he sells me them nonetheless. I accompany them with a few corn fritters, ears of sweetcorn tossed in batter and fried on a griddle by an amiable smiling woman. Together they make one of the best little meals I've had in Cuba. And one of the cheapest.

There isn't a lot of meat on display. At least, not dead meat. Over in one corner, leaning idly against a pillar in a blue T-shirt, baggy Bermuda shorts and with a baseball cap on his head proclaiming 'I ♥ Jesus' is a paunchy middle-aged bloke holding a piece of string with a chubby black pig on the end of it. Quite a little pig, but chubby enough, and at this moment – wholly unaware of why it's been brought to the market – cheerfully rooting around among the various bits of fallen fruit putrefying in the heat which didn't quite make it into the pungent-smelling waste bin.

While I'm standing looking at the pig a thirty-something scrawny black woman with a low top that shows up a bad rash of self-inflicted tattoos running across her shoulders and apparently down her spine, chunters something incomprehensibly at me. I haven't a clue what she's on about and give her my standard, 'No, no,' until she staggers off grumpily, at which the pig-flogging friend of Jesus bursts out laughing and indicates in no uncertain fashion, with use of his right hand and mouth formed into an 'O' that I was possibly being offered a blow job. Possibly for pesos! He seems quite excited by the idea and makes a show of whistling after her. I feel like telling him his pig looks a better option. But I don't want to offend the pig.

◆

By early evening Yanossi from the hotel still hasn't called, so I use Lissett's phone to call him. Happily he is still at the desk, but less happily he has not heard back from whoever it is has to issue my permit to enter the 'border zone'.

'It is not a problem,' he says. 'I will call you again,' ignoring the fact that I had to call him, finishing off with that word that is supposed to be reassuring but somehow never is: '*Mañana.*'

To drown my sorrows, I head back to the Ruina, once again taking refuge from the hustlers by opting for the peso bar. I order a rum and opt for Maria's recommendation of Mulata, made in Santiago at the original Bacardi distillery, rather than the ubiquitous Havana Club. I am surprised at how cheap it is, even in pesos. Yes, she nods, 'Much cheaper than in the shops.'

'What?'

'Yes, to buy in bar is 30 per cent cheaper than in shop.'

This makes no sense at all to me. Why? How can it be cheaper to sell it in a bar which has to cover its overheads, from lighting to staff costs, than in a shop when it's simply sold in the bottle it left the distillery in. She shrugs her head. Buying and selling are things the government does. Not for ordinary mortals to question. She does just does her job.

Then in a blinding flash of half-forgotten Soviet logic I remember that is what it comes down to. A main aim of communist society is zero unemployment: making sure everybody has a job. Not necessarily a useful job. Just a job. Maria has a job, just like the *babushkas* who used to sit at the bottom of escalators in the Moscow metro had jobs: just not jobs that served any purpose. The purpose of the jobs that Maria and her colleagues do – running a bar that is open twenty-four hours a day – is not to sell alcohol and soft drinks at a profit. It is to be a job for Maria and her colleagues. The job gives her a role, and therefore is an end in itself.

The fact the government which owns the bar and pays her does not make a profit is totally irrelevant both to her and to the government. It doesn't make a loss either: the rum is manufactured in a distillery owned by the government and sold, whether in a shop or a bar by people who are employed by the government, to people (with the exception of tourists) who are also employed and paid by the government. What goes around comes around, except that in what is effectively a closed circle economy with little exposure to the outside world, there is usually less of it second time round. The circle becomes a downward spiral.

It sounds like insanity until, with a bittersweet moment of humility, I realize I can think of quite a few people in our own society, still, post-Cold War misleadingly called 'western' though a long way east of Cuba, who do jobs that aren't exactly useful either if you dare to analyse them too closely. The difference is that when the money is tight, particularly as now in times of austerity, they get sacked. At which point the government has to pay them. Which is why, of course, the people who are best off are those who work for the government. Until the government, pretending it too feels the economic pinch, makes them too redundant, at which point it has to start paying them again, albeit at a lower level.

We all go mad in our own ways.

CHAPTER SEVENTEEN

The Cactus Curtain

The next morning, about 10 o'clock the phone rings. Lissett comes to fetch me. It is Yanossi, the guide from the hotel. If he says 'yes', I can be there in 20 minutes by taxi, ready to depart. I can be on the USA's 'final frontier' by lunchtime.

He says, 'yes'. My permit has been approved. But my initial celebration is restrained by something about the tone of his voice. 'But,' he adds, inevitably, 'there is a problem.'

'The man, he is not there.' Ah, the man. I'd forgotten about him. 'What man?'

'The man, the policeman who has to sign papers. He did not go to work this morning.'

Ah. My plans are going to be dashed because some lazy Cuban cop has thrown a sickie!?

'Can't someone else sign it?'

A long sigh on the other end of the telephone. 'No. Only him.'

'When will he be in?'

'I don't know. Maybe tomorrow. I hope so. Maybe tomorrow you can come to the hotel. Early. Maybe then we go.'

'Maybe?'

'Maybe yes. I think so. Very much.'

His sigh is nothing to my own. Already I'm getting to feel I've had enough of Guantánamo proper. There's only so much time a man can spend in a one-horse town full of hustlers with only one half-decent bar. Plus the *casa* has filled up and it's starting to feel cramped. After a couple of weeks on the road – or more specifically the railroad – in Cuba you begin to get a real feeling of what life is like for the ordinary native. And a real hankering for some creature comforts.

On an impulse, I decide to leave the *casa* and check into the Hotel GTMO for the night. At least that way if Yanossi's man actually bothers to turn up for work in the morning I'll be on the spot.

First though, I need to get a souvenir. I can hardly have come all the way to one of the most famous-named destinations on the planet, albeit not one on many tourist itineraries, without getting something with the name on it, and given that every town of any size in Cuba has a shop selling souvenirs aimed at the dwindling number of foreign tourists in order to squeeze a few extra CUCs into the government's ever-empty pockets.

And sure enough there is one. Right next to the main square, an Artex government-run souvenir and art store. And sure enough it has souvenirs. Exactly the same as you can buy in any other state-run tourist souvenir shop in any other town in Cuba; pictures of Che, posters of Che, T-shirts with Che on them, postcards of Che, even a few postcards of an old photo of Fidel swinging a baseball bat. There are Cuban flags, shoulder bags with the Cuban flag on them. And rum. Silly little Chinese-made plastic watches with fish on them. Ashtrays with pictures of Havana on them. But not one item that bears the name Guantánamo. Not even a postcard of the town square. Not even a CD of the bloody song they don't play here. *Nada*.

Disappointed, I wander back towards the *casa* to pick up my bag and head out when suddenly my eyes are drawn to a sports clothing store. Yes! There, in the back of the window, is almost exactly what I have been looking for. On sale for pesos even rather than CUCs. I wonder why it never occurred to me. In baseball-crazy Cuba, of course the one thing that would have the town's name on it is the local baseball team's shirts. There it is in big arcing orange letters on black: GUANTÁNAMO. I buy three, one for me and one for each of my kids. My dad went to Guantánamo and back, and all I got was this lousy T-shirt. Wear it with pride!

By mid-afternoon I have checked out and in. As far as creature comforts go, the Hotel GTMO isn't offering much. It has more Cuban guests than foreigners – as on the trains, they pay in pesos, we pay in CUCs – and feels rather like one of the old Soviet Intourist hotels from the early 1980s: more like a field hospital than a place of recreation, with uniform grey painted interior walls and no functioning lift. But it does have one thing that after weeks of sweating on and off sticky trains seems like a gift from heaven: a swimming pool.

It may not be exactly a five-star lido, more like a blue-tiled pit full of water set in the middle of an expanse of partly cracked concrete, but hey it's wet and cool, whereas everything else around here, including me, is wet with sweat. It looks inviting enough until I take a sudden turn when I spot, floating close to the edge, what appears to be a surreally large bluish dead frog. My stomach turns over until I notice a the shallow end of the pool a gaggle of eight- or nine-year-old Cuban kids splashing about and hurling other animals at one another, including a small pink plastic alligator, a bright green snapping turtle and a yellow bus.

Relieved, I leap into the water ready to give them a taste of their own medicine by hurling their mislaid toy over at them. I grab the said jolly smiling frog with its big popping eyes, only to find my hand closing not on hard plastic, but on swollen, slimy grey viscous frog flesh. What I had at first believed to be a bloated dead frog turns out to be . . . a bloated dead frog. It's all I can do not to empty the contents of my stomach on top of it, which would hardly make things better, and instead just manage to hurl the thing out of the pool onto the concrete surround. Somehow my enthusiasm for a swim has suddenly evaporated.

For the rest of the afternoon I manage to retain my composure with the help of a neat rum from the hotel bar, a couple of cold beer chasers a cigar from the CUC shop, and sit there in the shade like some pink-faced relic of British colonial days lost in the ruins of somebody else's empire, drinking and smoking and watching the bloated fog swell ever larger as it cooks on the concrete. It ought to be moved but nobody seems interested, and there's no way I'm going to touch it again.

In the evening the hotel bar fills with an unusually rowdy gang of what appear to be Cubans but a lot more affluent even than the emerging middle class I have noticed. At their centre is an elderly man who is obviously a paternal figure of some sort, though not as affluent as the rest of the family, with a surprisingly youthful pretty girl on his knee, whom he is treating in a decidedly non-paternal manner.

The kids, teenagers mostly, sport expensive trainers and gold or silver chains around neck or wrist, and smart shades. They are all, I slowly notice, substantially chunkier in build than any other young Cubans I have seen. That is when I suddenly hit on the truth, which with a bit of eaves-dropping is confirmed by their conversation: these are Miami Cubans, probably the old man's children and grand-children, come back maybe for the first time since their parents or grandparents did a runner maybe a generation ago. These are the first US citizens I have come across in Cuba and the first hard evidence that Obama's cautious thawing of relations by letting 'Americans' of Cuban origin visit their ancestral homeland. The bit of totty on the old boy's knee is his attempt to show off in the only way he can that he might not have their money, but there are still some things worth coveting in the 'old country'.

◆

At 9 a.m. the next morning I am standing at reception, after a breakfast of lukewarm weak coffee and a stale bun – 'fruit's off' – worse than anything served up in any of the private homes I have stayed in – waiting for Yanossi.

It is 10 a.m. before he shows up, looking almost apprehensive to see me standing there. Oh no, don't tell me his policeman or whatever he is has thrown another sickie.

'Wait, please,' he says in English. 'One moment. I make phone call.'

He picks up a vintage handset and begins dialling. Then his face grows sombre. He is speaking Spanish of course, and as so often happens when people revert to their native language after making an effort for a foreigner, he suddenly sounds a lot more intelligent. But what I am picking up is not good.

'I see. Oh dear. That is a great pity. How long? I see. Oh dear. That is a shame.' Then a long pause. 'Yes, yes, I shall tell him.'

He turns to me with a long face.

'He hasn't turned up again?' I venture despairingly.

'No, no. That is him. His mother. She is very ill. She had heart attack yesterday. This is why he not at work yesterday. It is very sad. He has to take her to the hospital.'

'But . . . ?'

'Hmm?' he looks up at me as if unable to comprehend that I might heartlessly have other matters on my mind than the regrettably poor health of the mother of a local police official. 'Oh yes, your permit. It is okay. You can go.'

A whoop of relief seems inappropriate for the circumstances, but within half an hour, both guide and taxi – a yellow Lada with a Grand Prix-style chequered spoiler on the rear – have arrived, and we are off, with a brief stop along the way for the guide to dash into a grey-looking office building where she picks up the all-important piece of paper with a scribbled blue line along the bottom of it, which I take to be the all-important signature. I could have forged it in a heartbeat. And maybe as a result spent as long behind bars in Guantánamo town as some of the men on the other side of the wire have spent there.

We roll out of town on rough roads for barely a kilometre before we come to the first checkpoint, a little hut by the side of the road manned by two officers of the *Policía de Carreterras*, traffic cops. They check the *carnets*, the identity cards of both driver and guide, and examine my all-important piece of paper, but bizarrely don't ask to see my passport to check that the one relates to the other.

It only takes a few moments and we are on the road again. It appears that the taxi-driver, a genial grizzled man in his fifties, knows more about the area than the bouncy twenty-something girl guide, who is there presumably because the state tourist office has to be involved.

'Everybody who lives in Caimanera has to have a permit,' he tells me. 'And anyone from Guantánamo who wants to go there, even just to visit for the day.' It would appear my permit is for all three of us. I had forgotten, of course, that once upon a time, before Guantánamo Bay came to stand for what it does today, the main reason Caimanera was so off-limits was that the Castro government feared its citizens would try to sneak into American territory to claim asylum.

Guantánamo Bay's strange status is one of the world's oddest colonial legacies. It goes back to what the United States still calls the Spanish–American War and Cubans call the War of Independence, in which US involvement was possibly helpful but neither asked for nor particularly wanted. It was, Cubans will tell you and it is hard not to agree, a war in which rebels fighting for their freedom were used by a new would-be world empire as an excuse to grab land from an older fading world empire.[10]

In 1898 the US fleet was attacking Santiago, then as now the capital of eastern Cuba, when one of the far-from-rare summer hurricanes hit. The fleet retreated from the open sea to the relative safety of the big, sheltered bay along the coast. They realized this was handy and when eventually Cubans achieved a form of independence in 1903, effectively as an American puppet, its first president Tomás Estrada Palma was obliged to sign a treaty granting the United States a 'perpetual lease' on the territory, a deal reaffirmed in 1934 by the Batista government that had come to power in a right-wing coup with US support. Under the terms of the original 1903 deal the United States was supposed to pay Cuba an annual fee of $2,000 and to this day it still sends cheques for the inflation-adjusted sum (now over $4,000 a year) to Havana. Castro keeps them uncashed – allegedly save for one which the US claims is justification for its continued presence – in a desk drawer. For years between the signing of the first treaty and the 1958 revolution most of the inhabitants of Caimanera provided the menial labour on the base, while the little fishing town itself became saloon bar and bordello for the GIs and seamen.

But the revolutionaries repudiated the treaty (probably

10. Guantánamo is not the only consequence we still live with. As a result of the quarrel on their doorstep, the US got into a general war with Spain. It finished by making Cuba a puppet state, seizing the nearby Caribbean island of Puerto Rico but also intervening on the other side of the world. The United States attacked Spanish colonies in the Pacific, aiding the people of the Philippines in an anti-colonial rebellion, then suppressing them in turn and turning a Spanish colony into an American one which brought them Japanese occupation and eventual independence in 1946. The United States also seized the formerly Spanish island of Guam from where its troops today nervously watch North Korea's military posturing.

correctly) as signed under duress, and gradually turned the screw on access to the 'occupied territory'. After some anti-communists claimed asylum there the Castro government in 1961 planted a thick border of sharp-spined cacti around the perimeter, which almost in parody of what was going on in Europe (the Berlin Wall was built the same year) became known as the 'Cactus Curtain'. But the real deterrent to any-one crossing was the thousands of mines planted not just by the Cubans but by the Americans too, although the lat-ter were eventually removed under Bill Clinton in 1996, and replaced by motion sensors. Needless to say, transforming Guantánamo Bay into the world's most notorious detention camp for untried prisoners has done more than Fidel in his wildest dreams might have to deter even the most dissident Cuban from trying to enter this little patch of 'freedom' squatting on the end of their island.

Nonetheless, a big red roadside sign we pass reads AREA DE ALTA SEGURIDAD PARA LA DEFENSA – Area of high defence security. The clear implication being that the threat is from the other side. But the road is noticeably better now, presumably military-maintained, and runs through a lush plantation of coconut palms.

A second checkpoint looms ahead of us: a concrete hut with two tank trap barriers in the middle of the road in front of it. We all get out and soldiers in green uniforms with insig-nia that mark them out as interior ministry troops open the boot and look inside. Our documents are inspected again, and this time the man in charge – a sergeant by the stripes on his arm – asks to see my passport as well. I feel a terrible tendency to lapse into Russian. It is something to do with the atmosphere, this sense of a strictly guarded frontier on the edge of nowhere. It reminds me of the Soviet–Finnish border circa 1985 except that instead of ice, snow and end-less pine-woods full of wolves, there is sultry heat, palm trees with cacti behind them and salsa music coming from the stereo in the Lada. A sign behind the guard hut proclaims that the village of Cayamo, which is where I assume we are, is an 'impregnable bastion of the revolution'.

We trundle on, the Cuban side of the frontier to the base now directly on our right. I can see Cuban troops in lookout towers beyond barbed wire training their binoculars on something in the distance. There is also a little railway that my taxi driver explains is still used for small gauge freight trains carrying fish or the salt taken from the salt flats now stretching away to our left.

'Guantánamo salt is famous. The best in Cuba,' my taxi driver explains. And there was me looking for a souvenir when I could have picked up a culinary delicacy in any state food shop. Maybe. My 'guide' has hardly said a word yet.

The land is low-lying here, partly swamp, which explains Guantánamo Bay's reputation as a breeding ground for mosquitos and tropical disease. Almost like an ill omen I spot a forest of small gravestones, an old cemetery on what is now effectively an island amid the salt flats and swampland. In the distance though, I can see the unmistakeable white golf-ball shape of a radar dome, the first US construction I have seen on Cuba other than 1950s cars. And tall stilts supporting a water tower. Somewhere over there I know there is also a Pizza Express, a Taco Bell, Subway, KFC and a McDonalds. It is rumoured that well-behaved detainees are rewarded with Happy Meals. Oh brave new world that has such fast food chains in it.

Meanwhile we have come to Checkpoint Number Three, which looks substantially more serious than the first two. For a start we not only have to all get out of the car, I am invited alone – at gentle gun point no less – into a little concrete cabin where an elderly army official with tremendous white moustache and thick glasses demands to see my

documentation. He spends what seems like ages scrutiniz-
ing my passport before eventually asking me to point out
where its number is. I show him and he checks it methodi-
cally against that on the all-important piece of paper signed
by the policeman with an ailing mother in Guantánamo
town before entering it by hand in a ledger.

The next question is more puzzling, to me at least. '*Su
nacionalidad?*' My nationality? The guy is holding my passport, right? I would have thought it was a bit of a giveaway.
'British,' I tell him, pointing to Her Majesty's crest on the
front of the maroon jacket. I am almost about to direct him
to read that guff about 'Her Britannic Majesty's Secretary of
State for Foreign and Commonwealth Affairs requests and
requires, etc. . . .' and to point out the bit about 'without let
or hindrance'. But he is looking at it carefully, nodding and
eventually says, '*Frances*?' Eh? And then it dawns on me that
the only words written on Her Majesty's crest are *Honi soit
qui mal y pense*. French.

For a moment I'm tempted to go with the flow and be
amused by presenting a British passport and being deemed
French. I believe strongly in the European ideal but even
the most fervent advocates of the EU haven't taken things
that far yet and there are more than a few old-fashioned
Europhobes in Britain who still regard the French as mor-
tal enemies. But on sober reflection I recall that getting
documentation wrong in suspicious communist countries
especially as regards nationality can be a very bad idea, and
feel reluctant to see my short-sighted Cuban colonel (or
whatever his rank is, I have actually no idea) end up behind
bars, possibly with me for his cell mate.

'No, no,' I tell him. '*Inglaterra.*'

'Ah,' he says, in a 'why didn't you say so in the first place'
sort of way and enters that too in his ledger, though not
without a second glance – in fact more of a second detailed

examination – of my passport. Not without cause, I realized, noticing for the first time that nowhere on or in the said document does the word by which most of the world still refers to our country appear: England. Scottish National Party, please note.

A big sign by side of the road informs us the sleepy little huddle of houses is the outskirts of Caimanera.

'Alligators,' says the driver. I stare out of the window eagerly. 'No, no. Not here, but the town, is named after alligator. Cayman.' How about that? A town in Cuba named after a Porsche!

Our own equivalent, the yellow Lada with go-fast stripes and its chequered spoiler skirts the seafront and twists up a hill to what has to be one of the country's nicest – and emptiest – resort hotels: the Vilamar, a pretty agglomeration of red-roofed chalets with an elegant hardwood bar and restaurant both fully staffed and both totally empty. Unsurprisingly. It is still illegal for foreigners to spend the night here, and all but impossible for Cubans. And in any case who would want to? Cuban shipping has access to the sea through the American-controlled bay but any sprawling sandy beaches there might be would lie on the shores of the Caribbean rather than the bay. And it is not as if Cuba is short on beaches. So until the day this last bit of Cold War frontier finally thaws, the Vilamar will remain a beautiful, fully-staffed, fully-functioning white elephant. Complete with mosquitoes, one of which, a particularly vicious little bastard, has just felt obliged to live up to Guantánamo Bay's unwelcoming reputation by tucking into a pint of my blood, the first mosquito bite I have had on Cuba.

As the sole visitor I feel compelled to please my hosts by posing for a photograph with them, cold can in one hand, straw hat on head and Fidel-style (before he quit) Cohiba cigar in the other. In the background is the inner bay, which is wholly under Cuban control, and the watchtowers – nearly all of which are clearly 'American' (the Cubans of course only ever call them *Estados-Unidosense*, making an adjective out of US). There is even one of those little fixed tourist binoculars on a stand which for a few CUC cents will let you spy up close on Uncle Sam, or at least get you a slightly less distant view of a US marine using a pair of binoculars to stare back at you.

It is one of the strangest feelings I have ever experienced in a quarter century covering the Cold War to what we all thought was its end. When I lived in East Berlin I would delight in taking visitors to the viewing stand next to the Reichstag from where they could look over, as over the 28 years of the Wall's existence thousands of tourists and hundreds of foreign dignitaries had done, to the supposedly frightening communist east beyond the walled-off Brandenburg Gate. Then I would load them into my car and drive through Checkpoint Charlie, turn left along Friedrichstrasse and left again down Unter den Linden to where the Brandenburg Gate stood floodlit from the other side, with the Wall almost invisible a hundred metres away, and try to tell them that there were two sides to every story.

The Wall was wrong of course, inhuman and by its very nature necessarily ephemeral, but the point I was trying to make, and still adhere to, is that history is what historians make it. Or as a greater wit than mine once put it, 'The only reason God tolerates historians is because they can do what he cannot: alter the past.' Just as journalists, and travel writers, do our best with perceptions of the present.

After all, here I am standing in an empty restaurant in a communist state with one party rule, which tolerates no opposition and insists despite the obvious economic quagmire into which it has led its people, that its system is fairer and more honourable than that of the country on the other side of this fence, which unselfconsciously styles itself 'leader of the free world'. It should be a bad joke, but the tragedy is that it isn't. Whatever the rights and wrongs of the US presence at Guantánamo Bay – and the obvious parallel is Britain's long but now relinquished occupation, under a similar treaty, of Hong Kong – it is the US itself which has turned logic on its head. The US regularly, repeatedly, systematically accuses the Havana government of a lack of respect for human rights, yet the continued existence of this greatest symbol of its own willingness to suspend those rights makes all else farcical.

Staring out at the watchtowers and radar domes on the low green tropical hills beyond the barbed wire I know that in camps over there, men in orange jumpsuits are imprisoned in cells without ever having faced trial; they have suffered what nobody disputes is torture by waterboarding. This makes it hard to believe there are – or maybe ever were – clear-cut sides in the Cold War or even now in its bastard child, the War against Terror. In all of this Cuba cuts an anomalous figure, like those apocryphal World War II Japanese soldiers holed up in Pacific islands decades after their war ended.

I know and like the United States. Many of my cousins are US citizens. In the year of Barack Obama's election I travelled 10,000 miles by train around that massive continental nation which prides itself, mostly rightly, on justice and liberty. Yet here in what most US citizens, including the bulk of Cuban emigrés in Florida, would consider the patch of weeds in Uncle Sam's well-kept back yard, I can't help feeling happy to be on this side of the fence.

In a small room next to the restaurant's unused swimming pool there is a small exhibition dedicated to the base. In fact the entire floor of the room, about the size of a small child's bedroom, is dedicated to a curious topographical map:

piles of sand in the corners of the room arranged to represent the hills beyond the forbidden frontier. On the wall is a hand-painted history of the bay, 'baptized by Christopher Columbus in 1494 as the Great Bay . . . illegally occupied by the United States'. On the walls are aerial photographs, decades old, of the base's desalination plant (Castro long ago cut off fresh water supplies), the hospital and streets of formulaic US suburban housing. They are all at least 30 years old, and all of US origin. For all that Cuba might want to spy on this cuckoo-like outpost of Yankee imperialism, they have had to get their photographs from *Newsweek*. They might have done better by using Google Maps. But then the problem may be not so much that this is a country where the government limits access to information, but that this is a country run by eighty-year-olds.

Back down in Caimanera town my minders are happy to let me 'escape' for an hour or so. The streets are little different to any other small Cuban town I have seen: dusty, hot, peppered with small dark cafés and shops with little produce. I drink a cold Mayabe at a corner bar watched with great curiosity by a group of three grizzled locals. Foreigners are obviously a rarity in Caimanera. The only thing that stops them staring disconcertingly is when I try to ask them about the base. They shrug their shoulders, mutter under their breath and turn back to their coffee.

Down by the shore a group of kids are splashing happily in the bay. The US watchtowers haunt the horizon several hundred metres away, but nobody pays any heed. Rather over-optimistically I ask a passing woman to take my photograph with the watchtowers in the distance but she merely shakes her head vigorously and points to a red sign nailed to a truncated palm leaning over the water. In big white letters it says ACCESSO CONTROLLADO. I take the point, though I'm not sure everybody does. Just beyond it two men are wading out into the water, carrying make-shift fishing rods.

And then beyond them I notice what has to be the main Cuban military guard post. Except that at first glance that's not what it looks like. Standing on a concrete base at the edge of the gravel beach is an absurd pantomime three-storey structure in turquoise blue with a white balustrade surrounding a second floor balcony. It could be the lifeguard station at some elaborate 1930s art deco swimming pool or the stand from which some Gilbert and Sullivan dictator would review his troops. The top floor is reached by a ladder from the second, but it is in any case empty. The supposed occupants, two of them, are lying in the shade by the foot of it, smoking, rifles by their sides. Whatever the state of per-manent alert on the Cactus Curtain, in Caimanera today it is clearly not red.

On a street corner next to the inevitable José Martí street, with a bust of the great man on a plinth, there is a swathe of supposed graffiti – obviously done by state-sponsored art-ists with official permission, like those on the walls in Santa Clara – showing a spit of red land, clearly intended to indi-cate the base, with a Cuban flag flying from it and the slogan in big bold letters: TE QUIERO LIBRE. I want you to be free. Next to it two teenage girls are sitting on a ledge, chilling. One of them is wearing a red T-shirt with the Stars and Stripes on it.

Che T-shirts may be Cuba's biggest export after cigars but nobody here wears them. Or almost nobody. On a previ-ous visit to Havana I did bump into a couple of characters at a parade dressed as Guevara and his late rival in Cuba's pantheon of foreign saints, Hugo Chavez. But basically they were just lookalikes having a bit of a laugh. A carefully polit-ically correct one.

The return trip to Guantánamo is something of an

anticlimax, back past the rusting rails, the distant US watchtowers and the strange little isolated cemetery. The checkpoints barely register us going in the other direction. This may be the last frontier in the Cold War but it is a stale, abandoned front line where both sides claim the high ground and moral values have become fudged. Down here in Guantánamo, Cuba's *Oriente*, for the time being, it really is all quiet on the eastern front.

CHAPTER EIGHTEEN

Da Coda: Santiago and the 'French Train'

The Moncada Barracks in Santiago de Cuba, the island's second city, capital of *Oriente* and chief rival to Havana, is the Castros' Dunkirk: the place it all went wrong, where the revolution might have ended before it started. But because in the end the disaster was not total, the failure is remembered as heroism and the place itself a national shrine to what was actually an almighty cock-up.

I had thought I would visit the Moncada on my way to Guantánamo but, like the start of World War I, the train timetables dictated otherwise. So I am here on the first leg of the return journey. I have already cheated, and not taken the train, not least because there is indeed no direct train link between Guantánamo and Santiago and doing the journey by rail would require that change in grimy San Luis, which it seemed the Cuban railway system simply wasn't prepared to accommodate unless I was willing to risk waiting up to two days at a railway station in the middle of nowhere.

Instead I promised myself a ride in the relative luxury of one of the state tourist industry's Viazul coaches, the sort which normally ferry hard-currency-paying foreigners from their Havana hotels to their gated beach resorts. I had bought my ticket for CUCs from the reception at the Hotel GTMO and taken a taxi to the bus station. Not taking any chances, although Viazul's reputation is much more reliable than that of the trains, not least because few if any Cubans can afford it, I arrive early only to find myself besieged by an army of alternatives: private cars hustling for enough fares to fill their vehicles. My taxi driver says I should take one rather than wait. The going rate he assures me is no more than 40 pesos, that despite the fact he has just charged me 4 CUCs, which is closer to 100 pesos for the short ride from the hotel.

We argue for a bit about the price. There is no way he is taking a gringo for 40 pesos. His starting price is 15 CUC. I laugh. He laughs back and says 10. I laugh again and say 5, pointing out I already have Viazul tickets. He looks disappointed, then laughs back and says 'Vale'. Okay. He ushers me into pride of place in the front passenger seat, then disappears for 10 minutes for a cigarette and to hustle enough other passengers, probably all paying 40 pesos at most, to fill the rear cargo compartment. And then we're off, with the sound of roaring rapper salsa howling from boombox speakers embedded in the leather upholstery above our heads, and every big round dial in the matching pillar-box red painted dash, from 'TEMP' to 'OIL' to the speedometer itself, set immutably at zero.

There is also the fact that I already have a ticket for what may even be an air-conditioned coach. But will it be real? The backpacker in me is shouting that it would be a cop-out now to take the comfy seat even if the middle-aged bloke with sore feet is hankering after it. Then all of a sudden the answer is in my face, in the shape of a huge great bright blue behemoth, an absolute monster of a vehicle with a great beaming monster of a man behind the wheel. With big brown arms the size of elephant's thighs, this genial giant in a singlet and shorts is only too proud to show me what he claims proudly is a 1951 Willys Jeep Truck, lovingly cared for, protected from rust by a thick coat of royal blue gloss paint and upholstered throughout inside in plush shiny red leather. There is even a magnificent curled ram's head motif on its nose though he admits that probably came from a Dodge.

Just forty-five minutes later after a thrilling rollercoaster ride over the hills that defeated the railway men he dumps me at what appears to be the unlicensed taxi clearing station in the Santiago suburbs. A cantankerous old bloke in a complete wreck of a 1950s Chevy – compared to the near immaculate Willys – offers to take me to my hotel, or rather his cousin's casa, which I have no difficulty turning down looking through the holes in the foot well at his clunking gears.

I have booked myself in at the San Basilio, am absolute haven of sanity in a city supposed to be Cuba's most frenetic. And it fulfils expectations, with a handful of elegantly decorated, blissfully high-ceilinged rooms around a little courtyard on the street of the same name, just a short walk from the city's main square.

The guidebooks paint Parque Céspedes as Santiago's thriving and just so slightly wicked heart, teeming with people high on hooch, fuelled by sex appeal and swinging to *son* or *trova* music. They must have been there on another day, because right now it reminds me more of Leamington Spa on a Sunday afternoon, with relaxed people enjoying cool drinks in the colonnade of the elegant Casa Grande hotel. There is a *trova* band playing outside but it's more background music than in-your-face hustle.

I also have a bit of compulsory sightseeing to do, the scene of Castro's classic débâcle. But first I need a new SD card for my camera, which I'm slightly worried might be impossible to acquire. But no, there is a shop off the main square which I am told has photographic equipment. Hmmm, I'm thinking Kodacolor rather than Secure Digital. But it turns out I'm wrong. They are available for sale, depending on who you are. The largest available is 2 gigabytes, the middle-aged lady shop assistant says proudly, which is almost the smallest available in most other countries, but it will have to do. But first I have to show my passport, then she has to fill out a form which I have to sign in duplicate and hand over a hugely expensive 30 CUC (£20/$30), vastly beyond the means of any native. But then so is the most basic digital camera. The whole process takes 20 minutes, including the time for her to write out a complex 6-month guarantee form without which she will not give me the card. Still, it's one-up on Turkey where I bought a 10-gig card for less than half the price only to discover it was phoney and didn't retain images.

And so to the Moncada, to see how the Castros' revolution nearly foundered on their almost adolescent over-enthusiasm. Having got to town earlier than expected, and reluctant to face another unpleasant Santiago taxi driver, I decide to walk it which turns out to be a terrible mistake. First of all it is further out than I thought, secondly because it is hot and Santiago is remarkably hilly, and thirdly because I don't recognise it when I get there.

Because the image hasn't been drilled into me since child-hood, as if has for most Cubans, I don't initially recognize the big yellow building for what it is. So I do what nobody would expect: I ask a policeman. He looks a bit surprised. We're standing next to the thing. There is also, just across the road a vast 30ft by 10ft banner adorned by the faces of both Castro brothers and the slogan: 'Santiago is Santiago, a rebel city once, a hospitable one today, heroic forever.'

Walking up to the door the evidence of the heroism becomes obvious in the spray of bullet holes around the door. The only trouble is that they don't actually date from the ill-fated action that took place here on July 26, 1953.

The relatively minor damage done in the Castros' attack was repaired soon afterwards. Then after the success of the revolution in 1958, Castro himself took a bulldozer to tear down the barracks' outer walls. It was only in 1978 that with an old man's eye to history and his legacy he had the outer walls rebuilt, the doorway re-'sprayed' with bullets and the building, which had been a school in the mean time, turned into a museum. Fidel may never have been to Disneyland, but that doesn't mean he can't take a lesson. A visit to the Moncada Barracks is a 'must' on the curriculum of every Cuban schoolchild.

The man on the door smiles at me – nice to see a foreigner come to pay homage to the birthplace of the revolution – and asks for two CUC. Feeling a bit cheeky I offer him two CUP, two pesos, which is what it costs ordinary Cubans. 'Aren't we all comrades?' I get a mildly amused look but he still wants his CUCs. No confusing history with the present here.

The history itself relates that the attack took place on July 26, 1953, little over a year after the military coup which brought dictator Fulgencio Batista to power. The gaggle of well-to-do young men and peasant farmers who had gathered themselves around the illegitimate farmer's son and Havana law student had deliberately planned their attack for the morning after Santiago's annual fiesta. Fidel was counting on the forces inside still being drunk.

He had been thinking about his move for a long time. Fidel and brother Raúl had been recruiting and training opponents of the regime under the guise of a clay-pigeon shooting club. The 153 rebels were clad in blue army uniforms that had been stolen by a relative of one of the revolutionaries from the laundry of a military hospital. On the night before they gathered at a farm in Siboney – as it happens the place where the jolly university librarian woman I met on the train from Camagüey lives – which was where most of them were informed for the first time of their target. The idea was to take over the barracks, loot its store of weapons and use its radio transmitter to send false messages to the army command while broadcasting revolutionary speeches urging the people to take up arms.

Equipped with a random and varied selection of weapons from shotguns, handguns, an assortment of rifles and one malfunctioning submachine gun, they set off at 4.45, before dawn, in a convoy of sixteen vehicles, hoping to give the impression of a delegation headed by a senior officer from Havana. They had three objectives: one group, including the then just twenty-two-year-old Raúl, was to take the Palace of Justice, a second smaller detachment of half a dozen was to seize control of the neighbouring military while the main party, led by Fidel himself, was tasked with the main assault on the barracks.

Unfortunately for them, Fidel's troops were indeed nearly all from Havana, or at least western Cuba, and they did the one thing that is absolutely unconscionable in a military operation: they got lost. Unfamiliar with the city, they ended up split into two groups, while the lorry carrying most of their heavy weapons never arrived. According to Fidel's own account the soldiers on duty at the barracks realized there was something fishy going on, refused to move aside and as a result he drove his car straight into them. His dilettante colleagues, poorly armed and hopelessly outnumbered, thought they had broken through the gates and jumped out of their vehicles. In the ensuing firefight fifteen soldiers and three policemen were killed and two dozen others wounded. The rebels suffered nine dead and eleven wounded, four of them by friendly fire from their own colleagues.

The aftermath demonstrated a gruesome and astoundingly incompetent mixture of atrocity and leniency on the part of the Batista regime: within a few hours of the failed attack, eighteen captured rebels were summarily executed in the barracks' firing range and their bodies strewn around the grounds to make it look like they died in combat. Of those who fled, a further thirty-four were murdered after admitting their participation. The remainder were rounded up but allowed to live to face trial, when a panel of three judges were harangued by Fidel presenting his own defence and complaining loudly about the 'murder' of prisoners.

As a result, nineteen of the rebels got off scot-free on lack of evidence while the ringleaders including Fidel and Raúl (who had actually succeeded in his own allotted task of capturing the Palacio de Justicia) were sentenced to thirteen years, later commuted to two. When they were released the pair wisely fled to Mexico where they continued to plot revolution now under the name Movimento 26 Julio, also known as M-26-7. As with Dunkirk, a disaster wisely handled can become a source of inspiration. Winston Churchill famously declared, 'History will be kind to me, because I intend to write it.' It was while he was in prison that Fidel wrote his famous manifesto 'History Will Absolve Me', and in the Moncada of today, he made sure of it.

The most remarkable thing about the museum to someone visiting it for the first time is how successful it is in making the visitor feel close to the actual events. Not just because it was just over fifty years ago, but because the artefacts on display still feel alarmingly contemporary, in the very real sense that they were 'of the moment' then, and surprisingly still don't look too terribly dated today.

A glass case contains clothing worn by some of the impoverished farmers drafted into Fidel's raggle-taggle army but rather than smocks from some peasant uprising or even Soviet-era army uniforms, they are denim jeans that look like they might have come from a retro stall at London's

Camden Market. Why wouldn't they? I can't see the label but they might well be Levis. These men, after all, were contemporaries of Elvis.

Perhaps the most poignant exhibit are the items of clothing belonging to the failed mission's most celebrated martyr Reinaldo Boris Luis Santa Coloma: nice brown brogue spats and a pair of gold cufflinks. Impeccably middle-class. Even Cuba had its champagne socialists.

Two elderly Cuban women come up to me and ask me in English what I think of the museum, obviously just slightly apprehensive as to what a foreigner might see in it all. I nod at the display in front of us, the brogue spats, and say, 'Nice shoes. Expensive.' They smile to one another, not simply but knowingly. They can take a joke, these Cubans. Even at their own expense.

On the way out you are faced with one whole wall devoted to a photograph of Fidel in fatigues with backpack standing on a rocky crest gazing out boldly into his brave new world. If it weren't for the superimposed background of the national flag and the profoundly nineteenth-century image of old José Martí, he could be some unshaven Aussie backpacker.

The Lenin Museum in Moscow which flourished from his death in 1924 to the dissolution of the Soviet Union in 1991 was subsequently transformed into Moscow City Hall for many years and is now the Russian Historical Museum, in which Lenin plays a dramatically reduced role. The Stalin Museum in his birthplace of Gori in Georgia was built around his tiny childhood home and filled with examples idolatry and hagiography. It endured more than 50 years after his death, though following the 2008 war over South Ossetia, the Georgian authorities announced plans to transform it into a Museum of Russian Aggression. What will become of Fidel's act of homage to himself and his apostles is something which history that hasn't happened yet will decide.

I have the vicissitudes of history firmly in mind as I make the trek back into town, thankfully mostly downhill.

The other great memorial site in Santiago, subject of my main interest the next day is thankfully only a short stroll way. It too is in many ways homage to a single man, one of the earliest of genuine globetrotters and will soon have endured half a millennium. The house of Diego Velázquez diagonally across from the Casa Grande on Céspedes Square is an unassuming building at first glance, just two stories high but built of ashlar stone with a Moorish grille balcony at first floor level, and a huge, square and rather imposing columned entrance. But then it is entitled to be imposing, given that it is the oldest building in Cuba and arguably the oldest European-erected building in the whole of the Americas.

Dating from somewhere around 1519–22, this was the home of Diego Velázquez de Cuéllar, the man who conquered Cuba for Spain and became its first governor, founding not only Santiago, but also isolated Baracoa, nearby Bayamo, as well as Havana itself, and incidentally exterminating most of the native Taino Indians and importing the first black slaves. With a record like that we perhaps don't need to feel too sorry that he died here in 1524 a bitter man after sending Hernán Cortés to conquer Mexico but falling out with him and getting none of the mountains of gold he captured.

The house today has been remarkably preserved and restored, given the general state of decay of most Cuban buildings of lesser historical importance, and features items used for forging gold on the ground floor as well as a recreation of how the rooms might have looked in the sixteenth century, as well as a restored nineteenth-century interior in the house next door. Wandering around its cool dark rooms feels more like exploring some palace in Córdoba or Seville than the Caribbean, an intimation of how the sixteenth-century Spanish took their domestic world with them around the globe in much the same way the British built cricket clubs in India.

The Spanish roots of most Cuban music, however, have been much diminished by the vast surging drumbeats of Africa, the influences from French Haïti, especially down here in *Oriente*, and of course the remarkable, and purely Cuban evolution of the musical styles and cultures its natives have imported and invented. Perhaps the most dominant is *son*, with its derivative *salsa* which with its vivid syncopations, short choruses and swaying rhythms is perhaps the most distinctive Cuban sound.

Different but equally significant is *trova*, considered – just a little arrogantly – by the inhabitants of Santiago to be theirs. The word *trovador* has its origins in the mediaeval 'troubadour' which was a fair enough description of the groups of musicians who roved around *Oriente* in the nineteenth century playing music of their own composition, usually performing alone or in duos, as opposed to the bigger *son* and *salsa* bands. *Trova* songs are the classic Caribbean ballads, usually guitar-accompanied, romantic and slower than *son*, but still eminently danceable. But then it is a rule of thumb in Cuba that any tune is danceable; that's what makes it a tune.

The Casa de la Trova, Santiago's most famed music venue, with its galleried balcony hanging out over the street on the corner of Heredia and San Felix, is distinctly low-key and relatively relaxed. Famously Paul McCartney landed his private plane at Santiago airport back in 2000 and asked to be taken to the club where he hummed along with the resident singers, acknowledged a Beatles debt to their music style and left them a note of thanks still enshrined there amidst the many tributes left by artists from all over the world.

'*Muchas gracias, señores y señoras, y señoritas*' it reads, in admirable Spanish, 'Paul McCartney *en Cuba, Santiago*, Jan 2000.'

But tonight that is about the height of the excitement. I pay my entrance fee, in CUCs of course, only to find the upstairs room has a motley three-piece band playing a little despondently to an audience of about a dozen, some of whom are clearly dancing girls employed by the establishment. The night is sultry and hot, the fans aren't working and even the girls aren't dancing much.

'It is not good,' Dolores, attired in a vast purple dress with frills and flounces tells me, puffing on a cheap cigarette as she leans over the balcony, ignoring the lacklustre music inside and sipping a warm soft drink: 'There are not so many tourists now. I think maybe nobody has any money any more.' It seems that even isolated communist Cuba is suffering from the global crisis of capitalism.

For the sake of it, I try a desultory twirl with Dolores on the dance floor, but the only others are a middle-aged Canadian couple and the band are hardly rising to the occasion. I buy a tot of Santiago's famed rum and sit with it for a while before it dawns on me that if I am not careful I shall be late for my train. And that would never do.

The time has come for my last train ride in Cuba. The big one. And supposedly the best. The fabled *tren frances*, the 'French train', the alleged luxury express that travels direct from Santiago to Havana overnight, at almost twice the speed of any other. Although, remembering that the average speed of most of the trains I have travelled on so far rarely hit 40 m.p.h., I am not getting overexcited about this just yet, even though I have already been down to the station earlier in the day and bought a ticket with – in Cuban terms – the greatest ease.

Santiago's station is the most unusual I've seen, a strange

modernist geometrical jumble of shapes, like something Frank Gehry might have designed if he'd been given lumps of concrete to work with instead of flowing titanium. The train is allegedly on time, according to a piece of paper on the glass of the *jefe del torno*'s office, but I'm dubious about there being any food and drink on board even a so-called deluxe train that runs overnight. I ask the *jefe* if there are any good food shops nearby to get supplies. The one I am directed to bizarrely resembles a low-end Chinese super-market in Soho more than anything I've yet encountered in Cuba (I recognize lots of familiar soy sauce brands), albeit without the fresh goods. In fact, beyond the option of tinned sardines from Ecuador which I can imagine being hard to open on a train and potentially both smelly and messy if I succeed, the only thing that looks reasonable is a can marked Jiang Lou Luncheon Meat Reliable Forever, Patent Number 200730094346 from the Jianglou Canned Food Manufacturing Co. Ltd. With some justifiable trepidation I buy myself what is effectively a tin of Chinese spam. And a dry roll to go with it. Yum, yum.

Back at the railway station with only two hours to go I am faced with three of the most obviously gringo lads I have ever seen, even if they are undoubtedly Europeans rather than North Americans. This blond, fair haired trio of tourists in shorts and panama hats turn out to be Czechs – Tomas, Martín and Karel – who have hardly been backpacking – other than a means of carrying their luggage – but travelling Viazul buses from one resort to another with a mild spot of catered camping in the mountains. I can only say they look like they've had a better time than I have. But I'm not really sure they've been to Cuba. For a start one says, glibly as if it is just an afterthought, 'I trust the train is on time.'

I find it hard not to crack up. Here they are, three lads from the heart of the old Soviet evil empire travelling around the most crocked communist country remaining – apart from North Korea – and they expect it to be like Europe. But then why wouldn't they with their squeaky clean EU maroon passports and their bundles of euros.

'Do you think we might have to share a compartment with any Cubans?' asks Tomas, somewhat apprehensively.

'Oh yes. Definitely,' I tell them to their obvious horror. I am sorely tempted to tell them that just twenty-five years ago 'westerners' – which of course they now unquestioningly consider themselves – travelling in Eastern Europe would have worried about having to share their compartment with any Czechs.

But they probably weren't even born when the Berlin Wall came down. One makes a bit of a fuss about not being that young, but then adds, 'My parents often say things didn't work so well back in those days.'

Which has a rich irony to it as at precisely that moment there is an announcement over the crackly station Tannoy (I suspect they still do actually use 'Tannoy') in Spanish. The Czech lads are blissfully ignoring it until I decide I really had better translate for them that the station master has just announced the train to Havana will be three hours late departing.

I can see the incipient panic. 'We have a flight tomorrow, via Amsterdam back to Munich, then the InterCityExpress back to Prague.' says one. This seems a bit optimistic to me. I'm leaving at least 48 hours clear for this supposedly thirteen-hour journey. But Prague these days is in the German sphere of influence rather than the extinct Soviet one. They are used to things working. It turns out they had enquired about flights but decided they were too expensive. Now they're wondering if they could get a cab to the airport on time.

By this time I am resigned to my fate and camp out on

a spot near the platform with my back to my rucksack and settle down for an extra three hours' wait. Three and a half hours later, with no further announcement and not the remotest sign of a train, I am starting to wonder if even my 48 hours was breathing space enough. To take my mind off it I do the only thing that in the circumstance was really likely to make things worse: I open the spam.

From time to time back in England I have been unamused to find bad Chinese takeaways using spam as a filler meat in anything from hot and sour soups to dumplings. I have always taken it as a hint not go back again. But that was before I encountered the sort of spam the Chinese ship to Cuba. The creature contained in the tin is a sort of slimy bright pink rubber smelling vaguely of pork you've left out of the fridge for a week. Even worse, I have managed to cut my finger opening it on the ridiculous unwinding steel spring thing which I remember from years ago on old corned beef cans. At least my pre-trip tetanus injection wasn't wasted. I staunch the bleeding with my bun. That'll add some protein to my dry bread meal.

There is not a bin in sight, so I surreptitiously move the spam to a kerbside near the road where over the course of the next half hour – yes, four hours after the original sched-uled departure time of the special Havana express – I notice one or two dogs come to investigate. None of them fancies it either.

By now the three Czechs are seriously panicking and wishing they'd got that flight. As the minutes tick into hours, I'm afraid the sight of their growing desperation is the only thing that keeps me amused. *Schadenfreude* may be a German word, but it is a universal emotion.

Eventually, a mere five hours behind schedule our train rumbles into the station. The pride of Cuba's railways has not completely let us down. Except of course that quite frankly it is a heap of shit. The *tren frances* is French all right, but it's a far fry from a 200kph TGV. In fact it is more like a train *regional*, the sort of decent slow clunker that connects smaller cities in France, or used to. This one has to be at least thirty years old. That said, it is almost literally light years better than any train I have travelled on since I came to Cuba.

The windows don't open – obviously – because the train is supposedly air-conditioned, not that any of the air conditioners I can see is emitting cold air. The automatic sliding doors between the carriages have long since given up on the automation idea. And the sliding. They are permanently stuck half-open and have to be physically forced apart, after which they are naturally reluctant to fully close again.

But the airplane-style seats are wide, far apart, upholstered in red leather – unripped! – and even actually recline a little, so it may be possible to get some sleep. Which is about all there is to do as barely half an hour after we pull out of Santiago station all the lights go out. An economy measure, apparently, but then I think back to *El Spirituario*, where through the early hours of the morning the lights were permanently on, and breathe a sigh of thankfulness for small mercies as I nod off.

◆

Morning comes early on a rocking, rolling train without window blinds. I have no idea where we are, but evidently nowhere near Havana. I wonder how the Czech lads are doing, stroll along a carriage or two and find them anxiously looking at their watches amidst a dozen snoring Cubans. They look glad to see me chiefly in the vain hope that I can reassure them they'll be in plenty of time for their flight. I have no idea how near or far from Havana we might be, not that even if I had it would be any guide as to how soon we might get there.

By the time I get back to my own seat I notice we are

passing through one of the smaller stations – where the 'express' of course does not stop – and realize the only news I could have given them would have been bad: we are scarcely half-way there.

Conversation with the young couple opposite me – a waiter called Mario and his young wife – shows that they clearly fit into the third of my Santa Clara baker's Cuban social classes. He works in a tourist resort and so they have access to CUCs. They also have property: and may soon even have more than one. They have been living in Santiago where with CUCs he bought the materials to build his own house. Now they are *en route* to Havana because his parents have just died and he has inherited their house.

The first law on housing instituted after the revolution contained the maxim that 'housing is to live in, not live from'. The state had first rights to buy any house on the market, effectively banning the sale of property to another individual. But it is one of Raúl Castro's most radical reforms that from November 2011, Cubans have been able to buy property from each other (exiles are still excluded) and inherit without having lived with the relative in question first. Mario and his wife now aim to open a *casa particular* and serve food. Foreign tourists are all they need to change their lives forever. As long as they keep coming.

My outward journey flashes past my eyes and the detail collapses into an overview that is far from heartening. There are whole swathes of central Cuba that more than anything else resemble the aftermath of a war, the general state of disrepair worn down and denigrated by the tropical climate. I am reminded of the Croatian district of Slavonia in the weeks after the withdrawal of the Yugoslav National Army: buildings in ruins, without roofs. The chief difference here is that there are still people living in them. For every one new building erected or restored in Cuba over more than half a century of communist rule, there must be at least 20 that have fallen down. There is a *ruina* bar in every town, roofless and worked by staff who don't earn enough to buy a drink there.

For the first time now there is an incentive to repair and restore property in the hope of selling it on or leaving it to relatives. It is an important step, as is the ability to employ another person who is not a relative. The beginnings of a more sensible economy, albeit one still under the aegis of socialist principles, are gradually beginning to emerge.

The question still to be answered is how far will it go, and what will it do to the countryside? Barely 10 per cent of the landscape visible from the railway is under any sort of agriculture. The nearest equivalent is the groups of wandering goats grazing where they can, and a few fenced off fields of scrawny cows.

We pass a tiny town half-built breezeblock houses roofed with thatch or corrugated plastic, populated by a few dozen kids, some sleeping adults, one ancient rusting Chevrolet and three horse carts. At one stage we pass under the concrete frame of a road bridge, neither end of which touches the ground. Not so much a work in progress, as a work forgotten about.

The hours pass by, hunger assuaged by some more mango juice and a man selling remarkably edible ham rolls. With my newly acquired facility for Cuban dialect I work out that what sounds like 'Doh pa sink' is actually in the Spanish I learnt at school, '*Dos para cinco*', and means he is offering two rolls for five pesos. *Nacional.*

Eventually we pass the outskirts of Matanzas, with the smart new bungalows of citizens class two crawling along the bay. I glance at my watch: 14.15. The Czech lads will make their flight after all.

And then suddenly, almost before I realize it, the view

from the window changes to ocean and container ships floating at anchor and we are pulling into the sprawling, incoherent, rambling suburbs of Havana. Past a goods yard we crawl, past coaches and freight cars that look like abandoned toys from some long-ago childhood. Then from behind me I hear that new global common denominator: a Nokia ringtone and a male voice says: *'Buenas . . . soy en el tren.'* Hiya, I'm on the train.

Aaaargh. Maybe the future is arriving after all. Just a little bit late.

Postscript

Cuba is changing. Slowly, so far very much at its own pace. Fidel Castro has been retired from government since 2008 and from the Communist Party of Cuba since 2011. He is approaching ninety years of age. His younger brother Raúl, who assumed both duties, is at the time of writing nearly eighty-two, but has nonetheless just been confirmed in a second term of office, though he has stated that he will step down when that expires in 2018.

Already he has introduced a limited degree of liberalization, including the right of farmers to sell a limited amount of produce in private markets, the right to buy property, the so-far limited right of one Cuban to employ another in what effectively constitutes a private business. Almost one million Cubans formerly employed by the state are being released with the option to set up small businesses of their own, without being taxed so heavily that they will not be viable, as has happened at times with the *casas particulares* and the *paladares*.

Tourism, therefore, is still seen as playing an important, if not dominant, role in the country's future. But above and beyond catering to the rich foreigners, there are now Cubans going back to old trades such as shoe repairing and hair cutting, as well as opening restaurants, such as that I visited in Guantánamo. In some ways, these legal relaxations are only regularizing a black market that has already been in existence for years; in others they are genuinely opening up new opportunities.

There is no longer the same paranoia about foreign travel – in either direction. Although there is still substantial hostility in the ruling Communist Party to those who went into exile and have tried to fund and encourage opposition in their homeland, modern Cubans are no longer so comprehensively hindered from applying for visas, travelling abroad, and returning home. Indeed, in many cases the biggest impediment can be getting a visa from the country they wish to visit rather than permission from their own government to go abroad. Mobile phones are already relatively commonplace, and access to the internet, though still rare, is no longer taboo.

These are rights and freedoms that we in the 'free world' take for granted, but in Cuba it is genuine change and completely unlike anything that happened in East Germany or the Soviet Union until right at the very end of their existence. If there is a parallel in old Eastern Europe it is probably Hungary where a greater degree of tolerance was always shown towards black market private enterprise and foreign travel.

Already more and more US citizens are ignoring their own government's already watered-down restrictions on travel to Cuba. The visit by megastars Beyoncé and Jay-Zee in early 2013 and the rapturous reception they received is proof that the artificial barrier is gradually disintegrating.

Certainly more and more Cubans are meeting foreign tourists who increasingly in their own way are no longer remaining restricted to the luxury enclaves to which the Communist Part of two decades ago once wanted to confine them. It is relatively easy to travel independently in Cuba, although the word 'easy' is hardly the one to use if you mean travelling like ordinary Cubans, as I trust this book will have made clear.

But the point is, you can do it. At no time was I ever troubled by, followed by (to the best of my knowledge) or hassled by any representative of the Cuban government, secretive or otherwise. The vocal arguments I heard about the regime on the trains and from individuals I encountered along the way were uttered with no obvious sense of fear; as someone who lived in East Berlin and Moscow, I think I have a pretty good nose for that.

The biggest issue for most Cubans is their continuing poverty, symbolized by the gross difference between the national currency in which most people earn their wages, the CUP peso, and the convertible CUC. But at least this parallel currency system, for all its harshness and inequality, works after a fashion and who knows, might even become a path to levelling the playing field: with the CUP wholly under control of the government with no foreign exchange markets to worry about, it might, just might, conceivably in time be revalued upwards towards parity with the CUC, at which stage they could be merged. That is a pipedream at the moment and I am no economist, but there are many ways in which Cuba's current political and social situation could evolve.

The United States may have long shunned Havana and nurtured the dreams of exiles in Miami of going back, seizing property confiscated from them and 'restoring' the old ways. Of course, most of the younger generation hankers after rapid change, but even they – as I noticed sitting in Matanzas where Cubans were watching adverts during US baseball games for horrendously expensive health insurance policies – are proud of certain aspects of their way of life.

It could be a mistake to assume, as many people do, especially in the United States, that when the Castros go, the system will collapse and rampant capitalism will return, bringing with it wealth and democracy. There are other options, other arguments. The lack of US influence has undoubtedly aided the Chinese to become vastly more influential in Cuba, providing buses and locomotives, and of course there has always been a small ethnic Chinese element in Havana since the late nineteenth century, adding just one more trace element to the exotic Cuban racial mix.

China still claims to be communist in name and operates a rigid one-party system but it has delivered economic development and relative riches. It is possible that the current leadership in Havana is already thinking along the lines of similar economic relaxation without necessarily allowing the sort of free-for-all that US involvement would likely witness. There is also the fact that – even at the cost of individual freedoms – it is only since 1959 that Cubans have genuinely felt free as a nation, other than a colony or a puppet state. Even during the days of their dependency on Soviet support, the USSR was a long way away; the United States is uncomfortably close and for now at least still the only military and economic global superpower. Of course, the Chinese may have something to say about that too.

How political change will come is uncertain. Raúl has admitted that his generation made a serious mistake in not bringing up a wave of successors. Of the fifteen members of the politburo at the time of writing, six were born in the 1930s, and four in the 1940s. This is essentially a government of pensioners born in the first half of the twentieth century trying to legislate for the twenty-first. But then the situation in the Soviet Union in 1985 was very similar when a group of out-of-touch old men elected the relative youngster Mikhail Gorbachev, then fifty-four. The rest is history.

And even if that history may not have turned out the way many Russians would like with the Putin–Medvedev dynasty hardly an exemplar of democracy in action, still that system too has provided a better economic and social lifestyle for the great majority of its citizens. In 1985 it was unimaginable that impoverished Russians might ever travel in numbers abroad, now it is impossible to imagine the cities and beaches without rich Russians in their thousands.

There is a thirst for greater debate in Cuba, particularly in intellectual circles, but amongst the broad mass of the population the real thirst, it may seem a shame to say, is just for a better lifestyle: food, drink and material goods. In eastern Germany today I still know many who, although they would in no way wish the Berlin Wall back, still hanker for the simpler, older world when the state had all the answers and life did not involve dealing with a complex, competitive world of bankers, lawyers, mortgages, insurance companies. They tell me that even as they flick their fingers across their iPads checking out the price of holidays in Turkey.

Nobody today can visit Cuba and not wish this beautiful island and its people well. But the more they are allowed to sort out their future themselves, the more interesting it will be. In one way or another. *Cu'a e' Cu'a*, after all.

Peter Millar was born in Northern Ireland and educated at Magdalen College, Oxford. He has lived in Paris, Brussels, East Berlin and Moscow, and has worked for Reuters, the *Sunday Telegraph* and *Sunday Times,* with a brief intermission as deputy editor of Robert Maxwell's *European.* He was named Foreign Correspondent of the Year in 1989, for his coverage of the latter days of the Cold War and Fall of the Berlin Wall. He is the author of four novels and four works of non-fiction, including *1989 The Berlin Wall (My Part in its Downfall)* and *All Gone To Look for America (Riding the Iron Horse Across a Continent and Back).* Peter has also translated Corinne Hofmann's hugely successful White Masai trilogy (*The White Masai, Return from Africa* and *Reunion in Barsaloi*) from German to English. He speaks French, German, Russian and Spanish and is married with two grown-up children. He splits his time between Oxfordshire and London, blogging on beer and sitting in the North Stand at The Valley with his fingers crossed watching Charlton Athletic.